"Unflinching in its honesty, intricately plotted, emotionally charged, and rich in characterization, Sklar delivers a novel that is both courageous and complex. A thoughtful page-turner for the sophisticated reader." – **Julie Mars,** author of *Rust, Anybody Any Minute,* and *A Month of Sundays*

"Atlas of Men is a provocative, unsettling, and ultimately redeeming story that addresses fundamental questions about American culture and its cruelties. Who counts, and who doesn't? How do we define success, both for ourselves and others, and how do we choose those destined for it? David Sklar's gifts for character and storytelling bring these questions to life in wholly unexpected and surprising ways. Ultimately, this is a wise, tender, and often funny novel that comes from the heart as much as the head, even as it asks us to examine, rather than to simply accept, the cold assumption that achievement alone provides meaning and worth in individual lives." – **Frank Huyler, MD,** author of T*he Blood of Strangers* and *The Laws of Invisible Things*

"Atlas of Men is a haunting, mesmerizing story about coming-of-age, of innocence lost and the search for redemption. David Sklar has skillfully crafted a story with achingly real characters who remain with us long after the story has ended. We join protagonist Robert Thames as he confronts a dehumanizing, dark past at a boys' boarding school and the dilemma it has wrought. Files that arrive at Thames' door are an eerie reminder of his own pain of dehumanization and exploitation and yet…the transformative, healing power of friendship and love triumphs, bringing renewed faith and hope for the future. Thames is indeed an "Atlas" of men with the weight of the universe on his shoulders, or so it seems. As he upholds what is true and just, he inspires us all." – **Hedy S. Wald, Ph.D**

"Something very sinister is happening at Dexter Academy under the guise of scientific research. More than a coming of age tale, this novel weaves together an intriguing story of love, loss and secrets. Transformation and truth telling transport us to another reality." – **Victor La Cerva. MD,** author *Letters To A Young Man In Search Of Himself*

Robert Thames, an infectious-disease doctor and researcher, was adopted as a child and brought to America from the Philippines. He attended Danvers, an elite private school, where he fell into a tight-knit bridge group. An unexpected delivery from an old professor reveals that Robert and his schoolmates were unwitting participants in a disturbing research study. On a mission to reunite his old friends, Robert takes a globe-trotting journey that stirs up old romance, scandals, and secrets, as he himself grows from a timid, nervous man into a strong-willed, decisive person who faces his fears instead of running from them.
– **Foreword Review**

Atlas of Men

A NOVEL BY

DAVID SKLAR

▲

VOLCANO CANNON PRESS

cover art: *Atlas of Men: A Guide for Somatotyping the Adult Male at All Ages*
by William Herbert Sheldon, New York: Harper and Brothers. 1954

While the Sheldon somatotypes study is based in fact, this is a work of fiction. The characters, incidents, and dialogues are products of the author's imagination, and any resemblance to persons, places or events is entirely coincidental.

Designed by Sarah McElwain

Author photo: Adrienne Helitzer/Still Productions©

First Edition

Publisher's Cataloging-in-Publication Data
Names: Sklar, David, 1950-.
Title: Atlas of men / David Sklar.
Description: Phoenix, AZ : Volcano Cannon Press, 2018. | Summary: Three boxes arrive unexpectedly on Dr. Robert Thames' doorstep, containing files from a secret research study conducted at his prep school decades ago. He tracks down four close friends from Danvers Academy, and together they uncover the truth that was buried by the faculty, the school, and the boys themselves.
Identifiers: LCCN 2018907327 | ISBN 9781732348400 (pbk.) | ISBN 9781732348417 (epub) | ISBN 9781732348424 (mobi)
Subjects: LCSH: Friendship--Fiction. | Human experimentation in medicine--Fiction. |Human experimentation in medicine--Moral and ethical aspects--Fiction. | Private schools--Fiction. | New Hampshire--Fiction. | Philippines--Fiction. | BISAC: FICTION / Action & Adventure. | FICTION / Thrillers / Medical.
Classification: LCC PS3619.K53 A85 2018| DDC 813 S--dc23
LC record available at https://lccn.loc.gov/2018907327

To Deborah

~

Despite the confusion now rampant in the social interrelationships of the species, underlying the social chaos is a matrix of organic order, which is to say, of beauty and truth.

> ~ William H. Sheldon
> *Atlas of Men: A Guide for Somatotyping of the Adult Male at All Ages*
> New York: Harper and Brothers. 1954

PROLOGUE

This research project landed in my arms like a small child I once caught off the top of a high slide while walking in the park. I remember thinking how odd as the child flew through the air like a football. I dove for him and caught his little head and body in my arms as we crashed to the ground. Instead of a medal or my photograph in the paper for saving the child's life, I met the wild eyes of his mother as she rushed me, seized the crying toddler, and scurried off to her car. And that's how it was with this research project. I never asked for it, but I did not want to drop it as it fell to me through the air, and so I caught it and cradled it in my arms.

What I found were photographs of boys with measurements of length and width, as if they were lumber or cloth for sale at a market in Cebu City, where I was born. Information about their school years, marriages, divorces, bankruptcies, illnesses, deaths, awards, and scandals, all run together like wet ink. I showed this research project around to people I knew, mostly my former classmates. Some thought it was interesting; others thought it was despicable. When I was alone at home at night, the boys in the photographs called out to me. At first I did not know what they wanted. Eventually I understood: They wanted me to tell our story, starting with the day those boxes arrived, right up until I decided what to do with them. So that's what I've done.

Book 1

I

When my father told me bedtime stories, he would instruct me to close my eyes and think about claws instead of fingers, a nose that could smell blood, leaves that could drink sunlight like water. I imagined how it would feel to have bark instead of skin, roots down into the ground, wind blowing through my leaves, sunlight nourishing me. My father encouraged these flights of fancy because he believed in the power of human imagination. He thought that there might be times when I would need to imagine myself a tree to escape from danger or pain.

Today I am not imagining myself to be a tree. I am imagining myself to be a fly. I am not just speaking metaphorically: Humans share 60% of their DNA with flies. So why can't I call myself a fly today if that is how I feel? Today I will be a fly and sit on the wall as my boss gives me the news that I have been fired. I know it's coming. The secretaries, janitors, and security guards pick up scraps of information like hyenas and vultures and other carrion eaters that subsist on the dead and decaying bodies on the jungle floor. The secretary who works for the director, Mr. Grundel, warned me.

At first I was anxious and scared. I have never been fired before, though I have often worried about it, like failing a test in school. Even after all the years of surviving as a doctor in the government, I still feared being declared an imposter. I wondered if it would hurt like a stab wound or a heart attack or an ulcer. That's why I have usually chosen the safer career path when I had a choice. I have tried to keep my eyes wide open, and if I have missed out on dreams, I have also avoided nightmares. Everyone told me that working for the government would be safe, that I would have this job until I retired at 65. But retirement is still ten years away.

It's not as if I did anything wrong. I have traveled the world – every place they sent me – looking for new antibiotics to replace those that the bacteria have learned to outwit. I have learned the languages of some of those places – Spanish, French, Swahili, Japanese, a bit of Thai. People smile at you when you try to speak their language. And I've studied the religions too. Even though I am a Christian, I have learned about Buddhism, Islam, Judaism, and even some of the indigenous religions of native peoples. Those are my favorites because their myths remind me of the stories my dad would tell me when I was a child.

Over the years on my trips, I have found some herbs or fungi that killed bacteria. Maybe someday a drug company will turn them into a pill. But when you work for the government, there can be budget problems and political decisions, and no one remembers what you discovered two years ago. Maybe it's for the best. I have been fully human for too long and maybe it's time to imagine being something else, like a bird or fly.

I have heard that they set out boxes of tissues in anticipation of tears when they have these types of meetings; they keep them in the supply closet. I will look to see if they are on the table.

I knock on Mr. Grundel's door at precisely ten o'clock, as instructed.

"Come in. Come in and close the door," Mr. Grundel says.

They always tell you to close the door when there's bad news. That's what I learned in medical school. When you have to tell a woman that her husband just died, make sure to close the door. And don't beat around the bush and talk about the weather or the score of the baseball game or any details about how long the heart kept beating before it finally stopped. Just blurt it out, "Your husband is dead," and then wait for a few seconds for the tears and sobs, before asking if she has any questions.

Fortunately, I have not had many occasions to be the recipient of bad news, except the time my parents died in a car wreck in the Philippines. I heard about that over the phone from my uncle. I was in the middle of rounds at the hospital, and I had to discuss the causes of lymphadenopathy and fever before I could find a room and close a door. It was the toilet in the men's room, and there was toilet paper instead of tissues. That was the last time I cried until today.

Mr. Grundel has black slicked-back hair on a balding scalp that always seems to have a few beads of sweat about to trickle onto his face. He mops at them with a handkerchief held in a ball in his fist. He transferred to our division two years ago from the information services and marketing office and is still trying to learn the names of the various tropical diseases and organisms our international office is supposed to be curing. He has always been pleasant to me, greeting me when we pass in the hall or in our lunch room. I heard that he could be a stickler for time sheets, but as one of the few doctors in the office, I have a privileged position and do not have to track my hours or activities like most of the rest of the staff. Mr. Grundel generally has left me alone, and I did my work as usual, with all of the necessary reports and documentation.

"Have a seat," he says, pointing to the small, green upholstered chair in the middle of the room. On the table next to the chair are two boxes, freshly opened, with tissues bursting forth. I take my seat and wait.

"Well, I guess we might as well get down to business," he says and smiles at me as if I know why I've been called here. "As you may have heard, there are going to be some budget cutbacks. Very unfortunate. Since they may involve you, I wanted to discuss the implications for your position here with the Agency."

"I am not sure I know what you mean."

"Well, Dr. Thames…"

"Robert is fine."

"This is as awkward for me as it is for you." I notice three discrete beads of sweat at the top of his forehead, preparing to descend to his nose and eyes. He lifts the balled handkerchief to his forehead and dabs at the droplets. "Another part of the Agency misspent its budget on a controversial project, and now Congress is punishing us by reducing funding for the entire department."

"Really? Which project?"

"It's not really relevant." He wipes his head again and continues. "But unfortunately, now we need to reimburse the account. It's not as if we can go out and sell cookies! Our only option is to cut programs, eliminate most of the funding for sexually transmitted and infectious diseases next year. Unfortunately, your project got caught up in this net. The cut will be implemented in six months, so you will have time to look for a job and relocate if necessary. There's a nice severance package – three months of full pay. As an infectious disease doctor you're in a much better position than our Ph.D. researchers. They'll probably be teaching biology in high school! And who knows? If you discover a new Penicillin mold during your next trip, we could make a strong case for continued support." He rustles some papers in his hands. "But lately…the specimens you've been bringing in have been duds."

I exhale slowly. It was true. The juice from the flowers I had brought back from Madagascar that was supposed to fight skin infections had not killed any bacteria or viruses, though everyone thought it had potential as a perfume. The Mexican cactus pulp that was a native remedy for burns had actually served as a growth medium for Staph aureus. But that was the nature of research: There were always more dead ends than freeways. I had always assumed that my superiors understood that. I was patient and had a ten-year horizon, just like many of our budget estimates. I had not imagined leaving my position at the Agency until my retirement. The pay was not great by doctor standards but for me, as a single man without a wife or children, it was enough.

"So I'm getting fired?"

"Fire you? No... Your job may be eliminated. Completely different! To fire you, we would need cause. That's a long process with a grievance procedure that could take years. You'd have had to do something illegal, like steal a computer or sell a drug to a private company or foreign country."

"I never imagined this…" I say.

Of course this is not true. I always imagined it would happen. I expected it my whole life. Deep down – in spite of my degrees and experience – I always have felt the imposter. Even now I can hear my mother's cautionary echoes about my tenuous achievements.

I reach for the tissues and pull out a thick wad. The sudden flood of emotion surprises me.

"Oh, help yourself. That's what they're for," he says as I wipe my eyes. "No one ever imagines it will happen to them. But look on the bright side: Maybe there are places you've wanted to visit. Or people you've lost touch with – family, friends, and classmates from college or high school – who might like to see you. People decide to climb mountains or create a new computer program or write a novel. Some people go back to church. It's not really so bleak."

I sigh again. I want to be that fly on the wall now, staring down at the two people in the room. I do not want to be one of those people. "I don't climb mountains. I don't have any family, and I don't have any old friends or go to church."

"Pity," he says.

"I guess there are places I've visited that I might like to see again."

"See what I mean? Glass half full, not half empty. And in any case, the decision is not final. Your program has been one of our most popular among the funders and the foreign countries we visit. A real bright spot. You have a lot of friends out there. And there's still time for you to produce something that might change the equation. Maybe you can find some tree bark or fungus or seaweed on your next trip to Africa that will lead to a new antibiotic. I have the notes right here. A trip to Tanzania, in about a week. That would be a game changer! It's the ninth inning and you've struck out the last three times to bat, but you could still hit a home run. You know what I mean?"

"I do have a trip to Africa scheduled. There are some promising specimens I'll be collecting."

"That's exactly what I mean. Swing for the fences! Even if you go down swinging. That's the spirit. Unless you would like to resign today."

"Today?" I stammer. "Not at all. My work is very important. I've helped discover chemicals that we'll be using for drug resistant infections."

"Well that was some time ago, and the trials haven't been completed. I can't make that argument to Congress. They want real outcomes, lives saved, that kind of results. But perhaps you can find another antibiotic on your next trip." He pushes back in his chair. "Well, I believe that is all I have for today, unless you have any questions."

"Do you have any Tylenol?"

"What?"

"Tylenol… for my headache. I'm beginning to get one."

"Huh? Actually we're not allowed standard drugs in our offices. Only the experimental remedies from the herbs and plants that you bring in."

My eyes began to pulse with light, like when you have to look into the sun while driving. This is how my migraine headaches start. I need to go home and lie down before the symptoms become worse. When I leave Mr. Grundel's office, I sign a sick leave form and tell the secretary I'll be gone for the day. I deserve a day to recover from this meeting.

As I enter the Metro station, I notice everyone around me. Most are young, well dressed, on the move. Young men in dark suits, texting on their cell phones. Young women in white blouses with tan and gray jackets and dark skirts, wearing eyeliner and purple lipstick. Black and Asian and Latin and White, standing around waiting for the train. They all seem to have a destination. I am just headed to Dupont Circle, to the long escalator and the walk home to my apartment. This is a trip I make every day, and I haven't really thought much about it until now, as I realize that the familiar routine might soon be broken.

I think about my retirement account. I've been putting money into it since I began to work, and the government contributed money, too. They send me statements, but I usually throw them in the trash once I determine they aren't bills. I remember reading something about how much money I'll get in ten years when I turn sixty-five – about a hundred and twenty thousand dollars a year. I could easily live on that until I die. And there's another two hundred thousand dollars in my investment account. But if I lose my job, there won't be any retirement money. The investment money will run out in about two years; three if I eat a vegetarian diet. Then what? I could probably get a doctor job doing physicals for insurance companies. That's relatively mindless work that would pay the bills until I find something better. Or I could call friends in the infectious diseases world. Sometimes there are openings for a year or two, visiting professor jobs. Over the years, international medical schools have invited me to teach for a year. I would always nod graciously and express my appreciation and explain how busy I was with my research. They would always smile at my willingness to consider their offers. That was part of the etiquette. But maybe now's the time to take them seriously, before I become tainted by the scent of failure.

If there were close friends to call, this would be the time to get some advice, but I've lost contact with most of them, and breaking the long silences would be awkward.

My head begins to pound as I get on the Metro. There are no seats. Two girls with purple lipstick listening to iPhones, two young men with briefcases, and a sweaty, bearded man reading a *Politico* newspaper all jostle and press against me. It's all I can do to hang on to the metal bar near the door and keep myself from vomiting and passing out.

Fortunately, it's only three stops. I push my way out of the car like a football player running through the line of scrimmage, seeking open space. There are the usual people who cluster around the Metro entrance – the newspaper hawkers, the shoe shine boys, the pickpockets and bums, the flower sellers, the disabled people with their dogs, the maids and busboys going to their second jobs. Usually I hand out some quarters to the homeless, but today my head's throbbing; I'm preoccupied with my own future.

When I get home I take off my shoes and lie down, pressing my fingers softly against my eyeballs and seeing bright yellow patterns of geometric shapes – triangles and hexagons and stars all floating on an ocean of black and gray. My head gradually loosens and I can feel my forehead and eyeballs without recoiling in pain. That's when the doorbell rings.

I'm tempted to ignore it, but I stand up shakily. The UPS driver in his brown suit seems surprised to see me, or perhaps I look strange as I open the door and squint in the light.

His eyebrows lift. "Dr. Robert Thames?"

"Yes."

"Could you sign here?"

I could go months without scrawling my signature on a document, and now I've done it twice in a few hours. I sign the form and watch as he removes three large boxes from the truck on a dolly and carries them up the short flight of stairs. My apartment has only one bedroom, an office, a living room, kitchen and den. The hallway from the door connects it all together. The boxes are too big to fit in my office. They're each about the size of a large microwave.

"Where would you like them?" he asks.

"What are they?"

He smiles and pats the stack. "Boxes."

I peer closer. My name has been clearly typed on the labels. The origin is Danvers, New Hampshire. I don't know anyone at Danvers who would be sending me packages now, unless someone found an old trunk from the high school I attended forty years ago. Maybe they're old clothes, a typewriter, or posters from my Danvers dorm room.

"Just leave them here in the hall," I say. There's no storage space in my apartment.

After the UPS man leaves, I lock the door and go back to bed. I dream about my childhood in the Philippines, my years at Danvers, my old friends from high school, and my colleagues at the office. It is a strange jumble of past and present with unresolved anxieties and problems that often accompany my migraine headaches. I've learned to slow my breathing, close my eyes, and let the present fade into the past where I can view it safely from a distance. I sleep as if the day never happened.

A few hours later, I wake up and check the hallway. Sometimes during a migraine, I have vivid hallucinations and imagine events that never took place. I wonder if the boxes might be one of them. But they are still standing by the front door. I find a sharp knife in the kitchen and cut through the tape on the top box. Inside are multiple sheaves of paper with cardboard dividers. I pull some out. They're reports – quite old by the look of the typing and the faded color of paper. The names seem familiar. I look through several until I recognize a few – former classmates at Danvers Academy.

I push the tower of boxes away from the front door and against the wall. The boxes are heavier than I imagined.

I haven't thought about or visited Danvers for years. It's not an intentional disregard for the place, because it helped me succeed in college and medical school. It's just that I had never really fit in; I hardly qualified as a traditional prep school student, having grown up in the Philippines. I made few friends, except some boys I played cards with on weekends. Even they had dispersed like billiard balls at the break, speeding off in different directions in search of some promised corner pocket. We all knew our friendships might be transient and sacrificed to the exigencies of our future education and other opportunities, just as they were limited by the daily centripetal forces of assignments, tests and grades.

When I arrived at Danvers as a fifteen-year-old, I spoke with an accent that the other boys mimicked, mispronouncing words and laughing at me. I worked hard at losing that accent, so as not to stick out more than I already did. Unlike most of the Danvers boys, I had dark skin. Not exactly black, but coffee colored – definitely not white – and I was neither tall nor muscular. I had no unique athletic talents which might have led me to befriend recruited athletes. I was a quiet, small, studious, international student, a relative anomaly at Danvers, which had a tradition of preparing the children of the American wealthy and cultured classes for future leadership. I was tolerated like an exotic herb in the garden, allowed to exist and contribute some unique aroma as long as I did not threaten the carefully tended plants and flowers around me. There were a few others like me – the African Americans, the Jews, Chinese, Latinos and the other members of the "diversity" club from India or Saudi Arabia – to demonstrate to the outside world that Danvers was forward-thinking and inclusive. I was the only Filipino.

I suppose Danvers served a purpose in classifying and developing our talents and sorting us for placement into a proper college. It was a dialysis system for America's elite colleges, removing those who would not succeed, further purifying us as we soaked up the rules, values, and skills necessary for admission to an esteemed undergraduate college and later, law, business, or medical school. Most of the boys at Danvers came from private elementary schools or elite public schools with programs and courses that fit like puzzle pieces into the Danvers curriculum. In between classes, they discussed golf or skiing or their vacation homes on the Cape; they could not imagine a life that lacked such essentials. But the boys I got to know at Danvers were mostly like me: intense strivers from the lower rungs of society, trying to climb out of our social class by working harder than our privileged classmates. We met through required scholarship jobs in the dining halls – washing dishes, serving ice cream, cleaning tables. We acknowledged each other with a nod on the pathways between classes, a silent gaze into each other's eyes; we had little time to talk or socialize.

I could not imagine why anyone from Danvers would send me anything. I never wrote notes to the alumni magazine about my achievements, and I had no wife or children to advertise, no books to promote. My articles about plants that might provide the next antibiotic were published in esoteric infectious disease journals of no interest to my former classmates. I was not a very good alumnus, only donating $50 to the annual fund, but at least I was consistent.

I have always prided myself on consistency. I am the turtle in the race with the hare – slow but sure, a long distance runner – able to endure frustration and failure and delay gratification to achieve my goals. I am not the type of person who gets noticed in a crowd, and so I have to wait until the competition thins. I become visible and make an impression through loyalty and hard work. As I stand leaning over the boxes wondering what to do next my back begins to ache, and I grab a chair out of the kitchen so that I can sit comfortably as I explore the boxes and consider their contents.

It's not as if I never veered off the path back at Danvers. It was difficult, day after day and week after week, to maintain a focus on a prize that was years away and might never arrive. I played cards on Saturday nights – mostly bridge – when I should have been studying, sometimes late into the night, and even gambled for money. My parents would not have approved, but I have always enjoyed card games, and I am quite good at them. The boys I played with shared the same zeal for games even though we were otherwise quite different. I would read books about bridge and study the games of experts when I should have been studying for my classes because I enjoyed the beauty of a well-played hand. For me, it was almost as much about the aesthetics as the winning, and I had so few other opportunities to appreciate beauty at Danvers that the card games became my escape. I sometimes feared that it was becoming an addiction that might endanger my other goals, and tried to resist the urge to participate in bridge and other games through an exercise of will power. Will power was something I learned from my mother, who believed that through denial of our desires we develop moral strength.

Now I feel the need to pace, and I get up from the chair and walk into my kitchen. I pour myself a glass of apple juice which I find can prevent the dehydration that can accompany my migraines. I walk back to the boxes and sit down again, sipping my juice. As I think back about Danvers, I realize that I was not a typical Danvers student. We all yearned for beautiful girlfriends who would orbit us like planets until we pulled one into our gravitational field and established a passionate relationship. I've had relationships with women who were beautiful, intelligent, creative, and compassionate. Really, they were perfect. And yet I broke up with them, and I don't know why. One day we were laughing and holding hands, and the next we were fighting and crying. This made me avoid close commitment. I never understood when or why it suddenly ruptures into a toxic spray of invectives and recriminations instead of love and harmony. I would make it worse with my own sudden outbursts of anger out of frustration. These vacillations of my emotions were like the ocean tides that can become wild during a storm and overrun a beach, snatching up houses and carrying them off to the sea only to resume the normal quiet pattern a few days later. Is the ocean responsible for what it does during a storm? Aren't the waves that crash onto the beach expressing the laws of their own nature? It's not as if I meant to be misleading, mean, or dishonest. Perhaps it is just part of Filipino culture to be romantic and not confront a pending conflict head on, or perhaps it was my own survival skill, absorbing criticism without responding and then running in the opposite direction. I always, eventually, retreated to a familiar and safe solitude – my books and music – apologized for any pain I might have inflicted, and swore to avoid such commitments in the future – until the next time it happened.

Now I play card games online with people named Overlord and

Yaz67 and Boris7 who could be from anywhere in the world – old or young, male or female – I don't mind. I have watched my friends suffer through divorce, or struggle to pay for college education for their children, or complain about the lack of time to read a book because of social commitments. Certainly there are times like today when it would be enjoyable to have a wife for the support she would provide, but I usually prefer the peace and silence of my home and the choice to walk out my door and down to the street and meet women from all over the world.

I suppose my Eurasian looks are part of the attraction for women. I'm "exotic"; they can't quite place me. I have slightly angulated eyes, smooth skin, brown wavy hair, an aquiline nose, and a cleft jaw. I could be from Istanbul or Kiev, Manila or Caracas. At times I have stared at my face in the mirror and asked myself, "Who are you? Where did you come from? Where are you going?" because I feel that question in the eyes of others as they observe me.

At Danvers, being different meant not being one of them – the boys from wealthy families in Connecticut or New York with pale skin, ruddy cheeks, and blond hair. I tried to downplay my differences, talk like them, and cut my hair like them. Perhaps I was accustomed to adapting because my parents did not look like me, and growing up I would notice our differences in photographs or when I stood in front of a mirror with them. My father had a round, pink face, puffy green eyes, and thin blond hair. He had bald areas just above the forehead that became red and scaly and always seemed to be peeling off like the skin of an onion. Sometimes children at the clinics would cry when they saw his face. He was a general practitioner in a small missionary hospital in the southern Philippines, and we would visit villages in the Jeep. During our trips to the villages he would let me help put on bandages after he had sewn up a cut, and once, after I helped him, he suggested that I might become a doctor too. When I agreed that I would like to be like him, he said that I would need to study harder, but that maybe someday I could go away to a school in America that would prepare me for medical school.

When I told my mother about the conversation, she rubbed my hair and told me how sweet I was and how much she loved me. But she worried that the medical training might be too much for me, that there were years and years of schooling and tests that piled up like too many people trying to cross a foot bridge that could collapse. I had seen that once with my dad at one of the villages near a river. The foot bridge hung in two pieces from the sides of a cliff and there were bodies at the bottom with bags of rice and jackfruit strewn on the ground. I did not want to turn out like one of those bodies that overloaded the bridge.

Mother had very pale, almost translucent skin that reminded me of the jellyfish that would sometimes wash ashore after a storm. She always kept covered in white and gray silk shawls, white cotton blouses, and blue or green skirts. This was her daily uniform, which she only altered on Sunday when she wore a long charcoal dress. She complained about mosquito bites and how they itched, and she would scratch them and raise red and bluish bruises and scabs in spite of Father's admonitions. Her head turned like an owl's, always watching me. Her pouty red lips gave her face a dour, unhappy expression most of the time, but it could suddenly open, like an Origami cut-out, into a great smile when I came home from school with an A or she won a bridge hand. She kept her hair in a bun on top of her head because once a beetle had flown into her hair and gotten tangled in it, buzzing and flapping its wings, causing her to curse for the first time in her life.

Mother taught English to some of the women and helped them read the Bible. She instructed them on cleanliness, hand washing, cooking, and hygiene. I also became one of her projects. She taught me to read stories and psalms like "The Lord is my shepherd, I shall not want," which I could recite to her before bedtime by the time I was five years old.

Sometimes even now I find myself repeating a psalm without thinking, and I wonder if it is my mother calling out to me from the grave. I suppose my religious training was of some value: It taught me discipline and the importance of patience and delayed gratification. But I have not been to church in more than 25 years, not since my parents died. I have watched too much random tragedy to believe there is a purpose to suffering or a god who would allow it.

Dr. and Mrs. Thames adopted me after my real parents died when I was a year and a half old. They described my arrival in biblical terms, like Moses floating down the river to them to achieve God's greater purpose. They had no children of their own. I don't know whether infertility or some sexual incompatibility affected them. I regarded my presence in the family like any fortunate pet adopted into a wealthy family – with cautious relief and constant vigilance against the moment I might be returned or replaced by something newer or better. I was happy to work for my treats, the little candies my mother would give me when I completed my studies or chores. As it was, they set the bar high for me. Mother was more uncertain about my prospects, but Father would laugh at her and tell her that good doctors only needed to be able to hear the melodies and rhythms of the body and coax them along when they got out of tune. He thought I had an ear for the music of medicine. His confidence in my capabilities helped me persevere during the many times when I felt like giving up at Danvers and later in college and medical school.

I'm not sure how I would have felt about my real parents if they had been alive. My biological father was an American soldier who died in a motorcycle crash shortly after I was born, and my mother was a teacher with some mix of Malay, Chinese, and Spanish blood, like most Filipinas. In the Philippines, female teachers would sometimes supplement their salaries by hosting tourists or visiting soldiers, and that was what my mother might have been doing. But I'm not sure; her family never contacted me, and I was never able to find out about them. So my real mother is a fantasy that I have created, based upon the known fragments of her life and the limitations of topics in our home. I was brought up with strict taboos about discussing anything sexual – kissing, petting, nudity. And yet personal hygiene and cleanliness were part of our household rules.

The Thameses discouraged questions about my real parents, as if such information might tarnish the imprinting and loyalty they had carefully been nurturing. But I did learn that my real mother died of some kind of sickness – pneumonia or TB – and that she had no family, only a grandmother who died when I was still a baby. I remember that Mother let some information slip out when I came home after drinking Philippine coconut wine called Tuba with a neighbor boy when I was thirteen.

"Do you want to turn out like your parents?" she had demanded.

I was too sick from vomiting to say much at the time, but later I got her to tell me parts of my history: My father was very handsome and popular with his military friends and the local women, and my mother worked in one of the clubs on the weekends as a hostess. They lived together for a while, and then he had a motorcycle accident after drinking at the bar and died. When I was born, my mother almost died from the labor and never fully recovered her strength. She got to know the Thameses from her frequent visits to their clinic. She suggested the idea of my adoption one day after a visit with Dr. Thames because he told her that God was going to take her soon. My real mother had no other family who could take me and somehow my adoption by the Thameses became a part of God's plan.

When you're adopted, your new parents do not want to take responsibility for your mistakes and bad behaviors. They blame them on your genetics. So you're constantly adjusting your identity to conform to the expectations of your adoptive parents and trying to anticipate and repair the genetic flaws that might make you unacceptable. You become an expert at shapeshifting and storytelling. I continued this behavior at Danvers and in college. The women I have known have sometimes complained that they never knew who I really was, so they could not trust me or know if I was capable of loving them. For a while I tried therapy to understand what they meant and to see if I could learn how to have a real long term relationship. But my relationships seemed to become shorter and shorter over time until now I have become used to my solitude, platonic friendships with women, and the occasional, intermittent companions I meet on foreign trips or here at clubs and bars.

I once visited a psychiatrist. He wanted me to regress to my infancy and try to imagine emerging from my mother's womb and visualize my real parents at that moment. He thought that it would begin to cure my instinct to camouflage myself like a chameleon and help me to discover what was really true and constant and unique about me. He said that was why I had never experienced true love; I was always hiding, seeking cover like an animal on the lookout for predators. But I decided against the therapy, mostly because I have been content with my life and molding myself into whatever people around me want me to be.

I have great respect for the people who adopted me. They stretched my horizons far beyond anything that might have been possible for me with my real parents. The Thameses believed in me and set aside money for my private school and college education. They were the only parents I ever knew and I loved them very much. Many years later, when they died in a car wreck in the Philippines, I didn't know if I could go on living. I received a letter from Father's brother a few weeks later, describing the will and my inheritance. I received enough money for my medical school training and a Bible that contained some baby pictures. He invited me to visit him and his family in Oregon, but we never found a good time.

I thought that if I could be a success, it would be the best way I could honor my parents.

It all went well enough, except now I am facing the loss of my job, and I'm afraid that their spirits might become unsettled and unmoored and begin to wander, as spirits sometimes can, according to our native beliefs in the Philippines. It is not that I believe in these superstitions, but I have heard stories during my travels that sometimes make me wonder.

2

I put down my glass of apple juice, got up from my chair and began to explore the boxes. I pulled upon the flaps of the boxes and started to rummage through musty papers in cardboard folders. I examined them with the same curiosity and caution I felt when I found exotic plant specimens on my foreign travels.

In each folder was a report that described the student's measurements: ratio of shoulders to torso and waist; waist to the length of the legs; distance between the eyes and length of the face. At the end was an endomorphy score, a mesomorphy score, and an ectomorphy score ranging from 1 to 7. While the scores meant nothing to me, I had some vague recollections of "endomorphy," "mesomorphy," and "ectomorphy" classifications from a college psychology class; the different body types presumably correlated to personality traits. It all seemed quaint and out of date, and I could not help but wonder why anyone would waste their time collecting this kind of information.

Next was a summary of the history of the boy's life prior to attending Danvers Academy, his progress through Danvers, and finally, a summary of subsequent achievements and milestones – college graduation, marriage, occupation, children, and so on. I quickly paged through the folder without reading any of the details. The folder in my hand belonged to a boy who attended Danvers Academy from 1965 to 1968, the same time that I had attended. Finally, on a separate page were photographs of the boy standing face front, side, and back. He was completely nude. I felt a cold chill of recollection when I looked at the photo. His name was typed above the picture: Howard Aaronson. His face was serious, vulnerable, tense – a bird caught in a net, awaiting its fate. His body was that of an adolescent – acne on his neck and chest, pubic hair, football bruises. Though I never shared any classes with him, I remembered he was at the beginning of the alphabet, the first name they called out in assembly, the boy at the front of the line.

It had happened to me, too – the embarrassment of nudity as I undressed in front of the curious eyes of my classmates, a flash of a camera like lightning in the night, a sudden blindness, sideways turn, another flash, and then one more before dressing and fleeing back to class as if nothing had happened. I never discussed the photographs with my classmates, and gradually I forgot about them.

But now they had returned, like dead bodies washed up on a shore. I looked at the boxes for some explanation and found an envelope taped to the inside of one of them. It had my name on it. Inside was a letter.

Dear Robert,

I hope this letter finds you well. I wish I had been able to contact you personally before sending you these files, but time was short. Recently, some events have forced my hand. By now you may have guessed that these records represent a research study. It is a study I have been working on for more than 40 years. I have always taken the utmost care to follow the original protocol and have maintained complete confidentiality until now.

I suppose I owe you an explanation. As you know, your father and I were classmates at Harvard Medical School, and before that we knew each other at Danvers, even though I was a year ahead of him. When I considered becoming a site investigator for the study originator, Dr. William Sheldon, I contacted your father. I told him about the study, and he agreed to collaborate with me. As you may remember, he had published several articles about tropical rashes he identified while working in the Philippines. I was looking for some general advice about research and backup in case something happened to me; my data needed to be protected. (It was something they suggested in the research protocol.) As you will see, the material in these files is quite sensitive and could be damaging in the wrong hands.

I sent your father updates every year or two, and he would write back with ideas and general encouragement. We maintained our contact for years until he and your mother died in that terrible accident. After that I was on my own. In the meantime, the funding for the study ran out and the original team retired or passed away. Most sites stopped collecting information and returned what they had gathered, but I kept going. The work of keeping it up was not much, just scanning the newspapers and alumni bulletins for the three years of boys in our files. Then came the Internet, which made things so much easier. I began to notice recurrent patterns – boys who had encountered disciplinary difficulty at Danvers losing jobs or getting arrested later in life. Every year I picked about 20 or so boys and tried to find information on them to fill in the gaps. I have never been one to give up on a difficult project, whether it is looking through rolls of pennies to complete a collection, weeding a garden, or pursuing a rare and complicated diagnosis.

In any case, the original research team forgot about me. I probably should have contacted them, but it was such a part of my daily routine to go down to the basement and review the files that I continued to collect information over the years. It was a fascinating avocation. I intended to summarize my findings and submit an article for publication, but never quite got around to it with all my other responsibilities. I kept the files locked in my basement and there was no problem until now, as my wife and I prepared to move to a smaller space in assisted living.

The study involves the measurement of physical attributes of students, documented in photographs. The goal was to predict personality and life events and achievements based upon these physical measurements. There were sites at Ivy League colleges like Harvard, Yale, and Cornell, but I believe we were the only prep school. We thought this could be a powerful predictive tool: No longer would a student pursue unobtainable goals and become depressed and perhaps suicidal when he failed. I have seen many such cases over the years. I wanted to prevent those outcomes with objective, scientific predictions. Using specific formulas, we could direct students to their best suited opportunities. It might also help us select students who would benefit from the Danvers experience and become future world leaders. Entrance examinations only predict academic and intellectual potential. But there are other important characteristics like courage, honesty, perseverance, self-sacrifice, and manliness that contribute to leadership and success, and we were looking for the clues to those parts of a boy's character in the measurements.

Every year I have attempted to update the files. Some of my updates are quite recent, within the last few years. Others are out of date. You might be surprised how you boys keep track of each other and disseminate information on your own web pages. I must admit I have enjoyed peering under the rocks and soil of the little gardens all you boys keep. I can honestly say that I have discovered something interesting about almost every one of our subjects. While many of the successful boys fit the profile for high achievers, there have been outliers who were also successful. Sometimes those outliers formed a cluster like you and your friends who played cards together.

Last year my wife fell and broke her hip. Our children have been encouraging us to move into an assisted living facility, and I had resisted, partly because I knew I would not be able to take the files with me. After so many years those files and those boys have become like family. (I suppose I should have converted them to electronic files, but I have not had any help and frankly I have never trusted computers.)

When I tried to secure a private, locked cabinet for the files in the campus library, problems came to a head. I received a telephone call from the President of the Board of Trustees, asking me questions about the nature of the project and whether I had institutional permissions to undertake such research. He wanted me to bring in all of the files for a legal review. Imagine! After 40 years they wanted to see the documentation of institutional review. (Of course we followed all of the regulations that existed at the time, but times change.) I also realized that they would not understand the need for absolute confidentiality. Some of the material could be embarrassing or even lead to blackmail. Information about drugs, sexual deviancy, discipline, and depression sometimes ended up in those files. Things went on in those days that are best kept quiet. I knew I had to do something to protect the files. That's when I thought of you, Robert. You are my dear colleague's son, a Danvers alumnus, and a researcher in your own right.

Should you feel unable to accept my invitation to keep the files and complete the research, I request that you burn everything contained in the boxes. I would not want to risk these files falling into the wrong hands. Although it would be a terrible loss, it would be preferable to compromising the confidential material.

I also would suggest that you read up on the work of William Sheldon, who identified somatotypes and who was the inspiration and leader for this research. Sheldon is much misunderstood these days, so I think you may need to go back to the source material. He developed the somatotypes that you have no doubt heard about – the thin sensitive, ectomorph; the overweight, jovial, lazy endomorph; and the muscular, energetic, decisive mesomorph. But these are the extremes. He thought everyone had a component of each element and that it could be measured with photographs of the body. Through these measurements we could identify personality, future achievement, and opportunities for leadership. (He even could identify an animal that reminded him of the somato-type – insects, dogs, lions, seals, elephants – as a sort of short hand to remember the characteristics of the somatotype. He seemed to have one for every somatotype. It made it easy to remember them, and I began to think of each boy as his ani-mal somatotype when I read the files.) His theory was criti-cized because it was far too simplistic and deterministic. No one wants to believe that their fate is sealed from birth. How-ever, no one said the basic idea was wrong.

My interpretation – which goes somewhat beyond Shel-don – is that the somatotypes are not tight, constricting molds, but, rather, costumes that can stretch like elastic to fit our individual variations and circumstances.

Well, I have gone on and on, far more than I intended. I suppose it is due to not having discussed any of this with any-one for so many years. I don't want to leave out important details. Please handle these files carefully and with utmost confidentiality. I look forward to hearing from you.

With best wishes for a fruitful collaboration and contri-bution to the future of science,

Sincerely,

Harold Hart, MD 603-828-5911

As I read the letter, I was tempted to laugh and throw the boxes in the trash. Why would anyone spend years studying the lives of Danvers boys? Why would someone weigh and measure us unless they were recruiting for an athletic team? But after a while I suc-cumbed to my curiosity and began to scan through the files. The lives of my friends and former classmates were open to me, but how much did I want to know about them? For some students whom I barely knew, I would be an innocent voyeur looking through an oddly shaped window. For others, with whom I had some familiarity, I might learn some interesting facts that would add dimensions to the faded memories I had of them, and perhaps encourage me to contact them and renew our friendships. And for still others, my closer friends, I might explore the fading of our friendships, and whether they might yet be coaxed back to life.

As I ripped open more boxes I realized I was also angry. I could feel the tension in my arms and hands as I grasped the cardboard edges and tore through the resistance of tape and paper. My head began to pound as I thought about the letter. I was furious at being an unwitting participant in a research project that had never been explained to any of us – stripped naked, the truth hidden from us. I remembered all the times at Danvers when decisions about us were made without our assent – our bedtimes, our visitors, our food, the privacy of our dorm rooms. But those photographs were the worst. Some Filipinos believe that part of their souls can be captured in a photograph. Even if I did not completely believe the superstition, I wondered who had looked at my photograph and what they had surmised. I imagined my classmates would feel the same way if they learned that the pictures from our first weeks at Danvers had been part of a cryptic, undisclosed study. There had been no consent process, no explanations to our parents, no awareness of the shame it would cause. The research had all been covert, and was still concealed. The pain in my head got worse as I got angrier.

I should have stopped right then. But I felt there must be some reason these boxes had come to me now. It was the same kind of curiosity and intuition that drove me forward on my quests for medicinal plants hidden among the weeds and refuse, and led me to my discoveries. And now I had to find out the reason these boxes of files had come into my life. As I pondered what to do, I found my own file, and suddenly I was no longer thinking like a researcher but as the subject of the research. I imagined Dr. Hart studying me like I was some kind of insect under the microscope and how surprised he might have been at the venom welling up in my mouth.

3

The subject of a research project can be probed, dissected, stimulated, and analyzed, and he is supposed to endure this without complaint. I had learned this during my medical training, when I cared for people with cancer on experimental protocols. Sometimes the subjects of research benefited from an experimental drug, but there were other subjects who received placebos. Their role was to demonstrate the natural course of a disease. There were African-American men with syphilis who never received treatment, while White patients got antibiotics. While this might have been scientifically useful, it was morally wrong. No one informed the African-American men about the possibility of treatment.

The report began with my name, date of birth, and a page with my photograph – front, side, and back views. As I studied the photograph, I began to sweat and my stomach began to churn, just as it had on that day. I looked so young, small, and helpless without my clothes. I had tried to blot out the memory of the photographs all these years, but now the shame flooded back. The report went on to describe my body.

The ratio of my wingspan to height was 1.01. This meant my arms from fingertip to fingertip were almost identical to my height. The distance between my eyes was 7 cm and the width of my head was 14 cm; my head length was 23 cm and the ratio of face length to face width was 1.64; the ratio or my forearm to hand was 1.6, and the ratio of my shoulders to my pelvis was 1.11. The ratio of my arms to legs was .83. I had no idea what the ratios meant and whether they indicated anything important, but they made me think about the people who studied my photograph and did the measurements. I wondered what they might have been thinking as they observed my body. Did I have the body of a cook? A waiter? A bank teller? What did they think I was meant to be?

An equation incorporated the measurements into a score for endomorphy-3, mesomorphy-3, and ectomorphy-4. As I understood it, these were assessments of the amount of fatty tissue, muscle, and nervous tissue and were presented in a range of 1 for low and 7 for high, based upon the measurements and an examination of my photograph. There was also a narrative description of my body: "Narrow facial bone structure with Oriental-shaped eye lids and orbits. Good facial symmetry and length to width ratio; symmetric eyes, narrow Roman nose and Semitic mouth, square jaw with cleft. Wavy brown scalp hair consistent with Arabic or Semitic origins. Body hair is typical of normal adolescent male distribution. Chest and shoulders narrow but appropriate width for height. Legs and buttocks more typical of Caucasian with ample subcutaneous tissue and mass. Genitals, Tanner 4. Posture loose and moderately straight. Overall impression: normally proportioned Eurasian male with appropriate physical development for age. Aesthetically above average with symmetric, masculine facial features and proportional body dimensions: 334.

Somatotype (Rabbit).

As I read this evaluation of my physical attributes, I felt an odd relief at having scored above average on aesthetics. Even though I knew that the assessment had no merit, I still cared about my score. At Danvers they taught us to care about our scores, regardless of the purpose, and never to be below average on any scale. Although we are born with our bodies, exercise, clothes, and grooming could improve our appearance. I have always attempted to improve my aesthetic impression with proper clothing selection and attention to hygiene and grooming. Even in college, when my friends had long, unkempt hair and wore torn jeans, I kept my hair combed and neat and my clothes clean and pressed. But I was still surprised to find myself aesthetically above-average in the analysis. I had always considered the blond, blue-eyed Danvers football player types to be the aesthetic model to which we should all aspire. I recall quickly dressing and escaping from the gym locker room after our workouts, lest I be unfavorably compared to my classmates. The reference to a Semitic or Arabic origin was curious, as I had considered myself Filipino. We Filipinos pride ourselves on the mix of races that has created our unique beauty. Perhaps I had a Spanish Moor ancestor? The Tanner score I remembered vaguely from my medical school pediatrics rotation as an evaluation of sexual maturity, with 1 meaning no pubertal signs and 5, complete adult maturation. A Tanner 4 seemed fair enough to me, a passing grade, though I probably would have liked to have a 5. I was not sure what a somatotype of "334" or "Rabbit" indicated, but Dr. Hart in his letter had mentioned that each boy had an animal associated with his somatotype. What did it mean to be a rabbit? I thought of rabbits as timid, with big ears, always on alert for a fox or dog. Now I stroked my ears and imagined the life of a rabbit.

A brief history followed the measurements and scores.

"Robert Thames was born in the Philippines, the product of an American soldier and a Philippine school teacher, both deceased. The American soldier (A. Berenson–Jewish) died in an accident shortly after Robert's birth. The mother died of medical complications of pneumonia, possibly tuberculosis. Robert was adopted and raised by American medical missionaries, Dr. and Mrs. Robert Thames. Dr. Thames is an alumnus of Danvers."

I paused in my reading as I pondered the information about my biological parents. Dr. Hart had included this information as part of his scientific data collection; he had known more about me than most students because of his friendship to my father. Yet he had never discussed any of this with me. He did not know that I had often wondered how different my life might have been if I had been raised by my real parents. Who was A. Berenson? I had known a student named Berenson in medical school. Perhaps we were related. He was Jewish and wore a small cap on his head. I had met some Jews at Danvers and later in college and medical school. They were supposed to be intelligent and studious. If I had known I was part Jewish, perhaps I might have worn one of those yarmulke caps and had more confidence in my potential for success. As it was, I always expected my brain to become overloaded and overheated by the demands of my studies.

"Robert grew up in the Philippines. He came to Danvers at the age of 15 after home schooling and attendance at Filipino and American schools. His initial grades at Danvers were marginal due to poor preparation, but he improved to graduate in the upper half of his class and gain admittance to Yale, and later, Tufts Medical School. He participated in protests against the war at Yale and went to Ecuador for an elective in international health in medical school, which led to his career in global health."

These few sentences hardly captured the terror of those initial weeks at Danvers when I thought I would fail my courses. I would hide in my closet at night after the lights-out curfew with a small light bulb illuminating my books, sheets stuffed under the closet door so that Mr. Shangly, our dorm faculty member, would not catch me studying after hours. I felt marooned on an island surrounded by sharks and monsoons, waiting for rescue but unsure who or what could save me. I had few friends until I found the boys in our card room. We would gather on weekends for some serious bridge and discuss money and girls, the most painful ways to die, or how the world would end – fire or ice. Regarding my visit to Ecuador, I never would have made that jump to global health doctor, but perhaps the researchers knew more than I did.

"At Danvers, he was noted to have a quiet, simple, cooperative personality similar to many of our other Oriental students. He completed his assignments on time and graduated with distinction in Latin. He participated in track and cross country at the junior varsity level. He was active in the Bridge Club and Chess Club. He had no behavioral or disciplinary problems, although he was a witness in the investigation of a Rule 7 violation with a young woman. The perpetrator, Mr. Steven Thompson, took full responsibility for the incident. Robert also participated in the Racial Understanding and Improvement Committee as a Vice Chairman, where he helped to develop guidelines for improving campus interracial communications."

I supposed my participation in the RUIC group helped me and the others get into a good college, though it was purely by chance – my bridge playing partners and I never discussed race or politics during our card games. But I read the reference to Steven Thompson with some trepidation, because even after forty years, I was still embarrassed at my complicity in the official version of what happened that night.

"After medical school, Robert pursued Internal Medicine, and then trained in infectious diseases at Mass General. Following his Fellowship, he joined the U.S. Public Health Service working for the Indian Health Service in Shiprock, New Mexico, for two years before joining the Centers for Disease Control in Atlanta, later moving to Washington, D.C. to join the Agency for International Development in the area of infection control and identification of new medication to combat multidrug resistant organisms. He travels around the world collecting specimens for future biochemical analysis, and is known for his mastery of indigenous cultures, multiple languages, and ability to communicate with native healers in identifying promising biological specimens. He is credited with identification of the recent class of drugs being used for methicillin resistant staphylococcal infection. He has also identified plants with activity against malaria."

I appreciated Dr. Hart's assessment of my contribution to malaria research and the development of new antibiotics; our lab was far more critical of my efforts. I wished that Mr. Grundel had done as complete a job of researching my contributions before dismissing them. I have always tried to contribute in some way to improving the lives of others, even if by chance, while I focused on surviving the various challenges life has set for me. My father would have enjoyed reading that part about me.

"He lives in Washington, D.C. He is not married and has no children. His health has apparently been good with only occasional migraine headaches and lumbar disc disease." How did he find out all of this information about my health issues? It was one more invasion of my privacy on top of all the others. Dr. Hart was supposed to be a friend, but his notes were cold, clinical, and without any emotion or signs of friendship. As I considered Dr. Hart's notes, I realized that I never wanted to be responsible for bringing children into the world, as they would add another obstacle to the safe and comfortable life always eluding me; it was an issue that my parents sometimes mentioned when they were alive. They had worried about who would take care of me when they were gone. They even offered to help find me a Filipina wife from a good family.

"The somatotype analysis suggests timidity, caution, and a tendency toward intellectual pursuits to compensate for a relatively under-muscled body type. He would have a preference for thinking rather than acting. His high success in medical school and in the public health service is a somewhat unanticipated result based upon our model. We would have predicted a lower technical and leadership level position such as nursing, where he would be directed by others. Although his body is underendowed for leadership, his good aesthetics and racial mix make interpretation of somatotypes difficult, and the high aesthetics could have compensated for the lower mesomorphy score and provided opportunities for leadership and advancement. We are also surprised at his perseverance in the face of adversity, which included the loss of his adopted parents during medical school, and his difficult academic transition at Danvers. His high perseverance trait and ability to delay gratification of his needs has undoubtedly contributed to his success, but could also lead to commitment to a hopeless cause. He might have difficulty adjusting to an adverse employment decision or job elimination."

I paused as I considered these comments. Was my current reaction to my job situation a reflection of certain genetic attributes? When I was younger, I had always been alert to threats and danger and was prepared to quickly react – smile, hide, negotiate – whatever was required to overcome a problem. Over the years I had let those skills atrophy, and grown more complacent with my life as I demonstrated loyalty and steadfastness to my employers – attributes they seemed to value. Did I have the versatility and confidence to adjust now?

"It is unclear whether he should be classified in the Asian subgroup or the Caucasian group subtype, Semitic. Students with mixed genetic contributions do not fit easily into the Sheldon categories and prognostications may be of lesser reliability. Robert was also noted to have a large mole on his back during the analysis of his photograph that may require medical follow-up."

As I read about the mole, I remembered visiting a dermatologist during medical school to make sure I did not have a melanoma on my back. The dermatologist explained that what I had was a typical medical student's anxiety about contracting diseases covered in my classes and that the mole was a large, benign nevus. One woman who had seen the mole after an intimate night suggested it looked like South America and suggested we travel to Rio for Carnivale.

Finally, the report concluded: "Robert Thames has achieved at a somewhat higher level than expected, most likely because of his focus on individual accomplishments, rather than long-term committed relationships with others. Based upon his physical profile and past experience, it would appear that such relationships might upset the delicate balance of the life he has constructed, and could create tensions that endanger the structure of his personality. Similarly, a sudden job change or retirement could create a cascade of mental and physical instability. He would likely resist such a change."

I dropped the report into my lap and stared out the window. Was I really so fragile and vulnerable, so flawed and damaged that I was constantly on the verge of collapse? Was it just luck that I could credit, a fortuitous lottery number against the odds? I shook my head and pounded the side of the box with my hand. Even now, years after leaving Danvers, the judgements about me from the study made me doubt myself and the decisions that had guided my life. Had I chosen a somewhat monastic, lonely life because I sensed that my body could not sustain love, family, and friendship? I never remembered making such a conscious choice, although I had moments of longing when I considered reconnecting with old friends like my bridge playing group. But I had foregone such activities as much out of laziness as self-preservation. And I felt that I got all of the social interaction I needed during my frequent travels and loose liaisons with various friends and colleagues at work and on the Internet. I reread the comments about the effects of a job change or retirement and wondered if they were true. I guess I was about to find out.

The report continued: "Based upon our analysis of the somatotype measurements and his past experiences, we predict that Robert will continue his solitary lifestyle without family attachments. He will resist any employment changes and maintain a stable position, even to his own detriment. We predict a normal life span with some increased health risks from exposure to infectious diseases and the stress of a solitary life style."

I sat there in my hall on the chair where had I started reading. My legs cramped up when I tried to straighten them. I rubbed my hands over my eyes and the back of my neck to massage away the lancinating pains of the migraine. Once I had begun reading, I had not even moved to the comfortable couch in the living room where I read my journals and books. As I stood, I felt nauseous – about to vomit – although I wasn't sure if this was due to my migraine or my file. I wondered how the other Danvers alumni would feel about their photographs and predictions.

As I settled on the living room couch, I thought about the way the summary had traced the various training, jobs, transitions, and promotions, as if my life had all been plotted out on a smooth, linear course. Each point seemed destined to reach the next point. But to me, there was a moat surrounding each destination. There was no hint of the apprehension I endured, wondering whether or not I would get accepted to college or medical school. I had been performing above expectations and now I understood that my anxieties were justified: I was over my head and didn't know it. I had thought the questions from the admissions interviews were because I looked different, but now I wondered about the letters of recommendation from my teachers at Danvers. I could feel the skepticism in the eyes of the college admissions officers. Were they thinking, Is he safe to become one of us? Does he have what it takes? There were so many times I felt I was teetering, about to fall. But each time, I refused to surrender to the fear. I gathered my strength, the way I would as a child when my father would stare into my eyes and chant, "Breathe, slow breath, slow breath…" to show me that if I could control my breathing, I could control my fear. Those sleepless nights before tests were torture, but I recognized them for what they were – part of the test. You had to get through the night to reach the daylight.

Yet the only recognition of the difficulties I overcame in my file was surprise at my perseverance in the face of adversity; my measurements had predicted failure or capitulation when things got difficult. In any case, I had surprised them. I had not failed. A rabbit would have hopped away at the first sign of danger, so perhaps I was not a rabbit and the somatotype theory or numbers were wrong.

Who did not have flaws? True, I had made choices to avoid the entanglements of relationships, but I had not done so consciously. I pined for my girlfriend, Sarah, for months at Danvers after we broke up, and for years later in college. A rabbit would have married her and had many children. I had navigated the rapids of my life successfully up until now by keeping low, holding fast, and avoiding the rocks. Suddenly, my head began to ache again and I closed my eyes to calm myself.

4

As I lay back on the couch, a few clusters of sparkling lights and the wave of nausea dissipated, and I began to see my room at Danvers: the single bed against the wall, the window looking out to the pathways where students would walk to class, and my desk where I would compose essays and work out math problems. Down the hall were the rooms of my classmates, but we would not usually gather in the hall or in our rooms. Mostly we would meet downstairs in the common room where we could make noise, drink Cokes, and play cards.

When I arrived at Danvers on my first day, I met the faculty advisers, Mr. and Mrs. Shangly, who gave me keys and my class schedule. Mr. Shangly taught English and anthropology and had a cherubic face with a small mustache and beard. Mrs. Shangly had deep blue eyes and a tendency to stare when talking. She taught art; her paintings hung in their apartment – canvases of red circles on white and yellow backgrounds that reminded me of my drawings as a young child. Mr. and Mrs. Shangly had recently served in the Peace Corps in New Guinea and had ceremonial masks and shields on the wall. I remember Mr. Shangly asking if I had seen such masks in the Philippines, and telling me that when you wore a mask, it was like jumping into another body.

As parents and the other advisers milled around at the introductory meeting, Mrs. Shangly explained how men in New Guinea lived in one big house, and the women and pigs lived in another. She said that sometimes the house with the pigs was cleaner than the house with the men;

she expected us to keep our rooms clean. The parents laughed and clapped, and I knew that we would all like Mrs. Shangly because she was funny. The other faculty advisers were white-haired, unmarried men who discussed algebra, Latin, and poetry as they examined my class schedule, and asked me questions like whether I had read Ovid, or could estimate the square root of two. Mr. Goodson described the Latin epics that we would be reading and put his hand on my wrist, biceps, and shoulder to demonstrate how Roman soldiers threw spears. He advised that I would need to exercise my mind as those soldiers exercised their muscles, and that as my Latin teacher, he would be there to help.

Mr. Cheadle, the assistant dean, went over the rules of conduct and the honor code: "Truth, honor, excellence, and service are the four pillars that support our school." He continued, "If one falls, the entire structure collapses. These have been our principles for 200 years. Dean Maiser has asked me go over the rules of conduct with each of you, so that there will be no questions about what is expected of you." He shook all of our hands and looked into our eyes, and we each agreed that we would follow the rules of conduct. Mr. Goodson, Mr. Cheadle, and the other faculty men stood in a shifting circle that moved around the room like hungry birds feeding on our questions and class schedules. I remember thinking that Mr. and Mrs. Shangly did not fit that group; they seemed too young and hopeful.

My first weeks at Danvers, I had no friends. During breaks in my studying, I walked through the card room and observed students playing, but I never had time to join them, and they barely noticed me. One Saturday evening after I had finished an English paper, someone got up from the table as I passed by, leaving an empty chair. The others asked if I knew how to play bridge. I nodded. Sometimes my parents had needed a fourth person if one of their invited guests got sick or my dad was called away for a medical emergency in the middle of a game. But, in fact, it was much more than that: I was obsessed with the strategy and intricacies of bidding and playing. There were opportunities for subterfuge and rewards for memory and analysis. I had read every book there was on bridge.

I sat down at the table and looked at the other players. I had seen them in the dormitory and at meals, but you could say we had little in common. Tim Washington was a football player from New York with dark ebony skin; his biceps flexed each time he picked up a card. His close cropped hair, muscular limbs, and tenacious smile reminded me of the Mr. Clean genie drawn on bottles of liquid soap. I could imagine Tim racing through our dormitory, wiping away every piece of dirt and dust like Mr. Clean, just as effortlessly as he sped down the football field with players in pursuit. We had never spoken, though we had once been in the school infirmary together. Once we started playing, he treated me as if we had always been friends. His confidence was like a shared drug; he always expected to win. He was usually my opponent, but occasionally we would play on the same team. It was everyone's respect for Tim that allowed our bridge group to lead a racial understanding teach-in, not only solving a problem for the school, but helping to assure my future.

My regular partner was Richard Burris, also known as "the smartest boy at school." Tall and thin like a skeleton, with thick glasses and curly brown hair, Richard rarely spoke to anyone outside of class. The fact that no one could understand him when he did speak added to his mystique. He once explained to me that his mind raced faster than he could verbalize his thoughts; his mouth fell hopelessly behind. During our games he would say things like, "That king… reverse finesse… would not have made any sense…of course there was back up… trivial after the jack was played," jumbled together in a torrent. After a while I began to comprehend him like a new language. Our bridge games must have helped him, because his speech gradually improved over time, although he also saw a speech therapist. He figured that he was the best player, and I was the next best, so that if the cards were normally distributed, we should usually win. When we did not, he felt there was some kind of temporary aberration in the universe, a betrayal of the logical order. I admit some pleasure at having him as a teammate, even if he was derided for his poor athletic abilities. Because he was the smartest boy at the school, the other students respected him, just as they respected anyone who was the best at anything, regardless of what or why.

The other boy in the group was Mark Harrison, a portly, ruddy faced, blond-haired boy, whose family had a long history at Danvers.

Mark's father and grandfather had been Danvers boys and Mark was following the same path. He was a skilled card player, but he hated to lose. When he did, his face turned so red I thought he might burst like an overripe tomato. Mark knew everyone, and always had gossip to share with them, particularly the boys from private day schools who knew each other. His jokes always made us laugh, though sometimes I suspected that he used humor to distract us from the game. He liked to play cards at night when the other boys walked by, so they could see that Tim Washington was his partner. Even though there was such a marked contrast in their looks and coloring, Mark and Tim made an interesting team; they both enjoyed competing in the spotlight, reveling in the attention of the crowd. They were at their best when their energy fed off of each other. At such times, my own team's logic and consistency collapsed in a heap of confusion and uncertainty.

There was also an occasional fifth member of our group, Steven Thompson. Steven and I became friends shortly after I arrived at Danvers. Initially, I thought he came to our games because of me, but after a while I realized he was drawn to the entire group. He mostly watched us and brought us Cokes. He would sit next to me or Tim and whisper advice to us. He wore the strangest clothes – a multicolored sports coat that looked like someone had sewn together patches of different-colored fabric. I could imagine it on a circus or rodeo clown. He had white pants that glowed like a spotlight and a flat French beret his parents had sent from Paris. Steven could be a very good bridge player when he concentrated. Once in a while he would substitute if one of us had to leave, but he was usually too distracted to focus on the game for long. We often offered him the chance to take our places, but he was content to sit on the sidelines. I am not sure why anyone would want to sit and watch others play cards except to learn the game, but Steven seemed perfectly content to just watch and participate in the conversations between hands.

Our group's friendship was accidental. We wanted to play cards with players of similar aptitude, just as boys might go to the park for a pickup basketball game. But that first night we jammed like jazz musicians together, creating new riffs and melodies. Bridge allows you to see how someone thinks and behaves: You get inside their head. You learn how they react to disappointment and pressure and stress. I soon learned that Tim was a risk-taker who bluffed and intimidated, while Richard was cool and calculating, never varying from the best probabilities he had calculated. I could always count on his unflappable consistency; he would comment if I deviated from standard bidding conventions or made low probability gambles. But he got flustered if Tim and Mark made up imaginary theories that contradicted what he knew to be certain. Richard did not believe in luck; there was no way to express it mathematically. Mark enjoyed reading our emotions, and he would comment upon my posture or the way I was holding my cards when I had a good hand. He based his play upon hunches and what he observed and he was usually right. I was the technician of the group, schooled on theory and the rules of the game and the approaches of all the great players. I could cite similar hands in my books and describe how Sheinwold – one of the great experts in bridge – would have played it. I liked having Richard as a partner because he didn't make careless errors, but we didn't have the creative impulse of Tim and Mark that could sometimes defeat our approach.

In between our hands we talked about our teachers, the onerous rules at school, the absence of girls, and whether we had girlfriends at home. Eventually, we talked about our families and what being away from them meant to us. Tim wanted to get a scholarship to play football at Harvard or Yale or Dartmouth. After that he wanted to play in the pros. Mark's family was pressuring him to spend a year in England before Harvard, to improve his appreciation of culture and prepare him for a possible career in politics. Even Richard eventually began to talk, though he seemed embarrassed to discuss anything about himself. I found out that Richard came from Princeton where his father was a professor of physics who had known Einstein, and his mother taught high school. He was the only child, and the family attended lectures on weekends instead of sports events.

Everyone was interested in my story, about how my parents were American missionaries in the Philippines. I didn't tell them everything. I told them the parts I thought they wanted to hear, like our Filipino love songs, and sang the words in the Cebuano language to prove it *(Na li mu ka ba sa manga sa ad ta ngano ba gyud na a ko gi sa kit mo)*. I described the beautiful women who won international beauty contests every year. I exaggerated about the girls, how many I knew, their characteristics and availability. Just like the other boys, I conjured up a girl-friend who was a potential beauty queen. I described the thousands of islands, where certain stone-aged tribes lived and practiced cannibalism, and tropical fruits with seed pods that had sweet creamy coverings like ice cream. I may have occasionally embellished because they encouraged me; sometimes people want you to fuel their fantasies. We listened to each other's stories with teenage skepticism and childlike wonder, glimpsing worlds we had not experienced ourselves, which now seemed within reach. This was the kind of mentality that Danvers fostered; many of the graduates were powerful men who had become senators, millionaires, writers, and even presidents.

Feeling the presence of my old classmates in the house, I walked back to the hall and reached into the box for the file on Tim Washington. Though my head still throbbed, the nausea was ebbing. I was curious about Tim. I knew he had gone into the professional football league after college and had played for several years. I had visited him once at a football game but there were too many people around to converse; he had waved and promised to get together outside of the locker room, but I never found him again.

The file included a news clipping of Tim Washington from his football days with a picture of him smiling broadly with teammates after winning a playoff game. I wondered how the clipping had landed in the file. Had Dr. Hart collected it? Had some alumnus sent it to Danvers? I briefly scanned the measurements of his body; his somatotype was a 2-6-2. He was a mesomorph with a high score in the second column and low scores in the others. The somatotype analysis compared him to a mountain lion – agile, athletic, strong – a hunter. That was how he seemed to me when I watched him playing football, particularly when he played defense. He would appear out of nowhere and clobber an opposing player in the open field, a lion tackling an antelope. It was also his style of play in bridge, although there was more subtlety and strategy in cards. He was six feet one and his wingspan was greater than his height. His estimated weight was 190 pounds. I could hardly imagine anyone with a body more different from my own. There were various ratios of his arms and legs and chest. I read on to the description:

"Mr. Washington is a 15-year-old Negro. He has typical Negroid features of small skull compared to body, thickness of the nasal and labial areas, high forehead, small ears, short wiry hair. He has good facial symmetry and strong jaw and lower face. His skin color is deep chocolate brown. He has a muscular torso and highly developed, muscular arms and legs. His overall body fat content is estimated at 7%. He is Tanner 5, fully developed adult male. His aesthetics are difficult to measure due to the small number of Negro males in our sample. However, based upon his facial symmetry, low body fat and highly muscular torso, we would estimate an above average aesthetic value. He would have good leadership potential in athletic endeavors and in business. However, highly mesomorphic individuals can be prone to violence and criminal activity."

When I read the comment about potential for violence and criminal activity, I wondered if it had been added because of Tim's race, as if someone had wanted to differentiate him from a mesomorphic white student who would not be prone to violence. I also noticed the terminology, "Negro, Negroid." These were terms that we no longer used. I continued reading.

"Mr. Washington successfully completed his three years at Danvers. He was recruited to Danvers primarily for his athletic talents and played on the varsity football team for all three years. He played quarterback, half back, and full back and also played in the defensive secondary. His grades were below average, but he did pass all of his courses. His behavior and social adjustment at Danvers were satisfactory.

"Mr. Washington was a leader in the Danvers initiatives for a more racially conscious campus, known as the RUIC, and became a leader of the Black Students Association of Danvers. Mr. Washington went on to a successful college career at Dartmouth and a professional football career with the Cleveland Browns. After the completion of his football career, he worked in financial services with Merrill Lynch and started the international charity Upward Movement for African youth athletes. He retired from Merrill Lynch in 2001 and has continued to build the charity and address community development and education. His charity has sponsored students from Africa to attend Danvers, and Mr. Washington has provided scholarships and mentorships to these students during and after their time at Danvers. Mr. Washington is unmarried and has no children. He now lives in Nairobi, Kenya, and Boston, Massachusetts."

As I read the summary, my first thought was that perhaps Tim had been thinking about creating the charity for a long time, even at Danvers. At the bridge table he had mentioned that he wanted to create something to assist poor Black African children. I felt sad that I had not spoken with him for years, since we were both interested in international development, and maybe I could have contributed to his project in some way.

When Tim was at Danvers, he had covered himself with a thick shell, like the padding of his football uniform, and did not want anyone to penetrate it. I suppose we all had a self-protective shell. We had each been on our own trajectory, concerned that someone might knock us off course. We had not recognized that we could boost each other forward. Struggling to emerge from our lower and middle class backgrounds, we did not recognize the power of the Danvers network like the other private school boys. Tim had asked me years ago, when we were about to graduate from Danvers, to reconvene our bridge group when we were ready to do something important together. Maybe now was the time, and the files were a sign? I had an upcoming trip to Africa and would be passing through Nairobi on my way to Tanzania. It might be possible to find Tim Washington there and talk about his charity, my job situation, and the files that filled my hallway. I suddenly realized that I missed Tim and the easy socializing that filled the space between each hand as we shuffled the cards and discussed the events of the week.

We played cards almost every weekend through our sophomore and junior years. Usually, we played for a few hours from about ten to midnight, sometimes even later. People would come by and watch for a while, and we would hear about the results of college football or basketball games, or stories about teachers drinking. Mr. and Mrs. Shangly lived just down the hall and would sometimes greet us on their way to, or from, a party. Mr. Shangly would usually watch us for a few minutes, commenting about how games and competition were important for the fabric of society in cultures around the world, and why our card games were as important as our study of math or Latin. We would nod and feel relieved that he was not critical of us for taking time away from our studies. We also enjoyed observing Mrs. Shangly as she leaned over us, looking at our cards. Mrs. Shangly, as one of the youngest and most attractive women at Danvers, was one of our favorite diversions and a lively topic of conversation for several hands after she left. We debated about which French perfume she wore – Eau Savage, Vetiver, or Y – and who among us she fancied most.

Our card table also became a fixture, a centerpiece, a social gathering point for other students, and we the sage oracles to whom they came for advice. A student would ask Tim how to intimidate a football player, or Richard to explain a physics concept. We generally welcomed such interruptions and enjoyed them as evidence of our growing status as experts and leaders.

I rubbed my eyes as I closed Tim's file and replaced it in the box. There was a faint smell of mold that made me sneeze, and I smiled as I realized that the relatives of these paper molds irritating my eyes and nose had helped me discover antibiotics and cure infections. Now they seemed to be trying to keep me from the secrets that had been buried in the pages of old files. I reached my hand into a box and I pulled out Mark's file to see what had been written about him. I was surprised at his photo in the file – the large chest and hefty bulges of stomach and buttocks normally obscured by his well-tailored jackets and pants. In the photograph, Mark expressed no signs of embarrassment. He smiled at the camera as if he were posing for a political campaign photo. But I felt ashamed for him: I could imagine the jokes and laughter if anyone were to see it. He was scored at a 5-5-2. Next to his somatotype numbers was a notation that he fit into the Sheldon category of mammoth or elephant. I could imagine him lumbering through the forest, just as he lumbered through the Danvers hallways.

He had mass, muscle, and momentum, and no one wanted to get in his way. I read:

"Mark Harrison is a 14-year-old boy. He is five feet ten inches and his weight is 190 pounds. His wing span is less than his height. He has an ovoid skull with protruding elephantine ears and straight blond hair. He has a rounded forehead with thick orbits and fleshy cheeks and chin. His light hair color gives the impression of absence of eyebrows which provides less expressive eyes than normal. He has slight facial asymmetry with increased labial fold on the right. He has moderate gynecomastia and stomach folds that are consistent with his endomorphic measurements, but he also has powerful shoulders and legs consistent with his mesomorphy. He is a Tanner 4. He has moderate acne on his face and neck consistent with his pubertal stage. His aesthetic impression is average."

I wondered which criteria Dr. Hart had used to arrive at that conclusion. Beauty and ugliness were culturally defined. In some cultures, obesity was associated with good nutrition and wealth, and thinness with malnutrition or illness. How had Dr. Hart generated an aesthetic impression for Mark? Did it have anything to do with his popularity in school and subsequent successes? Did he get extra credit for his family background, the previous generations of Harrisons who attended Danvers before him?

"Mr. Harrison is an affable young man who entered Danvers a bit younger than his peers. He became a popular participant in various clubs at Danvers, including the Young Republicans, Bridge Club, Chorus, Student Council and the Social Committee. His behavior and social adjustment were satisfactory except for minor infractions in school policy (possession of alcohol and *Playboy* magazines during his first year in residence). He was a member of the Racial Understanding and Improvement Committee that led a schoolwide initiative. He was elected class president his senior year, a position he maintained through each cycle of alumni homecomings. He attended Harvard and then Harvard Law School. He has practiced corporate law, worked at the Shawmut Bank in Hartford, and manages a small investment fund. He lives in Connecticut with his wife, Ann, and his four children. He has taken on social responsibilities for his Danvers class and has led the annual fundraising drives. He was a class representative to the Danvers Board of Trustees. He also serves on the boards of directors of the Red Cross, Boys and Girls Clubs, and the Chamber of Commerce. He and his wife have sponsored numerous international students for Danvers and provided holiday homestays. He is the son of Mark Harrison Jr., class of 1941, and grandson of Mark Harrison, class of 1905."

I had to chuckle about the *Playboys* because Steven told me that he and Mark sometimes got together and compared centerfolds and traded magazines. Steven had wanted me to participate in whatever they did together, but I had refused.

I got up and walked into my kitchen to make a cup of tea. I wanted a tea with a little caffeine so I made green tea. Then I went back to open Richard Burris's file and read it. I had almost forgotten how odd and stork-like he appeared with his eyes peering out from behind a large beak of a nose. I had usually seen him with glasses, but he must have taken them off for the photograph. His somatotype was a 2-3-6 (Whippet), and next to it was the note, "A strained, defiant temperament; a lonely hunter." I remembered seeing those slender dogs racing on tracks. Although they were thin, they were not frail. The photograph captured none of the brilliance of his intellect, but in his eyes there was defiance. I read:

"Richard Burris is six feet two inches tall with an estimated weight of 130 pounds. His wingspan is greater than his height." I noticed how long and thin his arms were.

"Mr. Burris is a fifteen-year-old Caucasian male. He has a large skull with enlarged orbits. He has moderate facial asymmetry; his left eye lid droops moderately compared to the right. He also has moderately increased facial creases on the left compared to the right. This asymmetry leads to a below normal aesthetic. He has moderate acne on his face, chest, and back. His poor muscular development and hyperextended fingers and wrists suggest possible Marfanoid characteristics. He has a pectus excavatum of the chest and narrow pelvis. He is a Tanner 4 with normal hair development. Based upon his physical attributes, we anticipate that he will engage in intellectual pursuits and be prone to anxiety, paranoia, and nervous disorders."

"Mr. Burris had the highest grade point average for his class during all three of his years at Danvers. He won the mathematics award and the physics award as a graduating senior. He tutored local junior high school students in mathematics and received the community services award for his tutoring activity. His behavior was at all times exemplary. However, he had some difficulty with communication, which was attributed to a speech impediment or a minor coordination problem, and he received speech therapy with some resolution of the problem. He attended MIT and received a Ph.D. in theoretical physics. He has written widely about chaos theory and other advanced mathematical concepts. He is a physicist at the Santa Fe Institute and the Los Alamos National Labs. He is married to Ann Hing and has two children. Mr. Burris is a sought-after speaker for national and international conferences. Although his opinions are considered controversial, he has been mentioned as a possible future Nobel Prize winner for physics. He heads a laboratory with 25 employees and has been acknowledged as an excellent leader for his group. However, his communication problems have been associated with lack of respect for hierarchy and authority and have created some controversy."

In addition to our lunches and card games, I sometimes saw Richard at the gym. He would dress, lace his running shoes, and grimly run laps as if each step might upset his precarious equilibrium. The track coach would scream at him: "Come on, Burris. You run like an old lady!"

I wondered how much his body and its apparent instability contributed to his views about the world and people. If you could never find a stable pattern in your movement, perhaps you assumed that instability and chaos characterized other physical phenomena. His was a body that would not have fared well during the thousands of years that humans depended upon hunting and gathering. He would not have been able to easily bend down and collect berries or climb trees to find fruit. And as for reproductive fitness, he would not have the physical appeal to attract female admirers. But in a world that valued intellect and rewarded it financially, he now had a certain appeal that could not be identified through the lens of physical analysis. I felt increasingly irritated at the portraits in the files, which maligned the identities of my peers under a pile of supposedly scientific measurements.

Now I reached into the box again and pulled out the chart next to mine – Steven Thompson's. As I gazed at the impish smile on his face, I remembered that he had been one of the defiant ones: His middle finger was slyly exposed in his hand.

He was five feet eight inches tall, a bit taller than me. His arm span was slightly more than his height. He was a bit less developed sexually than I was, though he had been the one with the girlfriend. He had been an endomorphy 4, mesomorphy 3, and ectomorphy 5 (white tailed deer). I thought about a deer's physical presence, the noble silhouette in a field at sunset. But a deer was also vulnerable, a victim of wolves, lions, or humans.

The written description followed:

"Steven Thompson has a well formed skull with a deep orbital ridge, dark mahogany eyes, high forehead, straight black hair, high cheek bones, and a cleft chin. His chest is well developed for his maturity level. His torso is long and well developed and his limbs are proportionally appropriate. He is a Tanner 3, two standard deviations from chronological age. He is symmetric and his overall aesthetic impression is high. Based upon his physical attributes and development, he has good leadership potential. The lag in Tanner development is of some concern as it has been associated with immature psychosocial development."

I remembered how Steven had always seemed young and undeveloped for his age. This might have been an embarrassment for some boys, but Steven had not seemed to mind and would often joke about his stage of pubertal development. He retained the childlike willingness to suspend disbelief that most of us had lost. Steven's world contained witches, superheroes, ogres, magic, beauty, miracles, and grace. Even his card playing displayed a kind of fantastical wonder: His eyes would sparkle and his mouth would open into a gaping grin when he observed a team win all the tricks in a hand and score a grand slam. It was something I always enjoyed about Steven, although others considered him naive and silly. I skipped through the anatomic descriptions to the section on Steven's background and later history.

"Steven Thompson came to Danvers from Brewster Country Day

School where he had performed well, receiving all A's and B's. His father is an attorney in Boston and his mother serves on the Board of Directors of the Boston Symphony. Steven was an above average student at Danvers and participated in numerous clubs and sports activities, earning two varsity letters in swimming. His grades were likely affected by the distractions of his extracurricular activities. He was recognized for his writing skills on the school newspaper and also served as a representative on the Danvers committee for support of underrepresented minority students. He had one disciplinary event associated with a Rule 7 violation (a young woman visiting him on campus without permission). He received religious counseling pertaining to this behavior from Mr. Goodson, with satisfactory completion. He was placed on temporary probation and had no further disciplinary issues. He attended Harvard and Harvard Law School, after which he practiced law and became a partner in his firm. He married Sarah Brand. She is a prominent civil rights attorney. They have no children."

These were all details that I knew except for the religious counseling, which he never mentioned to me. The visit that led to his probation was my fault, though Steven took responsibility. The file did not detail how Sarah showed up to visit me and how we had been caught. I resumed reading information less familiar to me:

"Mr. Thompson has continued to support Danvers with donations. He was nominated for membership on the Board of Trustees at Danvers, but turned down the nomination. In a recent letter he informed the Academy that he had received the Volunteer Attorney of the Year award from the Boston Legal Aid office for his provision of free legal services. Based upon his physical attributes and his high aesthetic score, we expect a high propensity for success. His delay in maturity may have led to faulty decision-making at Danvers. His early disciplinary experience was likely the combination of endomorphy, ectomorphy, and the low Tanner score which may have created a personality instability. It is likely that the instability has mostly resolved. In his withdrawal from the Board of Trustee nomination he suggested unspecified medical problems as the cause."

I looked at Steven's photo again. He stood there with his hand by his side and his middle finger raised ever so subtly toward the camera. Most of us had marched like sheep to slaughter with neither a protest nor a whimper. Steven mocked the entire enterprise. To him it was just a game, an opportunity to entertain, or perhaps an exploration of defiance. For me, the photo session was an invasive searchlight exposing my nudity and shame. I acquiesced with little resistance; Steven was one of the few who put up some fight.

I picked up the photograph of me as a 15-year-old, remembering how I had tried to put myself into a trance to manage the anxiety of standing there in front of other students. My lip had started to twitch, the way it sometimes did when I was anxious or frightened. I felt like it was a blinking neon sign, betraying my emotions to the world.

But my lip looked normal in the picture.

I continued to scan the photograph, noticing that my arms were thin but muscular, and that there was no fat around my waist, in contrast to my present bulge. I had no wrinkles around my eyes as I now do, and my hair was thick, almost black, and wavy, with none of its present streaks of gray. My current body was a distant echo of the robust, adolescent image in front of me.

That night I had a dream about a powerful force known as *barang*. Other cultures believe in God or fate or Allah, but native people in the Philippines claim that *barang* is the source of inexplicable behavior, illness, or crazy events. If a typhoon hit an island that had never weathered a typhoon before, it was due to *barang*. If a peaceful man got drunk and hacked off his neighbor's limbs, it was due to *barang*. My parents told me it was just a superstition, but as a child I believed that barang could make the stomach bloat or the memory fail. Other medical explanations were not as convincing to me as *barang*.

Our house man in the Philippines stayed up at night to protect us from *barang*. He would sit or sleep on a bamboo mat by our front door at night with his machete, guarding us from the entry of bandits, thieves, or any wandering spirits. He worried about food barang, wind *barang*, noise *barang*, and people *barang*. He had wary, narrow eyes, and spoke of *barang* in half whispered tones in his native language of Cebuano. He had learned of *barang* from his grandparents when he grew up in a mountain village in the forest, where people still spoke the native dialect of Manobo, and believed in the gods of the trees and the mountain. *Barang* could enter a baby's body in the night from a bottle of milk and leave it dead in the morning. *Barang* could appear in the guise of a wind through the house, causing a woman to cry uncontrollably, until she was taken away to a mental hospital, or cause a man to wander in the night with a machete and hack off the head of a passing stranger. *Barang* emanated from witches, sorcerers, or the dead – the last thoughts left behind when the spirit departed this world. *Barang* explained why people behaved completely out of character, why good people did terrible things. Some people could say there is a scientific explanation, a chemical imbalance of the brain, a hormonal overload – or that it's just human nature – a regression to primate behavior, but I still believe in *barang*. As I dissect some of the inexplicable things I have done in my life, it gives me some solace that I might not be entirely responsible for my actions, that *barang* compelled me.

In my dream the large boxes of files carried *barang*. When I opened the boxes, the *barang* entered my life. I could not be sure who had placed the *barang* in the boxes – a witch, Mr. Grundel, a former classmate; it did not matter. *Barang* forces you to do things until it has achieved its end, whatever that might be. Suddenly you are not fully responsible for your actions; you have lost some control. Events and surprises pass before you, and you cannot know if you will be a participant or observer, just like in a dream.

I woke up and drank a glass of water and tried to fall back asleep. But then I had another dream that woke me. It was about Sarah, my girlfriend from my Danvers days. We were sailing on a small boat past islands. We noticed green and yellow tropical fish and mauve shells in the clear water and then the water would become cloudy and murky. On one island were a Minotaur, a satyr, and a cyclops. They called to us and we ignored them, fearing their powers of violence and mind control. The winds picked up and the boat began to list to one side. I noticed Sarah on the side of the boat holding a rope as we tipped closer and closer to the ocean. I reached out my hand as she fell over the side; I could feel just the tips of her fingers as she slipped out of reach. And then the Minotaur and satyr came to the water's edge and began speaking to a mermaid. Was it Sarah? If the mermaid had turned, I could have seen her face; I would have gone to them. But she never turned. And then the cyclops began to chase me. I sailed away as fast as I could, and eventually they all disappeared behind me.

I'd had this dream many times over the years. I called Sarah once, years after Danvers, when I was in medical school. She and Steven Thompson were already married. I called because I wondered if the dream meant anything, if she was okay or if something had happened to her. We had lunch a few days later, and I remember how there came a moment when we looked into each other's eyes, and I knew what we were both thinking. I wanted to grab her hand, just as I had on that sailboat. And just like in the dream she reached out and I felt the heat of our fingertips touching. I cannot remember who pulled away first, but our hands pulled back, and just like in the dream, she disappeared.

5

In the morning I called Dr. Hart. I wanted to understand why he chose to send the boxes to me, of all people. A receptionist's voice answered: "Elm Street."

"Hello, I'm looking for Dr. Hart. Is this the correct number?"

"The doctor? Yes, I believe he is over in the Solarium. Let me see if I can get him for you." As I waited, I realized that Dr. Hart and his wife must have already moved from their home.

"Hello?" It was a long, deep, old man's greeting, uncertain who or what would respond.

"Dr. Hart? It's Robert Thames. I received your files."

"Robert! Hello. Thank you for calling. I'm glad they've reached you. I'm sorry I wasn't able to contact you ahead of time…"

"I've just begun to look at them. They're very…disturbing." I laughed, in spite of myself.

"I'm sorry to mix you up in this business, but I didn't know what else to do. Your father was so kind over the years in assisting me. And so I naturally thought of you."

I took a deep breath. "Dr. Hart, I will always be grateful for how you and Mrs. Hart helped me when I came to Danvers. You were one of the influences in my becoming a doctor – "

"I'm very proud of your accomplishments, Robert. Traveling around the world, discovering new antibiotics… It's the kind of work that I might have done had I been of your generation."

"Thank you. But I had no idea that our photographs had been part of a study. No one ever mentioned that to us." My throat was dry; I took a sip of coffee.

"Well, yes," he chuckled. "At the time we didn't really consider some of the issues that are important today. Sheldon was a big name in the science community. In those days we could do almost anything, as long as we weren't administering experimental treatments."

"But taking photographs of adolescent boys?" I squirmed in my chair.

"There was nothing remotely unsavory about it, I assure you," his voice deepened even more.

"I wasn't suggesting that – "

"Those of us who fought in the war were used to foregoing modesty. We considered those photos no worse than nudes displayed in museums around the world. We used them to assess posture, malnutrition, obesity, and genetic abnormalities, as well as for the project data; they had many purposes."

"Shouldn't someone have informed our parents? Or us?"

"Danvers was considered *in loco parentis,* in place of the parents, if you recall your Latin. We felt that they would have agreed to your volunteering for the study. The public had faith in us – not like these days. Scientists were on great quests for knowledge."

I stood up from the table and paced around the room, more agitated. "I just remember feeling quite embarrassed at being photographed nude my first week at Danvers."

"Well, Robert, we had the full accord of your father." He let that sink in a moment and then conceded. "Perhaps we should have informed the other families, but no one seemed to be concerned until recently." He paused and his voice faltered a bit. "I've just received a call from Tillman Hobson, the President of the Board of Trustees at Danvers. He wants to visit with me tomorrow. I'm very worried, Robert."

"Why?"

"Once people start looking into this study, they'll find other things best left alone – suspicions and rumors and the like – materials that are not exactly part of the research project..."

"What do you mean?"

"Reports on drug and alcohol use, sexual deviancy. If anyone were to read through them, it could be a great embarrassment. Especially to those in public office."

I was silent. I was already complicit, having read through a few.

"There are confidential letters from the dean about student infractions. Reports from psychologists. Anonymous letters that contained rumors about inappropriate relationships, some of them involving teachers…"

This reminded me of Mr. Goodson. He used to make us stand up on the table like Roman statues, and describe our pectoral muscles and hamstrings as he lifted our arms and legs. Sometimes he invited boys to his apartment for extra tutorial training. I remember one of those boys returning from his apartment late at night and crying about how he hated Mr. Goodson. I thought it was because Mr. Goodson was so eccentric.

"Is that why Hobson wants to meet with you?"

"He's worried about lawsuits. What the administration knew."

"What did they know?"

His voice softened. "It was hard to verify these accounts. We tried as best we could to remove the teachers who crossed that line, and we did it quietly. I hadn't wanted that information in the research files, but actually it helped me develop a more comprehensive picture of some students. I probably should have taken them out before I sent them to you, but there was no time."

I tried to think of what to say but took another sip of coffee instead.

Dr. Hart continued, "There were so many examples of boys who turned out exactly as Sheldon would have predicted. Of course, there were exceptions, like you. We need to understand them all."

"I never knew I was an exception."

"You weren't a typical Danvers boy."

"No, I guess not. Maybe it was just luck."

"I suppose luck plays a part – and God. Perhaps He selected you for some special purpose. Perhaps this purpose. Scan through the files and draw your own conclusions. There are some sad stories – suicides, cancers, accidents. Not everyone is blessed with a happy or successful life. But that's the purpose of studying them! Find the individual threads and tie them all together. My mind is too clumsy now, and my eyes are dim. Read Sheldon's *Atlas of Men*. It will explain the theory. And the *Grant Study* of George Valliant, and the *Glueck Study*. You know if your father were alive, he would be so proud. In fact, he would want to work alongside you."

"Dr. Hart, having these files in my house is...." I paused, trying to find the right word: *creepy, sick, malignant, evil?* I did not want to pick the wrong one. "They're very unsettling. I'll think about the project and call you tomorrow, one way or the other."

"Mr. Hobson will have come and gone by then. He's going to pressure me to turn over the files. Robert, you're going to have to be strong."

"Strong?"

"They're going to malign our best intentions and discredit the work."

"Let's just see," I said. "See what he says. I'll call you tomorrow, Dr. Hart."

I thought of my low score on mesomorphy and my somatotype: A nervous rabbit. Yet I had been strong, year after year, collecting specimens in humid, malaria-infested jungles all over the world. I had been strong in forcing open the doors of institutions that did not believe that I belonged because of the way I looked.

I waited until the silence on the receiver became a dial tone, and the dial tone a series of beeps, the rhythmic punctuation of lingering questions.

6

I had to pack for my upcoming trip to Africa. We'd received an intriguing letter from Dr. Tukutuba, who worked in a rural clinic in Tanzania. He had been doing research on some new treatments for AIDS, as well as collecting native medicines that might contain active ingredients that could be synthesized and turned into new antibiotics. There was a blue-green fungus that grew on the acacia that had been used as a folk remedy for skin injuries; it seemed to cure infections on the skin of his AIDS patients. It could be a fluke or the possibility of something new. It would be a long trip but I would have some time to think about my conversation with Dr. Hart. I called my department to tell the secretary I'd be working from home.

"I'm still recovering from a migraine. I may be in tomorrow. You can call me or page me if you need anything."

"Certainly, Dr. Thames."

I ate breakfast and then began flipping through the files again, reading about the boys and their somatotypes; Sheldon's reduction to animals, fish, or insects. One boy was a wasp, another a whale, another a porpoise, another a lion. Who would question the superiority of a lion over a wasp? Or the beauty of a gazelle compared to a pig?

The boys in the photographs gazed out at me, no escape from the lens. They had endured the moment with anger, bewilderment, acceptance, amusement, defiance. Their posture gave clues to their personalities – a slouch, a tilt, a military stance, a crouch.

A memory suddenly veered at me. I was perhaps four or five years old. My mother held the towel as I got out of the bath, and I pushed it away, exposing myself to her view. I was conscious of my body, the beauty and the miracle of it, like an actor on a stage as the curtain rises. But the look on her face – horror, anger, disgust – startled me. "Shame, shame, shame!" she uttered with a choked laugh.

I was wrong. My naked body was wrong. I reached for the towel to cover myself and ran into my room, weeping. I am not sure if it happened exactly that way, but it was the first time I was fully aware of my naked body, and registered that it could be the source of many emotions – pride, desire, fear, humiliation.

I know I still felt that confusing mix of emotions, ten years later at Danvers. But there was no towel, no escape. I stood there defenseless, scrutinized and measured, judged and dismissed.

Later in the evening, the telephone rang. I was in such a stupor, I almost didn't answer it. The voice on the other end was soft, feminine, familiar. "Hi, Robert, this is Sarah."

"Sarah?" my mouth fell open. I quickly closed it, relieved she couldn't see me. "How odd! I've just been thinking about you."

"Really?"

I didn't really want to tell her about the project, but felt I needed an explanation. "Some research files from an old study of students at Danvers were sent to me, and they brought back memories of all of us when we were kids – I mean, you and me and Steven and the others from the bridge group. So how are you?"

"Not good, I'm afraid. Steven's sick. That's why I'm calling."

"Is he all right?"

"No, he's got end-stage liver disease." She began to cry softly. "You wouldn't recognize him, Robert. He looks awful!"

"I'm so sorry, Sarah. When was he diagnosed?"

"A while back. He didn't want anyone to know. But lately he's been mentioning your name, and I thought it would mean a lot to him – to both of us, actually – if you would visit."

I fumbled for a chair and sat down. "I have to go to Africa this week, but I'll come up as soon as I get back."

"Will you be gone long?"

"A couple of weeks."

"Steven told me that you're quite the world traveler," she mused.

I remembered how Sarah and I used to fantasize about places like Shangri-La, Tahiti and Bhutan. Each of those words seemed to be magical. But my trips were more like walking through a Toyota factory with new people to meet and new products to inspect.

"Mostly it's airports and hotels and lots of meals with strangers," I said. "I eat a lot. I've gained too many pounds."

"Hard to believe – you've always been thin. In any case, there are new sights and smells and languages," she said wistfully. "A trip to New Hampshire is a long ways for me."

I looked around my apartment at the photos I had collected of the places I had visited. There was one of me in front of a temple in Cambodia: The roots of a tree had invaded the walls of the temple and had become a part of temple. Another photo showed me with Mia, a young doctor from South Africa. We had visited Cape Town together after a conference and had begun an intermittent, long-distance romance lasting two years before she announced that she was getting married to someone else. I kept her photo in my hallway to remind me of the possibilities.

"But what about your work?" I asked. "Isn't that still engaging?"

Sarah represented immigrants who had committed minor crimes and were facing deportation.

"Oh, I like what I do, and most of my clients. They need someone who believes in them and is willing to fight…but lately it's been hard with Steven being so sick. Robert, his prognosis is not good."

"I'm so sorry. It seems like yesterday we were kids." I looked back down my hallway at the boxes with the files. "I recently received files from Dr. Hart, the school doctor at Danvers. It turns out that Danvers and some other schools had been doing research on the students, which included us. Part of the research involved taking photographs, nude photographs, and analyzing them. No one ever told us about the research or that the photographs were part of it. We thought they were posture photographs. Dr. Hart has been continuing to gather information since then about each of us, and now he wants me to help him complete the research. It's so strange. And there could also be information about relationships between students and teachers buried in the files. I've read about it at other prep schools, but nothing ever has been proven about Danvers. It's all very disturbing. I don't know what to do."

"That sounds disgusting. But I'm not surprised. That place was full of assholes and pedophiles. That may explain the nightmares Steven used to have. He told me that teachers had their favorite boys. They practically worshiped the boys. I thought Steven was making it all up or exaggerating, but if they took pictures, they all should be reported to the police. That was probably illegal. I once did some work on one of the Catholic Church abuse cases. There's usually much more than what's on the surface. It also sounds like there were violations of the research rights of children, who are supposed to have special protection. Research law and ethics are not exactly my areas of expertise, but I could probably aim you in the right direction. And there may be cover-ups of illegal behavior. When you come up here to visit, we can talk about it," she said.

"Thanks. But don't worry about any of that now. You have your hands full. I shouldn't have even brought it up. I'll see you soon," I said. "I'm so sorry. I promise to be up there as soon as I can."

"Thank you, Robert. We appreciate it."

When I hung up, I walked to the window. There was a couple walking a dog on one side of the street, a teenager with blue hair on a skateboard on the other. A normal day in the city. And yet I felt like my life had been split in two: There was yesterday – before the files – and today, where I was suddenly, inexplicably, needed and wanted again.

I found my suitcase and began selecting my clothes for the trip. The government measured my success partly by how many expeditions I took, how far I went, and what I brought back. Africa was far enough that I got extra points for the journey; the reviewers liked to know I was giving the continent ample attention. But now, with budget cuts and the potential eradication of my job, finding a successful product was my most important goal.

I packed my anti-mosquito shirts and pants, even though I would be covering myself with plenty of DEET. I packed short and long-sleeved shirts, shorts, and long pants. I packed my medicines. I had to make sure the anti-malarial medications were included, as well as all of my other medications for possible parasitic and bacterial infections. I had my migraine medication, as well as a full-strength pain reliever, in case the long hours on the plane set off my back.

As I packed, I remembered again that Tim Washington was in Nairobi. I could probably take a bus down to Tanzania if I did a stopover. It would be fun to surprise Tim in Africa. I was curious about how he looked now, compared to the photo in his file. I could tell him about Steven, and maybe he could give me some advice about my job. Tim was never afraid of being handed the ball.

The last thing I packed in my bag was his file.

7

I called Dr. Hart back the next day. The woman who answered seemed hesitant when I asked for him. Then another voice came on the phone.

"Hello, I'm Margaret Hay, Elm Street manager. May I help you?"

"I'm Dr. Thames. I'd like to speak to Dr. Hart, please."

Sometimes the title of Doctor eliminates interference.

The woman's voice changed as I had hoped. "Oh, Doctor, I'm very sorry, but Dr. Hart passed away late yesterday afternoon. It was quite sudden and unexpected. His wife is not taking calls at the moment."

"What happened? I spoke to him yesterday. He seemed fine."

"Heart attack or stroke. He was walking down the steps and just fell over. Unfortunately, this sometimes happens here with our elderly residents."

"Was anyone with him?"

"We found him at the foot of the stairs and called 911, but it was too late. I'm very sorry. Mrs. Hart will be receiving visitors tomorrow afternoon if you would like to visit."

"I'm from out of town, but thank you."

"I'm very sorry. You're welcome any time."

These words – uttered by a stranger – made my eyes sting with unexpected tears. I had not seen the Harts for several years, but felt the loss like a deep ache in my chest, like when my parents died. The couple had been generous to me during my time at Danvers, inviting me for dinners and encouraging me when my initial grades were poor. Mrs. Hart had reviewed my essays on Thomas Wolfe and Faulkner and my proofs in geometry. Dr. Hart had taken care of me in the infirmary when I was sick. They both had championed my idea of going to medical school. Even though we had not kept in touch over the years, I had always thought of them fondly.

And now I had inherited Dr. Hart's files like an orphaned child.

I could catch a plane tomorrow morning and be back by that night. I felt I needed to be there for Mrs. Hart and to pay my respects to the doctor, who had entrusted me with his life's work.

8

I arrived at Danvers at noon from the airport. The cab dropped me at the edge of the school campus where the town and school meet, and I decided to walk around the campus before going over to the Elm Street Home to see Mrs. Hart. Students were walking briskly between classes; I noticed how the addition of girls seemed so natural, and yet so significant. We had all dreamed of having girls on the campus, but it had been an adolescent boy's fantasy – Renoir paintings, bathers at the swimming pool in bikinis, surreptitious glances around the seminar tables, romantic intrigues after dark, notes passed hand-to-hand in classes. That was what we imagined. Not real girls dressed in preppy sweaters and slacks with heavy books in backpacks, discussing Plato and Aristotle on their way to the cafeteria. The day was warm with the sun creating sparkles on the ivy-covered brick buildings just like it had when I was a student there, and I felt some anxiety and some sadness as I thought of the students and what lay ahead for them.

I wandered over to Elm Street and found the address of the residential home. For a while I stood outside, observing the residents limping or walking slowly with fragile hips and knees and canes in their hands. What a contrast to the adolescents I'd just left – their limbs still developing, gathering ligaments and muscle – blissfully unaware of how they would degenerate, diminish, and come to this. I knew I was somewhere between the two, nearer in age to the residents, but closer in spirit to the students.

I followed a flower delivery man into the home. When he asked at the front desk for Mrs. Hart, I surreptitiously trailed behind him, up the stairs to apartment 212. I watched from a dozen feet away as he rang the bell. Mrs. Hart answered the door in a black and gray checked dress and a white jacket, her back stooped. Her hair was completely white and her skin was the pale pink color of a cloud at sunset. She received the flowers and smiled as if she were receiving a Mother's Day gift rather than condolence flowers. The delivery man stepped back and started down the hallway.

I moved forward so that she could see me before she closed the door. "Mrs. Hart? Hi, it's me, Robert Thames."

"Who's that?" she said, straining to see. Her eyes were gray-blue and cloudy with cataracts. Her face was a map of blood vessels and yellow patches in loose skin, and yet she was still very much the Mrs. Hart I remembered.

"It's me, Robert Thames,"

"Robert? Why, yes! There you are. My eyes aren't as good as they used to be. You're in a sort of a mist. Harold died yesterday. Just keeled over."

"Yes, that's why I'm here."

"Why thank you, Robert. Thank you for coming. We'll have a visitation in an hour. Lots of people. Why don't you come in now before they all get here? I'd like to talk with you."

"I don't want to trouble you," I said, but she waved my comment away, and opened the door. I followed her inside. The tiny apartment was smaller than mine, overfilled with furniture, books, photographs of children, and household ornaments.

"You know, I spoke with Dr. Hart only a couple of days ago. He sent me several boxes of files," I mentioned as we took a seat together on the couch. She observed me with interest, but made no comment: "I'm so sorry for your loss. I want you to know how much Dr. Hart and you meant to me. I'm sorry I didn't visit sooner."

"Oh, I understand. You young people are all so busy." She hesitated for a second and added, "I have four children and ten grandchildren and I almost never see them except for Christmas and Thanksgiving. Now that Harold has passed, I'm sure they'll all pile in here and then go home until it's my turn to die." She grinned as if it were a joke, but I just tried to focus on her pale gray-blue eyes. "I'm forgetting my manners," she said. "Would you like something to drink? Tea or hot chocolate? Something to eat? Cookies?"

"No, thanks. I'm fine."

"Harold talked about visiting you in Washington soon. He felt that it was fate that he see you again."

"Because of the research project?" I asked. "He sent me some files. He wanted me to complete his work. I'm not sure I can do it. It's very disturbing."

Her jaw tightened. "Those damn files! I would've destroyed them long ago if I could have wrestled them away from him."

I was startled by her intensity. "Why?"

"It was an unhealthy obsession."

"You didn't like him working on them?"

"Oh, please," she said. "He studied those files as if he might find the cure for cancer."

"So are you familiar with the project?"

"I know it killed him!" I stared at her in shock. "The Board of Trustees wanted to take all of the files away. They were over here the day he died, and brought old Dean Maiser along. He should have been buried years ago. Horrible man!" Her voice began to shake. "Harold was in quite a state. I think it's what caused his heart to go out. Killed him just as if they had stabbed him with a knife."

"I'm sorry," I said sadly.

"Harold always felt he was cut out for something greater than just a school physician. When he was approached by Harvard for the project, it was like he came alive. He always wanted to do research. It was a gift from heaven for him. But..." Her voice trailed off.

"What happened?"

"Robert," she said, taking my hand carefully. Her voice lowered to a rough whisper. "I've never discussed this with anyone except Harold. But he sent the files to you so..."

Her thin bones tightened over mine. I knew that if I heard her out, I would find myself entangled in something I might not be able to escape, like the Philippine jungle, wrapping you in vines, distorting all sense of direction. I felt nauseated, the pin-pricks of my migraine returning, but nodded my assent.

"Harold was so proud of his work. One day he called a meeting with senior faculty and administrators. When he came home, he was terribly upset. He told me that…" She paused as if gathering her courage. "Several of the men who were there seemed more interested in the pictures of the boys than in the purpose of the research. There was a fascination that was deviant – unnatural – on the part of a few of the men. Snide comments – jokes about the boys in the pictures. They weren't taking the project seriously or scientifically. They were passing the photos back and forth like baseball cards. He said it was the worst moment of his life. Later, he told me the files were like Pandora's Box. Something evil was unleashed at Danvers. And it would never go back in."

I looked at the carpet, which was worn and stained in places. They laughed at us, appraised us. I felt the room starting to spin. I willed it to stop.

"There were more meetings. The deans and assistant deans and the house masters who discussed boys' issues. Harold was there to represent the scientific side because many of the boys had medical or psychological issues. These men… began to pore through the files at every meeting, insisting that the information might be useful during disciplinary and award meetings. But Harold never felt right about it." She shook her head as if to clear it. "I encouraged him to say the study was canceled or something, anything to bring an end to it. He finally did, though he kept working on it secretly on his own. It preyed upon him, what he saw at those meetings. It brought out the worst in some of the men. Of course, most of them are gone now, mostly dead, except Maiser. He was the worst of them."

"How so?"

"He was just plain mean. He didn't like any boy who was different. In his mind he had an idea of the perfect Danvers boy – 'athletic and intelligent and a good Christian,' he would say. He never approved of the changes in the admissions when we started to have the Jewish boys and the different colored boys like you – the Blacks and Chinese and Mexicans. Some of the alumni have tried to put him on a pedestal with all of his traditional values. They want to rename the Philips building after him. Can you imagine?" She paused for a moment, waiting for me to react, and when I didn't, she let my hand go.

"Anyway, Harold finally discussed all this with someone he trusted, one of the house masters, Mr. Shangly."

I nodded, urging her to go on. I had always liked Mr. and Mrs. Shangly, although their sudden departure, partway through my second year, had been a mystery.

"They were wonderful people. But Maiser got rid of them. It upset Harold so." She placed her hands on both knees and smoothed her skirt. Then she stood up and plucked at my coat.

"Robert, come with me. I want to give you something." I followed to the hallway closet. She pulled something metallic out of a white coat pocket, an old Hewlett Packard stethoscope.

"Wow, they don't make those anymore."

"It was Harold's, all those years. None of our other children became doctors; it would mean nothing to them. Harold would have wanted you to have it. He thought very highly of you."

"Thank you," I said, feeling the weight of it in my hand. The heavy metal bell at the end of the rubber tubing was smooth and shiny from use. "I remember this stethoscope. It will remind me of Dr. Hart whenever I see it. I'll take good care of it."

"I know you will. And one more thing." She went to a desk and opened a drawer, pulling out a letter. "This was a letter about the research he kept all these years. He gave it to me before the Board arrived the other day, 'just in case of trouble.' I haven't read it. You can see it's addressed to you. Why don't you give it a glance while I freshen up a little?"

She patted my arm and shuffled down the hall.

I opened the envelope and unfolded a letter, signed by Dr. Sheldon, authorizing Dr. Hart to lead the study at Danvers. The title was *The Danvers Adolescent Research Project – Body Somatotypes and Racial Factors in*

Personality and Achievement. The letter described the confidential nature of the research and the approval of various deans and scientists at Harvard, Yale, and Columbia. They had all certified to the scientific value of the study and gave permission for the research to be done on their students. The justification was for the understanding and betterment of humanity. The letter ended with a statement: "Please provide Dr. Harold Hart and associates all rights and privileges to which they are entitled as associate investigators." Signed, William H. Sheldon, Ph.D. M.D. Thomas Hutchinson, Ph.D. July 10, 1964.

I noticed that there was another sheet of paper in the envelope, separately folded and neatly typed. It read: *Memorandum of Agreement: Danvers Academy Release of Liability.* Beneath the heading there was a paragraph:

"As to the evening of October 3rd 1967, there was an incident involving Mr. and Mrs. Shangly, faculty advisors of Benson Hall, and four Danvers students: Tim Washington, Steven Thompson, Mark Harrison, and Richard Burris. The students apparently received alcohol from Mr. Shangly's liquor cabinet. There were minor injuries due to the alcohol. Dr. Hart was summoned and examined each of the students and Mr. and Mrs. Shangly.

"He found no significant injuries. He cleared the students for return to their rooms. Each student has signed this memorandum of agreement as a release of liability. The Academy has agreed not to pursue disciplinary measures against the students due to conflicting evidence about the involvement of the faculty supervisors. The liability release form will be kept in a confidential file until the graduation of the students, after which the form will be destroyed. Mr. and Mrs. Shangly have agreed to transfer from their dormitory supervision positions to an off-campus living arrangement. Comments from the students implicated Mr. Shangly for inappropriate and unprofessional behavior and Mrs. Shangly for violations of conduct. Mr. and Mrs. Shangly will be placed on administrative leave until a full investigation and final disposition is complete. All elements of this agreement are to remain strictly confidential. Any breach of confidentiality could result in further disciplinary action."

Under the paragraph there was a place for signatures, and I recognized the names of my friends signed in black ink. Beneath them were signatures of Dean Robert Maiser and witness, Dr. Harold Hart.

I could not imagine Mr. and Mrs. Shangly doing anything to hurt students or being unprofessional in any way. The letter mentioned my friends. Where had I been that night? Everyone else from our bridge group was there.

Perhaps I had been tired and gone to bed. Sometimes I would leave when the bridge game was winding down so that I could get some sleep in order to study the next day. I remembered a few occasions when Mr. and Mrs. Shangly had parties, and we would hear loud voices, laughter, music. Something must have happened after one of those parties.

Why had Dr. Hart kept the two documents together? Was it connected to the research project in some way? Why else would they be in the same envelope? Why had I never heard of any of it?

I folded the papers, put them back in the envelope, and stuffed it into my pocket. The doorbell rang behind me, and I turned to answer it. Two of Dr. Hart's sons, now gray and paunchy, looked surprised to see me.

I expressed my condolences as they filed in soberly, followed by wives and children. Later in the afternoon, one of the sons approached me.

"Robert, I think I recognize you now. Weren't you at Danvers? Didn't you use to tell us stories when we were kids?"

"Yes." I smiled at him, pleased he had remembered. When I was invited over for dinner, the children would beg me to tell them exotic tales set in the Philippines.

"Good always overcame evil in your stories," he laughed. "I wish that were the way the world really worked…"

"Me too," I agreed.

After I had said my goodbyes to Mrs. Hart and the others, I walked back through the campus and down the pathway, now filled with students changing classes. The old buildings in the central quad area and the ringing voices of adolescents transported me back forty years to the living, breathing boys whose lives filled my files. My hand felt the stethoscope in my pocket. I imagined that I had been given a tool to place on the files and examine the hearts beating within.

9

The next day, back in my home, I packed for my trip to Africa. Every time I walked down the hall to my bedroom to select clothes, the boxes of files were in my way. Even if they were an uninvited guest in my home, I was relieved that they would not be able to follow me onto the plane.

Today's taxi would take me to the international terminal. My mind automatically cycled through travel details: Did I have my passport, ticket, money, directions to the clinic, specimen containers, the name of the doctor I was visiting, and an introductory letter? I added Tim Washington's information. Back and forth, my mind oscillated like a metronome. The honking of the taxi finally forced me to stop. I grabbed my suitcase and backpack, opened the door, and waved at the driver.

"Where are you going, sir?"

"Africa: Nairobi, Kenya."

"Grand!" His accent sounded African. "Which airport?"

"Dulles."

"Yes, sir. Airline?"

"British Airways."

He nodded and put the bags in the car. His dark skin was deeply etched with lines around his forehead and eyes. I wondered about his journey from Africa and his life as a taxi driver in Washington, D.C. but resisted the inclination to engage him in conversation. I found myself thinking instead about my visit with Mrs. Hart and the photographs in the files. I let my head fall back against the seat. The day they had taken our photographs I was still new to Danvers and they had us line up alphabetically. That was when I met Steven Thompson, in line waiting for our photos to be taken.

10

We had only been at Danvers a few days when we received instructions in our mailboxes to report to the art building for a required activity at 3 p.m. A man in a plaid sports coat told us to line up alphabetically. I found the T's and gradually worked my way down to a boy named Thompson, Steven. As Thames, Robert, I stood directly in front of him. Preceding me was Thair, Paul. Paul had blond hair that hung down over his acne-covered forehead. He constantly brushed it out of his eyes, and I found myself wishing I had scissors so I could cut it off and spare him the need to constantly swat at it. When I introduced myself, I noticed his palm was cool and sweaty. He nodded at me, balanced on his toes, and turned toward the front of the line, considering our positioning of little interest or importance. The boy behind me in line seemed more social. He looked far too young for high school; I assumed he was probably a genius who had skipped grades. When I introduced myself, Steven responded in a high-pitched voice: "Thames? You don't even know how to pronounce your own name. It should be pronounced 'Tems', like the river in England."

"That's how my parents pronounced it: 'Thames' that rhymed with 'names'."

"You don't look like a Robert Thames either. You look like someone named Wong or Dong or Thong – since you're in the Ts." His voice carried an air of certainty, as if he deserved an explanation for this irregularity.

"No, it's Thames. I'm Filipino."

"So why don't you have a Filipino name? Aren't Filipino names Spanish, like Roberto?"

"I was adopted by American missionaries. I have their last name. We use the American pronunciation," I said emphatically – as if I were acquainted with American pronunciations for place names like Texas or Los Angeles.

In fact, I had no idea why we didn't use the British pronunciation. No one had ever asked about it in the Philippines. There were many words in the Philippines that were mispronounced: 'Sh' became an 's'. Words that started with 'f' got a 'p' instead. "Finish" became "penis," which usually elicited a lot of laughing among my school friends. "I'm finished already" became "penis already." Pronouns for 'her' became 'him,' because we did not distinguish gender in the pronouns of our Philippine languages.

"I've never met anyone from the Philippines or anyone who was adopted," he said. "All I know about the Philippines is the capital is Manila and there are Moslems and Christians who fight each other in wars. Did you have to convert to Christianity? Was that why you got adopted?" As he became more curious, his voice softened and became friendlier.

"No, we're mostly Catholic in the Philippines. There are some Moslems in the south and some native people who have their own languages and worship trees and spirits, but most of us are Catholic. I was adopted when my real parents died."

"Oh," he said. I could tell that he was considering what to say next. There was a long silence, and then he said, "Can you say 'fuck you' in Filipino? I like to know the curse words in every language. People respect you if you know curse words. They won't mess with you if you can cuss them out in their own language." When he said "fuck," it was so loud that other boys looked over to see what we were talking about.

"I don't know any curse words," I lied. I knew all of the curse words in Cebuano and Tagalog, but we would never use them in our home. I heard them on the streets when I played with the other boys or at school when the teachers couldn't hear us. When I was ten, my mother made me drink soap and water when she heard me use one. Neither of my parents ever swore, even when they got hurt. My dad would say "shoot" instead of "shit." My mother would say "Oh dear" instead of "Goddamn."

"How about 'Hello' in Filipino?"

"We might say *Maayou Buntag* in Cebuano, the language people speak in Mindanao and Cebu where I live."

"Wow, I guess you really are Filipino. I'm Steven...Steven Thompson. *Maayou Buntag*," he said. We shook hands.

"Where are you from?" I asked.

"Boston – Beacon Hill – not far from the Commons."

"I landed in Boston, but I haven't really seen it. It looks very beautiful with the ocean and the tall buildings."

"You could come to my house some time and I could show you all the neatest places in Boston. I don't think my parents have ever had a Filipino in the house before. It would probably be okay."

"Thanks," I said, looking at the line of boys ahead of us. "Do you know what we're supposed to do here?"

"It's some kind of identification card. That's why we're alphabetical. Afterwards do you want to watch the soccer team?"

"I have so much homework. I'm already behind. I don't understand anything in Latin class. Maybe another day."

"I have a book that has all the Latin translations into English. We aren't supposed to have it, but one of my friends on the soccer team gave it to me. You can look at it if you want. But I can't give it to you."

We were so immersed in our conversation that we quickly reached the door and got a glimpse inside. The art building had been transformed into a photographic studio with lights and a camera and a tripod. I had not been inside the building before, and was surprised at the modern sculptures of abstract shapes floating on thin wires. Everything else about Danvers Academy had emphasized the school's 200 year history, the classic, ivy-covered brick buildings, the famous graduates. It was proud to be an elite school where only the smartest, most deserving, best pedigreed students were admitted. I was an anomaly, and so was the art building with its modern sculptures and paintings. Ethnic and racial diversity and modern art were all part of Danvers's burgeoning modernization movement.

"What the – ?" exclaimed Steven, pointing over at the photo area. A nude boy stood motionless, arms at his sides, illuminated by the bright light. I stared at him in shock, expecting him to crumble into pieces, struck by lightning or God's hand. But he just stood staring straight ahead as the camera flashed once, twice, three times as he turned like a piece of meat on a skewer. Then he got dressed and left. I realized I was holding my breath. There were only five more boys in front of me.

I tried to think about what my parents had told me: America would be different. I would be tested. They were praying that I would succeed. But no one had told me about this kind of examination. The next boy in line was already folding his pants on a chair and pulling off his underwear. He had broad shoulders like a wrestler or football player, but he had a somewhat small, circumcised penis. That made me a feel a bit better, because I had heard that Filipinos had small penises compared to Americans, and I was already feeling very embarrassed.

"Why are they taking our pictures like this?" I asked.

"I don't know. Maybe they have to make sure no girls have slipped through."

"They could perform a physical exam by a doctor. They don't need to take a photograph."

"Maybe they need evidence. I once saw this boy who was kind of fat and had boobs and he walked like a girl. You could hardly see his dick. He could have been a girl." We watched as the next boy finished and now there were just three in front of us.

A boy with black curly hair and glasses stood looking at the chair. The photographer came out from behind a curtain and I realized that he was not much older than us. He seemed bored and tired of the questions that everyone was asking.

"I'll be taking your picture. Take off all your clothes. Everything."

The boy removed everything but his underwear and stood on the line peering at the camera lens.

"Everything comes off. Underwear, too."

We watched, hoping that this boy might start to protest, and that we'd be spared. We wanted him to stand his ground, refuse. I would be part of the rebellion. We could all fight together.

But he stared at the ground and took off the underwear. He was not circumcised. Perhaps that was why he had hesitated. In the Philippines, only very poor people are not circumcised. This boy stood somewhat hunched over, arms at his side.

"Okay, look at the red dot on the wall." The boy lifted his eyes and found the dot. Flash, flash. "Now turn and look at the other wall. Find the red dot. That's it. Flash, flash. "Turn again." Flash, flash. "Okay. Good." You can get dressed." And now there were just two ahead of me.

The next boy had a round red face and short black hair. When he removed his shirt, his abdomen hung over his privates, partly obscuring them. He reminded me of a pig, with his small extremities poking out of a pink smooth body and the fat jiggling on his chest and belly as he bent over to remove his socks. Even his high-pitched voice reminded me of a squealing pig.

In the Philippines, pigs would prowl around the villages searching for garbage and getting into whatever was left unattended. This boy began looking under the screens and lighting as if he was rooting for food.

"Leave that alone," said the photographer. "Just stand on the line."

"Sorry, sir. I was looking for my tie. I seem to have lost it."

"Don't worry about that now. Let me finish and then you can look for it."

"Do you remember if I was wearing a tie?"

"I don't remember what anyone is wearing."

"It belonged to my father. He told me not to lose it."

"Just stand on the line and look at the red dot."

The boy stood on the line with his face contorted, trying to hide the tears welling up in his eyes. Steven spotted the tie hidden under a placard. He pulled it out and waved it at the boy; a huge grin replaced the boy's grimace. "Thanks!"

"All right now," said the photographer, as he began his process again. "Look at the dot. Arms at your side. Good." Flash, flash. "Turn. Look at the dot on the wall. Okay turn. Very good." Flash, flash. "Okay, you're done. You can get dressed now."

Now it was time for Paul Thair. When he took off his shirt, I noticed acne covering his shoulders and the top of his chest. It was impossible to look away. He had red boils; some with white dots of pus. He kept sweeping his hair out of his face as he stood in front of the camera. I wondered if I would develop acne like that; I didn't want to get too close to him, just in case. I was very curious about the boils and what might have caused them.

"Arms by your side. Look at the dot," said the photographer. But Paul kept reaching up to his forehead and brushing his hair.

"Keep your hands down," yelled the photographer.

Paul complied for a few seconds. Flash, flash. "Good. Turn and look at the dot. Arms by your side. That's it." Flash, flash. And he was done. Paul and I were in English class together, and after this I always made sure to sit as far away from him as possible.

Now it was my turn. I pulled off my tie and unbuttoned my shirt and laid it on the chair. Then I pulled off my shoes and socks and my chinos. Then I hesitated: It just didn't seem right. "Why are we doing this?" I asked the photographer.

"What?" he snapped. He was a young man with a wisp of a mustache and a pale long face that looked as if it had never been exposed to sunlight. I imagined that if he smiled he would have exposed vampire teeth.

"These pictures. Why are you taking them?"

"It's a job," he said. "I was hired to take photographs, and that's what I am doing. Ten bucks an hour. Everything off."

"But what's the purpose?"

He shrugged. "I'm getting paid and that's all I need to know." He tucked in his black shirt that had come loose from his khaki jeans and wiped the sweat away from his forehead.

"In my country you couldn't do this. You couldn't take pictures of people without their clothes on. It would be against the law. And it's also against the Bible; ever since Adam and Eve left the Garden of Eden we've been wearing clothes."

"You want talk to the dean about it? Because I don't have time right now; I'm running late."

The thought of addressing the dean intimidated me; I didn't want to be a trouble-maker the first week of school. Danvers was a reputable institution; there must be a valid reason for everything they did.

I removed my underwear and glanced down at my body. I had thin arms and legs without any hair. Even my pubic hair was not very abundant. I felt my lip begin to twitch as I stood and tried to control it. In my mind I heard laughter mocking me, louder and louder. I felt voices approaching me from all sides, offended by my naked body. I tried to distract myself with meditation, imagining myself a tree with branches outstretched, leaves soaking up the sun. With each breath, I merged further into the shape of a tree, until I felt covered with a tough layer of bark.

In the Philippines, they believed the first humans descended from the trees and the sky. Although I was not sure of the existence of spirits, at that moment I became the spirit of a tree and departed from my own body.

I barely heard the words, "Look at the dot. Open your eyes."

I could feel my right eye squinting and my lip twitching. The flashes in my eyes were like the sun on my leaves.

"Turn, turn," became the wind through my branches.

I felt rooted to the spot; I could barely move.

Gradually, as if a soft breeze was blowing through my branches, I managed to comply.

When he released me, I returned to my human body, breathed deeply, and stumbled over to the chair where my clothes lay folded neatly in a pile.

Steven was next. He faced away from the camera and began to hum as if he were on stage, doing a strip tease. He swayed softly, slowly pulling off his clothes, and teasing his underwear up and down, over his pelvis. Then he started to dance, moving his hips and bobbing his head and neck. The boys behind us began to laugh and clap their hands to the beat of the humming. Steven turned and repeated his act again, now facing the camera. He smiled and his body undulated to the beat of the clapping and humming around him.

"There's always got to be a clown, huh? I don't have time for this. Let's go."

Steven laughed and pulled off his underwear with great flamboyance. He had barely started puberty and had a small, circumcised penis with just a sprinkling of pubic hair, but he did not seem embarrassed. As the photographer raced to take the picture, Steven raised his middle finger and then there was the flash, flash. The photographer did not notice or seem to care. Steven turned for the side view, back view and then he was done. We walked out together.

"What was that stuff you were saying about Adam and Eve and the Garden of Eden?" asked Steven.

"When they ate the forbidden fruit, they noticed their nakedness and lost their innocence. After that they wore clothes."

"Except when they have sex. When you fuck, you have to take off your clothes. Did you see me give him the finger?"

"Yeah, what do you think they'll do when they develop the pictures?"

"I don't know, but tough shit if they don't like it!"

"What do you think the pictures are for?" I asked.

"I heard someone in the line saying they were posture pictures to see if we had good posture. I think I slouch. I hope I don't have to wear a back brace."

"I don't understand why we must be totally nude for a posture picture. You can see posture with underwear on."

"Maybe someone wants to look at our dicks."

"Why would they want to do that?"

Steven gave me an odd smile. "Everyone likes to look at dicks. Let's go. I need to take a piss."

We stopped by the bathroom before walking back to our dorms. We stood together, talking and pissing into the shimmering white porcelain and marble urinals that Danvers students had been using for hundreds of years. Steven told me his dorm room number and offered to help me with my Latin translation. I nodded but quickly forgot what he had told me by the time I reached my own room.

I might not have seen Steven again after the photos, but a few weeks later I developed a throat infection. I felt hot and achy and groggy. I went over to the infirmary in the middle of the night because I couldn't swallow the saliva in my mouth without getting nauseous. A gray-haired nurse in a white cap greeted me at the infirmary door. She stood a head taller than me, with broad, powerful shoulders that pressed against the door to keep it from swinging open.

"Can I help you?"

"I think I'm sick."

"Have a seat." She pointed to a chair in the entryway, next to a scale.

As I sat down, my mouth filled with saliva and I could not swallow. I ran over to the sink and spat.

"How dare you spit in our sink!" yelled the nurse. "We do not spit in here." Her face turned red; she glared at me with steely eyes.

"I can't swallow," I explained. And then I vomited on the floor.

"Come with me," she said, and led me to another room with a bed and a basin. "You can lie here. I need to get the doctor."

"I'm sorry," I apologized.

She put a thermometer under my tongue and hurried out of the room. I drifted off for a few minutes and when I opened my eyes, Dr. Hart was taking the thermometer out of my mouth. He knew my father and had promised to look out for me at Danvers. When I had arrived, he had made it a point to come to my room and make sure I was settled. I felt happy to see him now. He had a kind, serious doctor-face like my father – though somewhat pink and puffy – with wrinkles in his forehead and around his eyes. He wore a white coat with a stethoscope.

"Well, Rob, looks like we have a fever here, 102 degrees." He called me Rob because that was what he called my dad, whose first name was also Robert. "What are your symptoms?"

"My throat is sore and I can't swallow."

His nodded kindly, revealing a receding hair line with light brown hair balding at the crown. "Well, let's take a look. Open your mouth." He put a wooden tongue blade into my mouth and shined a light into it. I began to gag and almost vomited again.

"Mmmm… Pus on the tonsils. Looks like strep."

He pressed his hands under my chin to feel for my lymph nodes. "Swollen nodes," he said. "So Rob, how's school been? You know your dad expects me to keep him posted about your progress."

"I'm sorry, Dr. Hart. I've been so busy with homework every night." I felt him tap on my chest and put his stethoscope on my heart and lungs. He had big hands. They pressed into my stomach as he tried to feel my insides.

"No sign of enlarged spleen. Since you have lived in the Philippines, we have to consider malaria, but I think this is just the garden-variety strep throat that's going around."

When he finished his examination, he said, "I think we ought to keep you here in the infirmary for a few days. We'll give you a shot of penicillin and that should take care of it."

He motioned to the nurse to get him the antibiotic in a syringe. "Now turn over. I'm going to inject it into your *gluteus maximus.*"

"Not in my arm?"

"No, this can only go in the buttocks."

When he was finished, he sat back and smiled. "So, Rob, are you going to follow me and your old man into medicine?"

"Yes, I'd like to."

"It's a wonderful career, but there's not much time for family. I know how important family is to Filipinos."

"I'm not going to have a family."

I'm not sure why I said that. My family had provided for me when I could have been abandoned, and I was grateful to them. I loved them. But my parents' constant lectures about the dangers of dating, which could lead to sex and pregnancy, which could ruin my life, had made me nervous about girls in general. I did not understand their drive to marry and have children.

The girls I had known in the Philippines giggled and put love notes into my hands. I met one behind a coconut palm one night after receiving a note from her, and she let me kiss her and touch her breasts. She told me she wanted to get married. My mother caught me coming into the house that night, and when I confessed what had happened, she cried and warned me that I would be poor like all the other Filipinos if I started kissing girls. I would never get to college.

"You think you're so smart. You're not. It's only because you work hard and we work with you that you do well in school. You have no time for girls. You have a chance to better yourself. But you can also ruin your life!"

I believed her, fearing that my brain would suddenly run out of gas unless I constantly primed it with hours of studying and preparation. I had to make up for my inferior intelligence and talent with effort, and that would require me to ignore the love notes and messages from friends about girls who wanted to meet me. Perhaps that was why my parents sent me to a boys' school.

Dr. Hart smiled. "Oh, you'll change your mind once a pretty girl comes along and begins to pay attention to you! Anyway, we can talk more when you're feeling better. Let's get you upstairs and into a comfortable bed."

The infirmary had a ward upstairs with eight beds, four on each side of the room. They were higher than my bed at the dormitory, each one with a white blanket and plump white pillow. Only one bed was empty, so I moved toward it. I could not distinguish the faces of the other boys in the dark. I quickly undressed and lay stiffly upon the mattress. After a moment, a shadow left a bed and crossed the room to me. It was Steven.

"What are you in for?" he asked, as if we were doing jail time.

"Oh, hi," I said weakly. "Strep throat, I guess."

"I got mono."

"Isn't that from kissing girls?"

"Yeah. I guess my girlfriend gave it to me. Hey, did you know that Tim Washington is in here with us, too? Isn't that cool?"

A dark fist, connected to a massive brown muscular arm, raised itself in greeting from the next bed. Although I had never spoken to him, I had seen him in my dorm surrounded by other football players.

"Hi," I said hoarsely. "I'm Robert."

"Hey," he answered peering out from his sheets. "Tim."

"We also have a guy from the wrestling team over there," Steven said, pointing to the far corner of the room. "And a writer for the newspaper over there." He pointed to another bed across the room. "These other guys, I don't know. They're not famous."

"I'm not famous," I said.

"Yeah, but you know me," he grinned, and went back to bed.

In the morning, Steven was watching me as I opened my eyes. "Hey, did you know you talk in your sleep?"

"Really? What did I say?"

"Oh, just some stuff in Filipino. I couldn't understand it. Want to go with me to take a shower?"

"I don't feel too great. I don't think I'm going to take a shower yet."

"I just need someone to be there with me so I don't fall because I almost passed out yesterday and the nurse said I couldn't go by myself."

I hesitated a moment, rubbing my eyes.

"Oh, come on. I won't spray you or anything."

"All right." I slowly pulled myself out of bed. We walked to the bathroom, just down the hall. It was a large bathroom with a toilet and a shower head over a bathtub. I sat on the toilet, feeling dizzy until Steven called, "Hey, you're supposed to be watching me." He was soaping himself up and washing his hair.

"Okay," I relented.

"Can you hand me a towel?"

I handed him a towel and averted my eyes as he dried off and got dressed.

"Hey, do you want come to my house this weekend? My parents are going to be gone, so I get to ask a friend."

"But we're sick. We might still be in the infirmary."

"That's not for three days. We'll be fine by then. It'll be great. My girlfriend Sarah is going to come over. She's great, even if she gave me mono."

"I still feel pretty sick, and I have a test in Latin on Monday."

"I can help you with Latin, remember? You can recover at my house. I'll fill out a guest slip for you today."

When I got back, two visitors had arrived for Tim. That meant that seventy-five percent of the school's African-American population was congregating around one bed in the infirmary.

"Where's that muffucker hiding that hit the brother upside the head?" said the one with buck teeth and black glasses. "He's going to feel some pain when I whup his white ass!"

They laughed and slapped hands. I was surprised when Tim introduced me to his friends: "This here is Robert."

The other boy, tall and thin with a man's deep voice, said, "What are you, some kind of Chinaman?" He laughed a loud, deep honking sound.

"No, he's a Flippo or some mongrel dog like you," said the boy with the glasses. "Chinese aren't brown; they're yellow. Haven't you ever seen a Chinaman at those laundries?"

I didn't respond, just climbed back into bed.

He shook his head and continued, "Sure as hell can't play football. Must be here to wash the floors."

The other friend laughed. "Hell, he's got a beak as big as a Jew."

The two laughed and clapped hands.

"Cut him some slack," said Tim. "We're all cooped up with a bunch of rich kids. I'm here to play football and help win some games so the alumni will give money. You're here to play the artist, and George is gonna teach these rich white boys how to play some hoops. And then we're all going to Harvard or Yale or wherever they need some color."

The thin boy nodded. "Hey, dude, we just messin' with you, gimme five."

I held out my hand and he slapped his hand against mine.

"I'm Jackson. And this here is my brother George Dodge, but we call him Slick 'cause he got a slick dick."

Now all three of us were exploding in laughter.

"So why you in the 'firmary, Bob?" George asked. "You get beat up like my man Tim here, who got his bell rung by some honky at the football game yesterday and couldn't remember his Mama?"

"Don't think he know'd her anyway," ribbed Jackson.

Tim threw back his head and laughed.

"I got strep throat," I said.

"You keep that shit away from me," declared Jackson.

"They already gave me a shot."

"They shoot you in the ass?"

I nodded and his eyes widened.

"Why the hell you let them do that to you? You got to have some self-respect! I won't let no motherfucking doctor give me no shots in the ass. Hell, I won't let them give no shots anywhere. I don't like needles."

Steven walked in and tried to slap hands with them, but they just laughed.

"Where'd they find this one, the nursery?" hooted Jackson.

"This here's Steven. He's a mean-ass motherfucker," said Tim Washington. The other two looked at Steven and then laughed and slapped his hands.

Dr. Hart walked into the room carrying his stethoscope. He was wearing a clean, starched white coat and his hair had been slicked down with water and some kind of smelly cream. The same gray-haired nurse followed him.

"If they can make this much noise, they can't be feeling too badly," she said.

"That's my visitors, Dr. Hart," said Tim. "They're a rowdy bunch."

Jackson and George got the hint and said their goodbyes. Dr. Hart examined Tim and pronounced him ready to return back to his dorm. Then he walked over to me.

"Let's see how my strep throat is doing." He took out a tongue-depressor and I opened my mouth. "Mmmm. Still red and still some pus on the tonsils. How do you feel?"

"Kind of weak."

"You'll need to toughen up. This is no tropical paradise. We have cold winters, snow. I'm not doing you any favors coddling you here in the infirmary."

"I don't need to be coddled, sir."

"That Negro fellow, Washington? He was knocked out yesterday and he's ready to run back on the field. That's grit. Life is a battle, and you need to be ready to fight and defend at all times. *Arma virumque cano,*" he recited: "Arms and the man, I sing."

I recognized this line from the text we were studying in Latin. Adults were always trying to show you they remembered the classics; I tried to look impressed.

"I'll give you some pills to take later. You can probably return to class this afternoon. And I'd like you to have dinner with us at the house this weekend."

"I'm going to Boston this weekend....with Steven." I pointed in Steven's direction.

"Ah, so you two have become comrades-in-arms? I suppose there are worse ways to get acquainted. You can learn a lot about a person by watching how he deals with pain and adversity. You can fool people when you are well, but when illness strikes, the truth emerges with the sweat of the fever, as they say. Well then, next weekend."

"Yes sir, Dr. Hart."

"Very good. Pack your things up and get ready for class."

"Okay," I said, having nothing but the clothes on my back. I moved slowly, waiting to see if Steven and I could leave together.

Dr. Hart moved on to Steven. "Any improvement from yesterday? Unfortunately, mononucleosis can hang on for weeks. Let's take a look at your throat." Steven opened his mouth and Dr. Hart shined a light into it. "Not bad. How's the energy level?"

"I want to go back to my dorm," said Steven.

"Yesterday you were ready for intensive care, and today you're well enough to return to your dorm! Another miracle of medicine."

"I feel better," asserted Steven.

"I don't suppose it has anything to do with your trip to Boston with Mr. Thames here? Frankly, I'm not sure it's good idea. You've fallen behind in your studies and probably could benefit by a weekend of catch up. But I'm only the doctor."

"We'll study at my house," said Steven.

"Somehow, I doubt that. Rob, your parents expect me to keep tabs on your activities. I don't want to hear that you have been led astray: No smoking or drinking or running around at night. I can't protect you if you break the rules."

"Yes, sir."

"Well, let's see how you feel after a few days of classes."

We walked back to our dorms as cold gusts of wind blew the leaves off the trees.

"We can take the bus to Kenmore Square and then we'll get a cab. My parents are leaving us the house," plotted Steven.

In the Philippines, it is insulting to refuse an invitation to someone's house. But it would be terrible if I failed my courses. "I'm behind on my English paper and I have to do my Latin and math…" I hedged.

"Don't you want to see Boston?"

"Sure."

"Well, this is your chance!"

I did not want to appear ungrateful, but I was still feeling somewhat dizzy and weak. Eventually, an old Filipino adage drifted into my mind: "No one should travel without the company of a friend."

I nodded my assent. "Okay."

II

I didn't think about the trip until after my last class.

"Arma virumque cano," read Mr. Goodson in Latin, turning to me like a searchlight. "Okay, Thames, translate."

It was the same line Dr. Hart had recited to me in the infirmary.

"Arms and the man, I sing," I said dutifully.

"And what does it mean?"

He gazed around the large, oval, wooden table. Twelve of us sat staring into our books, hoping the answer would become apparent.

"Why does Virgil begin his epic story this way? 'I sing of arms.' What kind of arms? And 'the man'? What man?"

Mr. Goodson was one of those theatrical Danvers teachers. He would jump onto a table, throw a piece of chalk at the blackboard, or shout some Latin phrase at the top of his lungs. He had a long body with a large bald head that turned red in moments of excitement. When he was animated, he looked like a glowing marshmallow on the end of a stick.

"I guess he's singing about arms because they are important in war?" I ventured.

"Good, Mr. Thames. And what about the man?" Now he leaped up on a chair, extended his arms upward toward the heavens and repeated, "And the man?"

No response.

He descended and walked around the table, looking for a victim.

He reached down and put his hands on the arms of blonde Peter

Tiel, whose face turned pink. "Is this the man?"

He moved on to another boy. "Are these the arms?"

"He was talking about weapons," I said. "The man must wield the weapons. Without the man, the weapons do no good."

"Correct, Mr. Thames. Our arms are useless if we do not have the capacity to use them correctly and intelligently." He put his hands on my shoulders and then my hands to demonstrate. "And why does he sing?"

"It's a story, sir," I said. "But he wants to share it with everyone, like a song."

"Like 'Twist and Shout'? 'Shake it up, baby'? Is that something he would have chosen?" He gaped at me and began to awkwardly swivel.

Everyone laughed and my face flushed. Mr. Goodson moved to the boy next to me and massaged his shoulders.

"Do you have the strength to defend yourself, to kill if necessary? To love your companions and die defending them?" He stared at the boy as he continued to massage his shoulders. The boy's face flamed red. "Each of you is that man."

Mr. Goodson turned back to me. "It is through the travels of Aeneas that we will find out who that man really is and how conflict will change him. This is what I want you to think about. Arma virumque cano. Remember it, Thames."

"Yes, sir," I said, relieved to be out of the spotlight.

Mr. Goodson always made me feel uncomfortable. I breathed a sigh of relief as I walked out of class. I was recovering my health, but I still was not eating as much as usual and felt tired each night, long before lights out.

But the anticipation of a new adventure provided me with a burst of energy. I began to think about the trip to Boston as part of a journey in my Aeneid. I found my tan suitcase in the closet, and threw in a pair of pants, a shirt, underwear, toiletries, and lots of books, hoping that by packing them, I would study. We had to catch the bus at two, but my suitcase was so heavy I had to rest it every fifty feet as I walked across campus. Tim Washington walked by and noticed me struggling.

"Hey, my little man, let me get that for you," he said, easily lifting the suitcase with one hand. He carried it to the bus for me.

"Thanks," I said, but he was already gone, running across the lawn toward a group of black students. Steven was wearing a long coat, waiting for me at the bus.

"You almost missed it. Good thing we know Tim, huh? I had to make the bus driver wait for you."

"Sorry. I didn't realize my suitcase would be so heavy."

We sat in the back of the bus and watched the scenery flash by – the river and surrounding farms, trees with multi-colored leaves, cars on the highway. School disappeared and I deeply inhaled through the open window. There were fumes from the bus and the traffic, but I was riveted by the sensation of speed and change of scenery. The bus was full of other students chattering about baseball games, teachers they hated, food they loved, and girls they wanted to see.

"Sarah is coming over tonight for dinner," Steven announced.

"Who?"

"Sarah. My girlfriend. She's so beautiful. I'm going to marry her someday. We decided when we were eight years old. I've known her since I was about three or four. She goes to Concord Academy and she's coming home this weekend, too. Her parents live a few blocks away from my house. You'll fall in love with her, but she's mine."

I considered this for a moment and then said, "In the Philippines some children marry at the age of eleven or twelve, particularly in the Moslem areas. I once had a girlfriend who wanted to marry me, but my parents wouldn't allow me to see her because they were worried that it would distract me from my studies."

"Your parents sound really strict. When you see Sarah you'll know why I want to marry her. And you should see her run. She's on the track team."

"I like to run," I said, not sure why I said it, because in reality I found running painful and embarrassing. What I did like was the satisfaction of overcoming the pain and finishing a race. It was something that at one moment seemed impossible, and then, after some time and effort, possible.

I was not afraid of pain. I feared failure or embarrassment. But not pain.

"You should run with her. But be prepared to lose if you race," he said. "She loves to beat boys."

We were rocked by the rhythm of the bus and the blur of the roadway. Soon we were dozing; occasionally I felt Steven's head on my shoulder, bouncing like a globe as we drove over potholes and cracks in the road. I tried to protect his head from striking a window or seat. Steven was my first real American friend at Danvers. I was glad I had accompanied him. I knew my parents would be proud of me.

He yawned when we stopped. "We're already here? I must have nodded off. I gotta take a piss and then we'll get a taxi."

I gathered our bags and waited for him to return from the men's room at the bus station.

12

We got into the back of the taxi and Steven gave the driver his address. The man was wearing a turban and spoke with a British accent. We could have been anywhere in the world.

I watched the meter click off dollars as we drove; it made me nervous because I did not know how much money Steven had on him. I had only brought $10 from the secret emergency stash my father had given me.

"Will your parents be at home when we arrive?"

"No, they're already off to the Cape."

"Do you have any brothers or sisters?"

"I'm an only child." He grinned. "I think I was a mistake."

I watched as the meter passed twelve dollars and then the taxi slowed.

The house was a grand two-story that stood back from the street. It had a red brick façade with large white wooden windows. Strange twists and spires of green shingles covered the roof, as if mischievous children had wrapped it up as a prank.

We stepped out on to the sidewalk and the driver unloaded our suitcases. Steven paid the driver from a roll of twenty dollar bills.

I dragged the suitcases up the brick stairs, and Steven passed me to unlock the front door. I followed him into a dark alcove with a rack of hanging coats and hats. A small table with mail and magazines stood at the entry. Steven showed me the first of several notes we would find in the house:

Welcome, dear,

Call us tonight at the cottage so that we know you arrived safely. I've left some blueberry muffins in the breadbox for you and your friend. And there's milk in the refrigerator. Make sure to drink some with the muffins. If you need anything, call Rosa and she will come over.

Love,

Martha and Bob

"Rosa is our maid," explained Steven. "She knows where we keep everything in the house."

"Why do your parents sign their letter like that? 'Martha and Bob'?"

"For a while they wanted me to call them 'Mother and Father,' but then I just started calling them by their names and that's what we do now. Let's put our stuff in my bedroom."

He led the way while, once again, I hefted both bags. I followed him through a hall and up another flight of stairs to his room. It had two beds, a desk, and a poster of a half-naked woman in animal furs.

"It's Raquel Welsh."

"I've heard of her. She's a famous actress."

I imagined the kinds of dreams I might have if Raquel Welch were the last face I saw before I went to sleep. "My parents wouldn't allow me to have a poster like that in my room," I said. "They don't allow me to put anything on the walls except paintings of Jesus or landscapes or maps."

"My parents don't come into my room. Just Rosa. They don't really want to be parents because it makes them feel old, so they let me do anything I like. We can drink some wine or beer if you want. I'm gonna call Sarah."

He walked back down the stairs, picked up a telephone, and dialed. I heard him murmuring on the phone and then he said, "Sure, come over now," and hung up. He turned to me and smiled.

"She wants to go running, but I told her to come over here first; you would go running with her."

"*Me?*"

"You said you like to run. Aren't you running cross country?"

"I'm just a beginner!"

I ran cross country because I needed to select a required sport and the other options were football, crew, and soccer, which I had never tried. Running was something I did to escape from the scrutiny of the teachers and coaches as I disappeared into the forest, and the trees would welcome me with their branches and leaves like family. I didn't care if I didn't do it very well. But I wasn't prepared to run with a girl.

"You'll be fine," said Steven. And then he took me on a tour of the house.

The living room felt distinguished and old, almost like Danvers Academy. The chairs sported beautifully woven needlepoint patterns of flowers and vines and seemed arranged to accommodate the conversations of intellectuals, with enough space to allow for the free flow of thoughts. Between them was a small table with a chess board and carved stone pieces, an invitation to combat. A long couch of dark brown leather stretched out opposite. It was the type of couch that allowed you to sink down deeply, as if sliding into a pool. A carved wooden table with lions' heads rested in front of the couch. On the walls, a portrait of a judge in flowing black robes gazed toward a portrait of a woman in a long white and yellow dress. A baby grand piano dominated a corner of the room, while bookcases with hundreds of volumes lined the walls.

The kitchen and dining areas were more modern, with a steel dishwasher and refrigerator, a gleaming faucet, a gray stone countertop that provided an informal eating surface, and a food preparation space across from the stove. A dining room connected to it through an arched opening. I could see an immense, rectangular walnut table and eight carved, high-back chairs.

On the refrigerator there was another note:

Steven,

There is chicken soup in the orange pot. Underneath on the bottom row I left a spinach quiche, which you might like for breakfast. Hamburgers and cheese are also in the meat drawer which you can grill or use in spaghetti sauce.

Love,
Martha

"Let's make spaghetti tonight," said Steven.

"But the soup is already made for us."

"Yes, but this will be more fun, and we can put wine in the sauce. Have you ever had wine in spaghetti sauce?"

"No, I don't think so. How would I know?"

"You would know."

13

The doorbell rang and Steven ran to answer it.

"Sarah!" he yelled, and threw his arms around a girl with blond-brown hair in a silver Concord Academy sweatshirt. She had on running shoes, sweatpants, and a sweatshirt. He pulled her close and hugged her, burrowing his head in her neck. Sarah was about my height, with gray-green eyes and hair pulled back in a ponytail. Her face was flushed, with a few droplets of sweat on her forehead. She had high cheekbones and her eyes became narrow slits when she smiled.

"Hi," she said, extending her hand to me. "I'm Sarah."

"Robert," I said, shaking her hand. Her fingers felt narrow and soft, but strong, like the tendrils of a vine.

"I have to do a run for my cross country practice. Do you want to come with me? Steven said you like to run." Her voice retained the tone of a younger girl, but the assurance of someone much older and more sophisticated.

I panicked for a moment, considering how to answer: just say 'yes', or provide a more detailed explanation of my running experience, or tell her I was ill or just recovering. With so many options I felt unable to speak and just looked into her eyes, which seemed to see deeply, past the practiced smiles and agreeable nods that satisfied most people I met.

Then my voice cracked, like the static of a radio between stations. She continued to smile at me until the words finally emerged, as if my brain had moved the dial and found the right transmission. "I'm not very good at running, but I'll go with you. In my country you never allow anyone to go anywhere by themselves. We consider it bad luck."

"Well, how chivalrous. Where do you come from?"

"I'm from the Philippines."

"I run by myself all the time so you don't have to go. But if you'd like to go, I'd be happy for the company. Let's get going before I cramp up."

"I'll be right back. I have my running shoes and shorts in my suitcase." I hurried upstairs, dressed, and noticed I had an erection. I worried about that and whether Sarah would notice. I also worried that she might talk to me and I would be too distracted to answer. When I returned downstairs Steven and Sarah were discussing dinner.

"Don't go for one of those long runs because I'll have the spaghetti ready soon," said Steven.

"What? You? Make dinner? I'll have to see this." Sarah gave him a playful sock on the shoulder.

"Ouch. That hurt."

"That didn't hurt. What a baby. Okay, let's go."

She pushed the door open and we started jogging down the stairs. "Just follow me. We'll run on the sidewalk for a while and then we'll come to a park and we can make a few loops around the park and then we'll see how you're feeling."

Sarah darted out ahead of me. In her sweats, the muscles of her thighs and shoulders stood out with each step. She took long graceful strides and I tried to emulate them rather than my usual short choppy stride. But it was difficult on the sidewalk, with all the cracks and obstacles – hydrants and barrels and people walking dogs. I bumped into a bicycle that someone had left standing on the sidewalk in front of a house. Sarah looked back at me. "Are you all right?"

I tried to lower my voice into a more masculine sounding range, rather than the higher-pitched gasps I used when I ran. "Yes."

"I can slow down."

"No, I'm fine. Really."

"The park is just up ahead."

I saw the entrance of the park – a brick gate with a sign that read "Robert Kelly Jr. Park." There was a plaque that described Robert Kelly, a veteran of World War II who had died during D-day and killed 35 Germans while saving his battalion.

Sarah began to quicken her pace. The sidewalk gave way to a dirt path. She seemed to bounce as she ran. She reminded me of an angel running on clouds, her hair soaring in the wind, and her arms extended out like wings. Her sweatshirt moved up her back, exposing the light skin of her waist as she stretched out her stride. From her waist you could just begin to see up her back and down toward her bottom and legs. The trail became darker as trees and bushes created a canopy. I felt myself beginning to gasp as we picked up speed, and I had to concentrate on breathing and stepping and not losing sight of Sarah.

As the vegetation continued to thicken, it reminded me of a kind of forest where you might find animals and perhaps murderers hiding. When I came through the dense canopy Sarah was waiting in a clearing.

"How are you doing?"

I was breathing too hard to answer. "You're a very fast runner." I finally blurted out. My heart pounded and sweat dripped down my forehead.

She smiled. "You think so?"

"Yes, like a gazelle." We stood in the clearing. There was a bench to one side of the path, and I sat down for a moment to take some deep breaths. Sarah stretched her legs as she leaned against a tree, waiting for me to catch my breath before continuing the run.

"Really? A gazelle?" She smiled again.

"Definitely. Or a horse. A racehorse. Even a horse with wings, a unicorn. Or a zebra." I added more animals to the list; she seemed to enjoy the comparisons, and I wanted to make her happy while I was recovering my breath. "Or a tiger or lion. I haven't actually seen them in person, but I've watched them in movies. Or an ostrich. Even certain dogs are quite fast runners, like the greyhound," I added.

She laughed and held up her hands for me to stop. I changed the subject.

"So, how long have you known Steven?" I asked.

"Oh, we've pretty much grown up together. Neither of us has any brothers or sisters so we've been like brother and sister to each other."

She sat next to me on the bench. "He's a bit of pain sometimes, spoiled by his parents, but he's also a lot of fun. He helps me have a good time and do things I wouldn't do on my own. When I'm with him I don't have to be so serious and worry about school or anything. We can be silly, like kids. Do you know what I mean?"

"Yes, I think so. I'm always worried about completing my assignments and my grades. I feel like I'd fail if I didn't work hard. My parents sent me here to the United States, and I don't want to disappoint them. But Steven doesn't seem to worry about his grades."

She was looking at me intently. It made me nervous. "Well, we can run again. I think I've caught my breath."

"Sorry. Sometimes I like to go fast through the trees. I just lose myself and all sense of how fast I'm running. I'm in my own world. Does that happen to you?"

"I don't think I'm fast, but sometimes I do feel like the trees are lifting me up and carrying me. Do you ever get a side ache or feel your heart pounding when you run?"

She nodded. "Sometimes, but I run through it. Pain is in the mind. I've tried meditating, but running is easier for me."

"Meditating?"

"My parents are into yoga and Buddhism. My dad used to be a lawyer but then he quit and opened up an ice cream shop. He's learning the guitar. My parents are thinking about buying land and starting a commune where everyone will share the work and food. They want to move to the Southwest and start a community."

"Where is the Southwest?"

"Somewhere out near Arizona and New Mexico. People ride horses and wear cowboy hats and have meditation teepees. I've seen pictures. And the Indians out there love to run in the mountains." She stood up and I followed her. "I don't really want to live in a commune. I'm more interested in politics and stopping U.S. imperialism. Did you know that the fighting in Southeast Asia is about capitalism? We want their people to work like slaves for our companies and then buy our products. It's about racism, too. I want to be a civil rights lawyer. It's really disgusting how we treat Negroes. They can't go to school where they want, or even sit on a bus where they like. I wish I could be a Negro so I could fight back. But if I were a lawyer, at least I could defend them if they got arrested. Do you ever feel any prejudice against you?"

"Everyone at Danvers is very nice to me. Sometimes they make a joke about my accent or my dark skin. But it's just joking."

"They may not be joking. Sometimes they might be saying what they feel," she said. "You need to stick up for yourself. Anyway, I think dark skin is beautiful." Sarah smiled, showing off her perfect teeth.

I got aroused again and worried that Sarah would notice. I started to jog forward slowly, and she followed. We moved through the park around to the entrance.

"Do you want to do one more loop?" she asked.

"Okay," I said, attempting to be courageous.

This time we moved slower, until the end when Sarah sped up, practically flying to the park entrance. Then we jogged slowly home on the sidewalk.

"Whew," she said, "that felt good. Thanks for going with me."

I nodded as we climbed the stairs to Steven's house. He pulled open the door with a flourish. I could smell the spaghetti sauce wafting out from the kitchen. He had also put on some music. The Beatles were singing, "I once had a girl or should I say she once had me..." He ushered us in like guests at a party.

"Here, have a glass of wine," he said, pouring a glass of red wine for each of us.

"Are you sure?" I asked.

"It's just one glass. Don't worry."

I looked at Sarah and she raised her eyebrows in a way that made me wonder if I should go along with his plan. But she also had a glass in her hand and began to sip. I tasted my wine and was surprised that it was not sweet at all, but smoky and fruity. I had tried wine a few times before at home and didn't really like the taste, but this was nice and I was thirsty from running. Besides, Steven seemed so excited to serve it; I wanted to be appropriately gracious.

Sarah slowly sipped from her glass and then asked, "Steven, what would your parents say if they found out?"

"They don't mind if I have a glass with dinner. Anyway they're on the Cape. It's no big deal. And it's really good wine. My dad said it was from France."

Sarah had another sip. "Mmm. It is good! I guess no one needs to know."

"The spaghetti is ready," Steven said, leading us into the kitchen. "Everyone grab a plate and then we can take it to the table."

I took my plate and grabbed a clump of noodles and spooned the sauce over them. There was also cheese to sprinkle over the sauce, with bits of tomato and hamburger in it that tasted really great. I finished my first glass of wine and Steven poured me another. He also poured a second glass for Sarah. By that time, I was beginning to feel the effects of the wine – a mild glow of warmth and a feeling of love for Sarah and Steven, my two American friends. I noticed that our conversation was animated and that we were all laughing loudly. This was unusual for me. Steven opened another bottle of wine and no one objected.

After dinner Steven suggested we play poker. He brought out the cards and dealt them to us at the cleared table. Although I was familiar with most card games, I had not played much poker.

"Are we playing for money?" asked Sarah.

"I don't have much money," I confessed.

"Okay," said Steven, "Let's pay strip poker."

Steven and Sarah stared at each other and giggled.

I looked to see if they were joking, but Steven dealt the cards and we began to play a hand. I had never participated in such a game. I could not imagine that Sarah would agree, since she risked exposure in front of two boys. But she seemed fine with it. I suppose it was the wine and my curiosity that allowed me to overcome my apprehension and embarrassment.

The first game, Sarah ended up with a pair of twos and Steven and I had nothing." Okay," she commanded, "take off your shirts."

"It's kind of cold," I said.

I was hoping to find an excuse that we could all accept so that we could end the game, but Steven had already pulled off his shirt, so I did too. I imagined that it was like being at the beach, where we could go without a shirt. I was beginning to experience a slight excitement along with my trepidation. Steven dealt the cards again. I began to calculate how many hands I would have to lose before I would be depleted of all my clothing, and I wondered if we were all wearing the same number of items.

How many layers did Sarah have under her sweatshirt?

This time I got good cards – two queens. I drew three more cards and got an ace, a nine and a three. Steven bet his shoes and his pants. Sarah bet her sweatshirt. Even though it was only one item, we agreed to let her sweatshirt equal two items. Our approach to the game was flexible. I bet my shoes and socks, and laid down my two queens. Steven and Sarah moaned. When Sarah took off her sweatshirt, I saw that she had a Concord Academy track t-shirt underneath.

Steven pulled off his shoes and pants and started to laugh. "Close your eyes and pass me another glass of wine," he demanded.

Sarah laughed. "You're the one who wanted to play strip poker!"

At this point I felt slightly numb, as if I were watching a movie in which the plot was becoming increasingly strange and thrilling.

Steven dealt the cards again. Steven bet his socks; Sarah bet her sweat pants; I bet my pants, I suppose to demonstrate to Sarah that I was not afraid. This time Steven won. I watched as Sarah removed her sweat pants. Underneath were gym shorts. I pulled off my pants anxiously, revealing my underwear.

Steven laughed. "Look at our boners."

I was embarrassed that he had made this observation; I had hoped it might go unnoticed. I had never had something like this happen to me with a girl; I was tingling and warm all over. My heart was racing, but I couldn't move.

"I'm going home," Sarah said. She began pulling on her sweat pants.

"You're such a chicken. I just won a hand, and now you want to leave," said Steven.

"That's not why. It's because you boys – " she stopped, her face red.

"It's not our fault. It's just our hormones," said Steven.

I was ready to collapse in a heap. It was as if a puppeteer were controlling my arms and legs. The wine had made us do things that we would never have done otherwise.

Sarah shook her head, sighing. "One more hand."

I felt powerless to stop, even though I knew that I should. Steven dealt the cards again and I won. He pulled off his underwear and shouted, "I'm naked!"

Sarah removed her shorts and laughed along with him.

I watched them both in a state of silent amazement.

"Steven, it's like a big pencil. It looks so weird!" she exclaimed. I realized she had never seen an erect penis before.

"You should see Robert's," Steven said.

"Why?"

"It's just different. More hair."

"How do you know?"

"We had to have our pictures taken without our clothes on. We were next to each other in line."

"You must be joking."

"No, it's true. Robert, show her yours."

"No," I said, shuddering. I could feel my face get hot and my lip begin to twitch involuntarily. I was aroused and terrified at the same time. I wanted to run away, but felt glued to my chair, waiting to see what would happen next.

"Okay," said Steven as he dealt the cards. "Robert's got a good hand. Look at him smiling."

Sarah frowned. "All right, show me."

I laid down my flush.

Without a word, Sarah slowly pulled off her shirt, exposing her breasts. Steven breathed in deeply. I felt myself falling out of my seat, mesmerized by her small, round breasts.

"Haven't you ever seen a girl's breasts before?" asked Steven.

I couldn't answer.

Sarah suddenly began to collect her clothes.

"What are you doing?" said Steven.

"I have to go," she said, and scurried to the hall bathroom. Moments later, she hurried out the front door and slammed it behind her. I felt like I was in a movie theater when the film breaks and the lights abruptly come back on, and you find yourself surrounded by mundane objects – chairs and soda and popcorn – the illusion of the fantasy ruptured.

"Should we go after her?" I asked.

"Nah, she'll be fine. It's not that late."

We dressed and began to do the dishes.

"How did you like her?" Steven asked. "Sarah."

"Do you realize what we did? We took off our clothes with a girl."

"Neat, huh?"

"It's terrible, a sin!"

"Is it?"

"In the Philippines you can't do something like this. There are always parents and relatives around and you can never be alone."

"Well, you're in America now."

"I have never done anything like this before."

He flicked some water at me, grinning. "But did you like it?"

I sighed and nodded. "Yeah, but I worry that she's upset."

"Nah, she was just mad because you won. She wanted to see you naked."

"Do you think so?"

"Sure! Girls are curious, just like boys."

We watched television for a while and then went up to his bedroom. Steven took the bed under the poster of Raquel Welch. He said he felt horny and was going to jerk off; was that okay? It was because of seeing Sarah's breasts.

I said "okay" and he handed me some tissues, "just in case." Then he shut off the lights.

I could hear him breathing heavily, but I all I could think about was Sarah and her body, running through the forest.

14

In the morning I woke up before Steven and did some homework, and then we went out for breakfast. Steven's parents had left him an envelope of money for food and taxis. There was a restaurant that served eggs, bacon and coffee. We talked about how to spend the day. There was a baseball game at Fenway Park; the Red Sox were not doing well so we'd be able to get good seats. Or we could go to a movie or a museum.

"Should we call Sarah?" I asked.

"She doesn't like baseball."

"Maybe she'd want to go to a movie."

"Okay," he said. "I'll call her when we get back from the game. I want to take you to Fenway Park."

The stadium was surrounded by a large brick wall in the middle of the city, so when we walked through the gates and into the seating area I was surprised at all the grass growing on the field. The walls were olive green with nets that collected the baseballs if they were hit too far for a fielder to catch them. The people who watched the game wore t-shirts and caps that had a "B" on them. Sometimes they screamed at other people who were wearing caps with a "C" on them. This reminded me about school and my grades and my struggle to avoid C's and get B's. I wished I had brought my homework with me because there was ample time to complete an assignment between the long stretches when two men stood throwing the ball to each other and everyone else seemed to be waiting for something to happen.

When we returned to his house, Steven called Sarah. She said she had to go shopping with her mother, but asked if I wanted to go running with her first.

I bolted upstairs to put on my running clothes and shoes. The doorbell rang, and I could hear Steven and Sarah, quietly talking down below. By the time I arrived, Steven had disappeared. Sarah was on the front porch, stretching.

"Hi," she said, without meeting my eyes. "Let's go."

She turned and started jogging away. I closed the door and hurried after her.

We started jogging the same route as before, but before we got to the park, Sarah stopped and began walking.

"I feel weird about last night," she said, looking at me nervously.

"I don't remember much," I said. "Sometimes when I drink alcohol, I completely forget events – as if my memory was erased."

"Oh, really?" she said, smiling a little,

"I remember we were playing cards, but nothing after that."

"Really? You don't remember anything?"

"No, I don't," I said, as sincerely as possible. I wanted to spare her the embarrassment.

"Well, that's a relief, because I think we acted silly and I didn't want you to have a bad impression of me."

"Are you and Steven sweethearts?" I blurted.

I'm not sure why I asked such a personal question. In the Philippines, we wouldn't have been so direct.

"Sweethearts? Do you mean Steven as my boyfriend?" she laughed. "He's really more like a brother than a boyfriend. We joke about getting married someday, but it's just a joke."

I was relieved to hear this, except that Steven was convinced otherwise.

"But what about you? I don't know anything about you," she asked.

"I don't have a sweetheart in the Philippines," I said, and then I told her a little bit of my personal history, and how I had ended up at Danvers.

"You're funny – different – I mean, from other boys. It's refreshing. Do you like Steven? He doesn't have many friends, but you seem to get along well."

"Most of the other boys at the school hardly see me; I'm like a ghost to them. Steven has been very kind. I hardly know him, but he invited me to his home. And then he introduced me to you." She smiled and looked into my eyes and stared for several seconds.

"Do you want to run again? You don't have to."

"Yes, I'll follow you."

We turned down an alley and jogged past a laundry and then past an old cemetery with fading headstones from hundreds of years ago. Sarah went striding over the curb and past an old lady with a dog. I almost tripped.

"Are you okay?" she asked, glancing back.

"Yes, yes. I'm fine." I would have followed her wherever she went – upstairs, across a road, into a ditch – the way I used to follow beautiful tropical fish through the coral. We passed a school and a post office and then went down another alley. Suddenly we were back at Steven's house and Sarah turned to give me a little hug before running off. Except that neither of us released our arms very quickly. For what seemed like an eternity, but was maybe only a few seconds, I could feel her lungs expanding and contracting as she breathed against me.

Steven and I mostly slept on the bus back to Danvers that night. He had a headache, and wasn't very talkative.

"Thanks for taking me to your house," I said, as we carried our suitcases across the quad. Mine felt lighter than it had a few days before. "It was really great, and the baseball game was too."

"And Sarah," he added.

"Sarah, too. She is a very beautiful American girl."

"You liked her."

"Of course." I felt my face get warm as I recalled her hug.

"It's all right. I can share her with you."

"What do you mean?"

He smiled. "She can be your girlfriend too."

Then he walked off towards his dorm with his suitcase. I watched him for a few minutes but he never turned back.

This was not a custom in the Philippines. Sometimes several men serenade one woman, but the woman chooses only one man. Even though we are generally peaceful people, we are competitive when it comes to love. There is only one winner. Sometimes there is even violence.

I was perplexed at Steven's attitude, but also grateful, because now I wouldn't have to give either of them up.

15

I didn't see Steven for several days. There were homework assignments and quizzes and daily cross country practice. Although memories of the weekend constantly intruded upon my study, I never made time to walk over to Steven's dorm. Finally, he showed up at my door Thursday evening. I was working on an essay for English class about "truth" and whether it was "an absolute or relative attribute." Was it like light and dark, with shades in between, or more like life and death, where you are only alive or dead? I was reading Plato, Aristotle, and the Bible to buttress my arguments.

Steven knocked on my door and came in before I could answer it. He plopped down on my bed as if it were his. "I can't take it anymore," he said.

"What?"

"Everything. It sucks."

I figured I better close my door and find out what was wrong. "What happened?"

"I flunked my algebra test, and I've got a fucking headache."

"Maybe you should go to the infirmary. They can give you aspirin."

"I've already taken aspirin. I just need to sleep."

"Do you want to rest here for a while?"

"Yeah. I don't want to be in my room by myself in case I get worse."

"Well…I can go study out in the hall and shut off the light here for you."

"No, I don't want to be alone. You can study. I'll just put the blanket over my head."

"Okay." I tried to return to Plato, but I was distracted by Steven's presence. I started worrying. Should I call Dr. Hart or the dorm master? I had some obligation to Steven because he had become my friend, but I also had to complete my assignments and prepare for class.

I felt badly that he had failed his test. I would also have felt ill.

I returned to my essay, writing, "Truth is an absolute. Something is either true or it is false. There is no middle ground. Just as a circle has a certain form and a name, all statements can be classified as true or false. But because of the consequences of the truth, we often disguise it and use deception to hide it, hoping that we can avoid the consequences. If you like your friend's girlfriend, do you tell him the truth or just pretend it is not so? If you lie, the friend may not become angry, but you will create within yourself a conflict between the words you say and the way you feel. If you tell the truth, you may lose your friend, and if the girl does not accept you, you may lose her as well. In the Philippines, we value harmony between people above all else. Therefore, we would not lie, but rather provide hints and clues about how we see the truth to the friend and the girl. We might bring in other friends and relatives who could help deliver the message. By revealing truth gradually and transforming what it looks like, relationships between people can be protected.

In America, people generally value a blunt confrontation over the truth. Although this approach creates a clear picture for everyone, there may be hurt feelings and loss of face if the truth is embarrassing or unpleasant. Some people believe that there is an objective truth that you can measure, like how hot the water is or how much someone weighs. And then there is subjective truth, like saying that all people are equal. You cannot measure it. The only way it is true is because of the relationships of power between people. This is called relative subjectivism."

I provided references for my statements and felt satisfied that I had covered the question. When I finished, I called out Steven's name, but he didn't answer. I checked under the blanket to make sure he was breathing; he was sleeping peacefully. Should I wake him up and walk him back to his room, or let him sleep in my bed? I was used to sleeping on the floor in the Philippines because we had sleeping mats. We also had beds because my parents were Americans. But sometimes I just liked to sleep in the Philippine style. Except I hadn't brought a sleeping mat to Danvers.

I finally decided that the bed was probably big enough for both of us if we didn't move around too much. We were both somewhat small.

I washed up and very quietly got into bed next to Steven. He moved to the edge of the bed so there was room for both of us.

In the night I felt his arm around my shoulder, pulling me close. I was not sure if he was having a dream, but I did not resist. Then I felt his hands begin to wander over my body. At first I nearly laughed because it tickled. Then I got embarrassed. I did not oppose sexual feelings between people of the same sex, but I did not feel them myself. I certainly did not feel that way about Steven. However, I also felt some obligation to him. His hand traced the contour of my back and down my leg, and then he reached inside my underwear. It was different from any other feeling I'd known, like being examined by a doctor. At first I was scared and tried to remove his hand. He rubbed my legs and back and I tried to move away. But then I gave in. It felt good to be touched in that way.

"Pretend I'm Sarah," he said.

16

Steven left early in the morning and I went off to class. We did not discuss the night. I felt uncomfortable and wondered what it all meant about me. I hoped that by not talking about it and not thinking about it, I would convince myself it had never happened. But three days later he returned and fell asleep in my bed again. I worried because any participation now would signal my conscious acceptance. And this was an infraction of the rules; the penalty was suspension or expulsion. Even though we had not been caught, I did not want to risk it again. I tried to awaken Steven by calling his name and moving his arms, but he just rolled like a dead body. And so I slept next to him again. And again in the night, I felt his hands on my back and between my legs, and there was nowhere for me to escape. When I awakened in the morning, his arms were around my chest. I felt like a captive.

The next day a letter arrived in my post office box from Sarah. I was happy to receive her letter because it contained her address, and now I could write to her without informing Steven.

Dear Robert,

I was just listening to the Beatles and it reminded me of the weekend at Steven's house. Now I'm back at school and we just had a cross country meet yesterday. I came in third for my team, which is pretty good for a sophomore. Classes are tough, especially algebra. English is not bad. We are reading Faulkner and his sentences go on and on for a whole page, and I can't understand how anyone can keep up with his thoughts, especially because they seem to change midway through the sentence. We have a dance coming up next month. Can you ever come down for a dance? If you could, I would invite you. Maybe I can borrow my parents' car in case you need a ride. Steven could come too, because I have a friend who could go with him. Or if you have a dance at Danvers, we could come up there.

Sarah

I carefully folded up the letter. It was my first letter from a girl. I tried to think about what I should say to her. I did not know how to dance, but I wanted to see her again, and the invitation suggested that she was more interested in being with me than Steven. But this was very awkward. She was different from girls I had met in the Philippines. I was not sure how I imagined a double date with Steven might work out. I should have analyzed these questions the same way I analyzed my algebra and geometry problems – with logic – but instead, I found myself imagining her hair as I followed her through the park and the revelation of her breasts during our poker game.

I wanted to be with her. She was fearless, independent, and tough, but could she guide me through this thorny thicket of feelings? I still had my courses and tests to consider. I decided that I would answer the letter, but not all of the questions. I wrote:

Dear Sarah,

I received your letter today. Congratulations on your race. I believe that we have a dance next month here at Danvers. I am not sure about the arrangements or requirements, but I will find out. I have something I need to discuss with you. It is somewhat personal. Do you have a telephone number and a time I could call you? School is difficult and we are beginning to have tests every week. I think I have mostly C's so far and maybe a B in English. But I have to work so hard to get these low grades that I am somewhat discouraged. My running continues to improve. I finished my last race in 16 minutes, which was an improvement of 45 seconds, and I was in the top half of finishers. But it is still not as good as I would like. I need more practice with you. Steven is fine. Thanks for writing me the letter. It is the first one I have received at Danvers, except for my parents.

Sincerely,
Robert Thames Jr.

After I mailed the letter, I worried about what else I could have said. I did not tell her that I thought about her every night. I even signed the letter formally, the way they teach you in school. I felt some relief that I had at least hinted at the situation with Steven, although I had not mentioned it exactly. I was hoping she would call me, and when I heard her voice, my thoughts would become more coherent.

I liked Steven and enjoyed his friendship, but his visits to my room had become extremely disruptive and upsetting. I did not want him touching me anymore. I decided I would sleep on the floor if he fell asleep in my bed. And he was disturbing my studying schedule. I would ask him about his own assignments and whether he needed help to complete them. I did what I could to help him, tutoring him in algebra, though I was far less capable in most subjects than he was. But thus far he expressed no interest in his subjects, or would laugh and explain that he had already completed his assignments and just wanted to discuss more important subjects like the utopian vision of Island by Aldous Huxley, and the nature of reality, and whether dreams or visions inspired by drugs gave access to a reality that we could not perceive during normal consciousness.

By the next weekend, I had gotten more exasperated with Steven and refused to let him spend the night. When I heard a knock at my door on Friday night, I opened the door brusquely. Then I noticed that there was someone with him wearing a sweatshirt with a hood and cap. When the cap tilted, I realized it was a girl.

"Sarah!" I gasped, nearly speechless.

I allowed them to pass inside, feeling surprised, excited, and anxious. We had very strict rules about girls visiting a boy's room. The penalty could be expulsion.

"Shh. Someone could hear you," said Steven, shutting the door

"But what are you doing here?" I felt paralyzed.

"I thought that you wanted to see me," she said nervously. "I borrowed my parents' car."

"But we could get expelled," I said, laughing.

"Didn't you want to talk to me?" she looked a bit dismayed.

"Yes, sure!" I didn't know what to do. I leaned forward and touched her arm. "But I'm nervous in case anyone should find out. Girls are not allowed in our rooms."

"I'm not a girl. I'm a boy."

She turned and showed me how the cap hid her long hair. It was true that in her sweatshirt and jeans and cap, she could pass for a boy. Just as long as no one saw her face.

"You worry too much," said Steven. "She parked downtown and we walked here."

"How long are you staying?" I asked.

"I don't know. What do you do here on Friday nights?"

"Usually I just study." I shrugged.

"There's a movie," said Steven. *The African Queen.*"

"I love that film," said Sarah. "Katherine Hepburn is so cool."

"I think so too," I said. "Let's go!"

"We just have to act like three boys," she said. She lightly socked me on the shoulder with her fist. "Isn't this how boys pal around?"

Once we left the room, I began to enjoy Sarah's presence and proximity. She was beautiful, even dressed up like a boy. She had fine features and full, prominent lips like Katherine Hepburn. Her high cheek bones and narrow eyes radiated the same kind of aura and intelligence. And she seemed to have the same combination of class, determination, and reckless courage as the character of Rose Sayer, fighting the Germans in a boat in the middle of Africa.

At the school auditorium, Sarah, Steven, and I sat in the last row, away from our classmates. We did not want anyone to notice her. We flanked her on either side, like eager lieutenants, although I was already plotting to separate her from Steven.

In the dark, her fingers stretched for mine. Our hands touched and then she grasped my fingers and thumb gently in her palm and rubbed them softly. This was a message that we were a "we," in a secret code without a word exchanged. We sat like that for about five minutes, and I hardly breathed until she withdrew her hand back to her lap.

Although the movie was very exciting and romantic, I could not concentrate on the story because I was pondering the next scene of my own life with Sarah.

After the movie, we walked back toward the dorms. There were boys walking and running all around us. One of them slapped my head and yelled something about leeches crawling on me, an allusion to the movie. I wondered how I might have some time with Sarah, but was afraid to say the wrong thing, so I just walked silently.

Sarah must have read my mind. "Robert needs to talk to me," she said to Steven as we approached the dorms.

"Okay," he said, oblivious to the implications.

"We need to talk alone, Steven, by ourselves."

"Oh…" he said. "Sure. I'll meet you back here later, in front of my dorm."

Sarah and I watched as Steven disappeared into his dormitory.

"That wasn't so difficult! I was going to call you, but then I realized I could get off for the weekend and drive up here. I wanted to surprise you."

"Well you did. I'm very surprised. And happy." I grabbed her hand and squeezed it and she squeezed back.

She smiled. "Okay, so what did you want to talk about? It sounded like something important," she said.

I hesitated a moment. She looked at me with concern. "What is it?"

"It's…Steven. He comes to my room almost every night now and falls asleep in my bed." I was too embarrassed to tell her the rest.

"In your bed?"

"He won't wake up."

"So what do you do?"

"I sleep on the floor." I was sure that Sarah noticed my embarrassment.

Sarah began to laugh. First it was a muffled chuckle, and then it grew louder. I stood watching until she finally subsided into a giggle. Then she said, "If he were a dog jumping on your bed what would you do?"

"I wouldn't allow a dog to sleep in my bed," I said.

"But if he did?"

"I would push him off."

"Or what else?"

"Kick him."

"Okay, that's what you need to do."

"I can't just kick him. That would hurt him. Or his feelings. It's not something I can do."

"Whose room is it? Whose bed is it? *Yours.* What can he do? Unless you want him to sleep with you. Do you?"

"No. Not at all. It's very awkward."

"Well, think of him as a big, playful pet – a mischievous dog who'll get up on chairs and sofas if you let him, who'll steal your food and wag his tail innocently. He's a loyal dog, but he needs discipline and training. His parents spoil him, you know."

"Really?"

"Yes, he's quite spoiled. That is why he does the things he does to you. But I've trained him to listen to me," she said.

"I don't think I could kick him," I said.

"You must, and hard. Then he'll learn."

We continued to walk, past the library and Dr. Hart's house, toward the infirmary, with its lights glowing out into the surrounding woods. The shadows of trees hid the path that we followed tentatively with our feet. When we were fully concealed, she kissed me. The kiss was different from any I had imagined, longer and more insistent her tongue moving inside my mouth. A French kiss. I had heard other boys talk about it and had often wondered what the appeal of it could be, but now I knew. I put my arms around her and pulled her close. I could not see her face; I only felt her lips and tongue and cool cheeks against mine.

"That's why I drove here," she said softly.

She pressed her face against mine again, ran her fingers through my hair, and hugged me close. Her hair fell out of her cap and spilled down over us. The rest was like a dream, passing in a blur. I remember the coldness of the ground, the wet leaves against my back, Sarah's hair and coat and the smell of her lavender-scented skin. The taste of her mouth and neck, soft and rich and sweet. Her hands racing over my body like a feverish pianist – I was the piano creating sounds and rhythms and crashing chords in response. Our fingers moved through sweatshirts, over backs, down hips and up to breasts. Her hands positioned me inside of her before I could realize what she was doing and ask her to stop. Our motion increased rhythmically, until it was out of control, swept into a whirlwind of breathing, clutching, and rocking. And suddenly, I felt that I would explode into a million fragments. I could not stop as it went on and on until she cried out. And then I felt a sense of quiet and peace, of floating above the trees, arms and legs intertwined as the moon began to cast a soft light as it rose. I felt that perhaps I had died and was floating in the clouds in heaven. Until that moment I had not imagined that I would ever experience such a feeling. But as I lay there, I could not imagine any feeling that could be better.

I don't know if it lasted ten minutes or an hour. Suddenly there was a man, running with his dog and his flashlight – a teacher from the school who saw us in the moonlight – calling out as the dog began to bark.

"Run!" Sarah said, and I jumped to my feet, pulled up my pants, and ran, faster than in any cross country race. I imagined a Danvers banner stood at the finish line, if only I could run fast enough. I passed by Steven on the path. What was he doing here? Had he followed us, like a dutiful dog? He started running too, but in the opposite direction, towards Sarah. As I looked back, the teacher had stopped both him and Sarah, the dog furiously barking and growling at them. More infirmary lights blinked on and students and nurses came out to see what the ruckus was about. I ran in the shadows, all the way to my dorm and quietly bounded up the steps to my room, my door, and my bed. I plunged, under the covers, into a world of whirling thoughts and fears and dreams until it became light.

The next day, when Steven's parents came to take him away, I heard the other boys yelling as he walked across the grass, "Hey, Thompson, you stud, how was she?"

I stood there, watching, safe in my anonymity. One of the boys told me that the girl was from Concord Academy, and had been collected by their Dean of Student Affairs the night before. "Get it? Student Affairs," he laughed.

Steven waved and smiled like a young politician as he got into his parents' car. He seemed to bask in the attention, while I nervously hid away in my room. I felt horrible. I heard he had been suspended for one week; he would have been expelled if his parents had not been donors to the school. The boys in my dorm talked about how it was guys like Steven, the quiet ones, whom you would never expect, who would surprise you. I listened and agreed. And wondered if I would be next.

What had he revealed?

I was terrified that I might be sent back to the Philippines in disgrace. My parents had scarcely acknowledged the existence of my sexuality, and the idea that I might be dismissed for something sexual would be an unspeakable horror. I had broken school rules, family rules, and God's rules. Punishment seemed almost inevitable.

All of that was compounded by the shame of leaving Sarah in the woods and allowing Steven to take the punishment that should have been mine. And I worried about Sarah and what would happen to her for being caught. Her parents would be furious and her school would punish her and I could do nothing. I prayed that I might be spared, and promised that it would never happen again, if only God would help me. Suddenly all my doubts about the existence of God were replaced by an allegiance to the power that could bestow upon me protection and the forgiveness of my sins. The theories of Darwin and the Big Bang were useless. Probability and relativity offered no solutions.

I watched and waited. I counted each hour and then each day, as one more gift from God. I imagined Jesus on the cross, dying for my sins, writhing in pain to free me from detection. Never again, I vowed to Him, even as I had dreams about Sarah and me lying together on the ground, bodies entwined. I could scarcely concentrate on my studies. I would just stare at the books and at the words on the pages that lay deaf and dumb, like stones on a field.

Finally, Dean Maiser came to our dorm to conduct interviews. Several of us had an appointment, and by the time it was my turn, I already knew the questions.

"Hello, Robert," Dean Maiser said as I entered the common room. He looked tired and bored. His short gray hair gave him the appearance of a retired military officer. He taught American history and religion in addition to his administrative duties. He was a strict disciplinarian who could discover the truth by peering through a boy's eyes, deep into his soul, and tearing it out like a hook in a fish's gullet. In former years, when corporeal punishment was tolerated, he had whipped recalcitrant boys with a leather strap. It was rumored that he still practiced this form of punishment.

"Hello, sir," I said, wondering if I should sit down.

"You understand our honor code?"

"Yes."

"And what does the honor code mean to you?"

"We must tell the truth about any violation of the rules. If we do not tell the truth we are as guilty as the person who committed a violation," I said.

"Sit down," he said, and pressed his gaze upon mine. "This is the code that governs everything we do. It's the basis for our education and the values we instill in each and every one of you, no matter what your experience has been before arriving here. It's more important than your grades. It's how we create gentlemen who will be the future leaders of our country. The code rises above your responsibility to your friends, even if your friend might be guilty."

"Yes, I understand."

"Do you realize that if you violate the honor code, you will be expelled?"

"Yes."

"Did you have any contact with Steven Thompson on Friday the 10th of October?"

I hesitated, as if I had seriously contemplated the question. I thought of the boys who had seen me walking back from the movie. I imagined what Steven might have said during his interrogation. My lip began to twitch, so I put my hand on my chin and mouth to mask it, trying to appear thoughtful and reflective.

"No," I concluded.

I felt Dean Maiser's unrelenting stare, trying to gauge the veracity my answer. I suppose if I had been the first of his interviews, I might have wilted and confessed. But he was tired, and I was the tenth boy he had already seen. He moved on to his next question.

"Do you know a young lady named Sarah Brand?"

"No," I said, and looked him straight in the eye so that there could be no doubt. Even then I convinced even myself that it was the truth: Who was Sarah Brand anyway?

"Never met her?"

"No," I said, wiping my memories clean like the plates from our spaghetti dinner.

Dean Maiser squinted his eyes as if he were searching for something, a bug perhaps that had landed on me. "Robert, where are you from?"

"The Philippines, sir."

"And in the Philippines do people tell the truth when you ask them a question?"

"Sir?"

"It's a simple question. Do people tell the truth in the Philippines?"

"Yes, sir, we tell the truth."

"That's interesting. Because when I was in the Army, I had a friend from the Philippines. He told me that Filipinos survived by telling the Japanese and the Spaniards and the Americans what they wanted to hear. They had no concept of the truth the way that we do here in America. That's why I never wanted any Filipino students here at Danvers."

I gazed at him innocently, without malice.

He shook his head. "But times have changed. You understand what the truth is, don't you, Robert?"

"Yes, sir."

"And you've been telling me the truth?"

"Yes, sir."

"All right, then. That's all. You can tell the next boy to come in."

I think he knew that I was lying, but his trust in the honor code and our obligations to follow it as gentlemen was more important to him than the truth.

And I was not a gentleman.

Later, I had moments of imagining that I would come forward and admit my guilt and prove myself to be a gentleman. I would stand up for Sarah and fight to keep her – whatever the cost. I would apologize to her parents and to her school. I might even be spared for my honesty. But such moments were quickly supplanted by my fear of discovery. Who had seen me at the movie? Would the man with the dog recognize me some night at dinner? Did Sarah despise me? Did Steven laugh at me? Had I failed the school by lying to Dean Maiser? Was I a fraud and a fake? Could I ever reverse a moral failing, or would I always be tainted by my acts of cowardice and deceit?

Numerous times, for many days, I wanted to see each one of them and explain. I wanted to write or talk with Sarah, but I was terrified of exposure and expulsion. And the fear overwhelmed everything else. When I thought of her at night, the ache I felt in the pit of my stomach was like an ulcer boring its way from inside to my outer layer of skin. I expected to wake up one morning and find a bloody wound on my belly, evidence of my guilt. But gradually the pains disappeared and a tough, invisible scar formed. When Steven returned to school a week later, he came to my room. I did not know what to say to him. He didn't look particularly angry.

"Steven, I'm sorry about what happened," I finally said.

"Why? Why are you sorry?"

"Because you were punished, and I was the one responsible."

"I guess you owe me," he said and smiled.

"I will always be in your debt. If you ever need anything from me…"

"Well, I don't want you to see Sarah anymore. Or speak with her. Or write any letters to her. I don't want to share her with you anymore."

"I promise you it will not happen again."

"Okay."

"Is there anything else?"

Steven looked down at the floor. "What I said to Dean Maiser… just remember I lied for you."

I did not know what he meant and did not want to ask.

We went down to the common room where boys had gathered after dinner. Steven was a hero for a while, adored by the other boys. Everyone wanted to hear his story. Even as he repeated the false account of his encounter with Sarah, I noticed details being altered. Where had he met her? How did they escape detection? How much had happened? Did they have sex? He said they had decided on the date when he saw her at home a few weeks before. He described a shower they had taken together at his house and how he had admired her body. That was when they hatched the plot to meet up at Danvers, with a bottle of wine, and have sex together. It was the wine and the noise they made that got them caught. The answers were embellished by other boys who claimed to have observed them drinking and singing. It was painful for me to hear the accounts, but I wanted them to be believable. I worried that the whole story would unravel.

Initially, I honored my pledge about Sarah. But she wrote me letters. And I wrote her back. I apologized for abandoning her. She wanted me to visit her, but I was afraid. Later she told me she was becoming more involved in civil rights issues. She had made friends with members of the Black Student Union at Harvard and wanted me to come along on a march and a sit-in. I used excuses about homework and tests. In another letter she told me she attended rallies against the war in Vietnam and met a college student named Dirk. After that her letters stopped, which was somewhat of a relief since I worried that Dean Maiser might see my mail. At some point she got back together with Steven, or maybe they never were apart. Sarah seemed tethered to Steven like a lifeboat even as she explored politics and traveled. We wrote a few more letters about college applications and summer vacation. She told me that she and Steven would be traveling in France for the summer. In a letter toward the end of school, I asked her why she stayed with him. She answered that he was her best friend. He was loyal and that he made her feel safe. He was also the only person she knew who was fully committed to her, and she cared about him. I suppose that between the lines, she was asking what I could offer. I wanted to tell her that I had loved her from the first moment we met, and still did. But it was too late. My response was to wish her a "happy summer" in France with Steven. I occasionally saw her during college, and for years after that. Our relationship gradually diminished to occasional letters and phone calls to "catch up." I attended her wedding to Steven. They both seemed happy that day. My consolation was that we had been each other's first lovers, and no one could ever take that away.

As for Steven, he would call at night for years, but there would be no voice at the other end of the line. I knew it was him. Sometimes I would listen to the silence and even talk aloud for a few minutes, telling him what I had been doing and that I missed him, waiting for a response that never came. Finally I would hang up the phone.

And there was the terrible day I received the call from the church informing me of the car crash in the southern mountains of the Philippines. My parents drove over a cliff trying to avoid a San Miguel beer truck that was sliding toward them through the mud after a torrential rain. It was the worst day of my life. I felt completely lost. I called their phone and left a message. That was the night I also found out that I had developed an allergy, or perhaps an increased sensitivity to alcohol, because I woke up in an emergency room on a stretcher as they were trying to put a red plastic tube in my nose to pump out my stomach from the six glasses of rum I had downed with some friends. Alone in the hospital room, I hallucinated that Steven Thompson was standing near my bed, wearing a long coat. I imagined that he put his hand on my head and wiped the drool from my mouth and told me I would be okay and that he loved me. I had not seen him in several years.

When I finally woke up alone in the ER, he was gone and my parents were dead. I realized that I could not depend on anyone. They all would leave me eventually and I would have to protect myself and get what I could from them to survive. Even my old Danvers bridge friends had disappeared from my life. Maybe we were only friends by coincidence, like the rocks and dead tree stumps kicked up and discarded by the plow of our lives.

That was what I had done. I had pushed forward into my future, and traveled to more than fifty countries in pursuit of new cures for global diseases. I had learned greetings in ten languages from botanists, chemists, and doctors who taught me that even the ugliest, smelliest plant could be the source of a chemical that might save lives.

I have never understood why memories arrive when they do.

There had been hundreds of cab rides to airports just like the one I was on now, on my way to Africa and whatever I would find in the clinic in Tanzania. Perhaps cab rides were a good place for memories to appear – a place between where I had been and where I was going. But these memories of Danvers and Sarah and Steven would not recede neatly into recesses of my mind.

The Departures sign at the airport jolted me; I tried to remember which airline and flight I was taking. There were gates for United and Aero Mexico and China Airline and British Airways. Had I already told the cabbie? I began to panic. I wondered whether we were on time or late and how long I had been day dreaming.

The cab stopped neatly in front of the British Airways sign. People were lifting suitcases out of cars.

I felt somewhat disoriented and stopped to make sure I had everything – my bags, money, passport. I reflexively opened the passport to look at my photo. It was the face of a dark-skinned, middle-aged man who looked surprised, as if someone had turned on a light in the night and woken him as he slept.

I waved at the cabbie, who still lingered by the curb, and he waved back at me. Then I began my trip to Africa.

Book 2

17

During the first leg of the flight, the plane bounced through air pockets over the Atlantic and I dreamed of playing bridge. I could barely make out the cards from one hand before another appeared. Then, for an instant, everything stopped and I could see all of the hands. Each player had the cards of a different suit. I had all the hearts. It was the best and worst of hands because I knew I would bid everything, risk it all, and lose to the hand with all the spades.

As we flew over Europe on our second leg, I dreamed of death. How would my life end? Who would be there with me? Maybe someone on a plane, like the old lady snoring in the seat next to me. Maybe it would happen in my office – an allergic reaction to a fungus from Africa. Mr. Grundel would be trying to remember what policy to follow, how to activate the automatic defibrillator, and what reports to fill out as I took my last gasp of air.

Over North Africa, I dreamed of love and sex. I thought of all the women I had desired but never had slept with. What if I had gone up to this one's room? What if I had tried to kiss that one? What would it have been like? Would we have fallen in love, traveled to Peru, climbed Machu Pichu together? Or would it have ended in rejection and embarrassment?

Over East Africa, I thought about Dr. Hart's research at Danvers. Wasn't it all just an elaborate game, and weren't we the pieces being moved on the chess board? Some kings and queens, some knights fighting bishops. Perhaps the teachers liked to watch the contest and admire the pieces, pick us up, turn us over, weigh us, measure us, and put us down again. Even the pawns. Most of us were powerless pawns lacking the size and strength needed for combat. Wasn't that the theory behind somatotypes? But didn't they realize that the occasional pawn could be transformed by moving slowly and steadily to the end of the board to become the new queen – the most powerful piece on the board? Didn't they realize that there were many more pawns than other pieces?

A few hours before landing, I filled out my immigration card for entry into Kenya and wondered whether my ruminations were a useless excursion through a haunted house of illusions, bent mirrors, and other deceptions. Wouldn't I be better off passing the remaining hours on the plane watching movies or reading a mystery novel or just resting my eyes?

Instead, I decided to examine Tim's file again. He was different from the rest of us. The photograph accentuated his blackness, blotting out most of the shades of light and dark that would have made his face recognizable. It was a black blur with dots of white around his pupils. Tim's neck and shoulders were like black cables and ropes stretching between the spans of a bridge. His body lacked the blemishes, divots, and scars that seemed to plague everyone else.

After our graduation, I had watched Tim on television. He never achieved stardom, but was a solid defensive back known for his steady and aggressive play. When he retired from professional football, I lost track of him. It was something I regretted, as he had asked me to keep tabs on our group. I had not even kept track of him. Well, this was my weak, belated attempt.

As I looked at his file, I figured that if anyone would provide support for Sheldon's theory about physical shape and personality, it would be an athlete in a sport where size and muscles were critical for success. According to his file, Tim had used his professional football credentials to launch a successful business career, and at some point had founded an international charity program.

As I returned Tim's file to my bag, I noticed the materials about the doctor from Tanzania about to fall out onto the floor. I grabbed them and decided to review them. Now as we sped over Africa preparing to touch down in Nairobi, the research in the report become less theoretical and I began to wonder how a rural doctor could have gathered data and analyzed it on his own. My colleagues were skeptical about the AIDS research because it had not been conducted with an approved research study design and protocol, but I was impressed at the tenacity and creativity demonstrated in the report and was willing to examine what evidence the doctor had collected. Over the years, I had learned to keep an open mind about even the most unlikely prospects.

I landed in Nairobi and checked into my hotel. I felt exhausted, but I could only nap for a few hours before I was awake again, staring at the ceiling and trying to figure out where I was. Since it was still light out, I decided I would begin my search for Tim.

He was not difficult to find. I asked the desk clerk at the hotel about Upwards Movement Foundation and mentioned his name. The clerk had a cousin who had received a scholarship from the Foundation, and she got me a cab and gave directions to the driver.

Nairobi pulsated with traffic and street hustlers hawking wood carvings, safari tours, and prostitutes. I was happy to enter the safety of the cab and I drifted off into a late afternoon languor as we bumped over potholes and past traffic jams caused by stalled buses and broken-down trucks. The driver asked me why I was in Nairobi, and I explained that I was a doctor.

"Dactari," he said, smiling broadly. "Will you stay here in Africa?"

"I'm only visiting," I said. "But we never know the will of God." I smiled the way foreigners have learned to smile when they say something that is likely false to avoid unpleasant answers – but raises the glimmer of possibility amid the harsh daily realities of rejection, which are so familiar in Africa.

18

Upward Movement Foundation was in a cinder block house not far from the bus station. Teenage boys in khaki pants and Upward Movement t-shirts kicked a soccer ball in front of the doorway, ignoring a man who was struggling to carry a burlap bag overflowing with rolls of brightly colored fabric. A faded sign proclaimed the office of Upward Movement and the address on 230 Rafiki Road. I paid the driver and walked up the steps to the door. I asked a man who seemed to be some type of security guard, "*Wapi Mzee* Tim Washington?" in my broken Swahili. The man motioned with his hands in the direction of stairs. The woman at the front desk had short hair, a prominent forehead, and muscular arms that seemed too large for the typing she was doing. I approached the desk and the woman barely looked at me as she continued typing. "I am looking for Mr. Washington," I explained.

"He is not here."

"Do you know when Mr. Washington will be here?"

"He is on his way."

I decided to wait and began to look around the office at the pictures on the wall. I found one with what looked like an older version of Tim in an African village with runners at the end of a race. There were photographs of various animals – lions, zebras, giraffes.

That moment Tim walked through the door. I recognized his walk, the swagger in it, and the way he carried his body, before I recognized his face. He had narrow eyes that were sunk into puffier cheeks than I remembered. He looked at me suspiciously.

I extended my hand. "Hello, Tim. It's me, Robert Thames from Danvers."

"Robert Thames? Damn, sorry, man! I don't know why I didn't recognize you."

"Maybe because about 40 years have passed?"

"But you look just the same!" He squeezed my hand and put his other arm around my shoulders in a brotherly hug. "Robert Thames," he repeated, "I'll be damned. What're you doing here, man?"

"I work as a doctor for the U.S. government on infectious diseases. There's a hospital in Tanzania I need to visit, and I remembered that you were here and thought it would be fun to visit. Remember when you told me that I was supposed to get our bridge group together again? Well, here I am."

"Ha-ha, the bridge club. I haven't thought of that game in years. Come into my office."

He walked me up the stairs. The room contained a desk, a small round table, a rattan couch with yellow and black cushions, and an orange pillow on the end. The walls were blue plaster with several hanging pictures. There was one of Tim in his football uniform, and another of Tim and several Kenyan officials signing a document.

"Sit down," he said, ushering me toward the couch. "Would you like some coffee or tea, a biscuit? You know they all drink tea here."

"Sure, thanks, tea would be fine." Tim called down to the secretary to bring tea.

I noticed a piece of brightly colored African cloth hanging over the window in Tim's office that said Chakula ni uhai.

"Food is life," I translated.

"So you know Swahili?

"Just a few words. I don't really know Africa all that well. "

"I'm glad you came by. I have a whole operation going on here. It's really amazing what you can do in a poor country."

I nodded. "I visit a lot of third-world countries, looking for new antibiotics based upon folk medicines."

The secretary entered the room and set down a tray with two cups of tea, sugar, and milk on Tim's desk. She still would not look at me, but smiled at her boss as she left.

"That's great, man," said Tim. "I don't keep up much with the 'first-world.' Once in a while I read the Danvers alumni bulletin, but…" He poured the tea gracefully and handed me a cup. "I never had much in common with them, if you know what I mean."

"Yeah, I do. Some of us didn't really fit in at Danvers. That's part of what I wanted to talk about." I described the arrival of the files, the photographs, the measurements. Tim's eyes widened and his jaw clenched, but he remained silent until the end.

"That's quite a story. But I'm not surprised. I never trusted those guys. "

"I brought one of the files just to show you."

I put his file on the desk and let it sit there. The cardboard had a musty odor from the years in Dr. Hart's basement. I watched as Tim reached for the file and opened it. He turned the pages and examined his photograph. Then he took a deep breath.

"Damn, Thames."

"What do you think?"

"I think I look pretty good," he laughed. Then he paused and became more serious and said, "Where did this picture come from?"

"Don't you remember? Right after we arrived. We had to line up and take off our clothes?"

"Damn, that's right. I thought maybe that's how they did things in private schools, part of our physicals. I didn't think too much about it. In football we're always running around the locker room undressed."

"It was research to measure our bodies."

"What were they measuring? Our dicks?" He laughed and reached over to slap my hand in a high five.

"They measured all kinds of things – arms, legs, head, face, eyes. I heard that the Danvers teachers would sit around and look at the pictures and laugh at us."

Tim shook his head grimly. "I'd like to see some of those old guys stripped naked, run around the gym five times, and then photographed.

Now that would be funny."

"I have boxes of files just like this. What do you think I should do with them? "

"I don't know, Thames. I've been trying to escape this kind of bullshit for years. People telling you that you're not qualified, don't know enough. It's all code for you're-not-White. Do you know that at Danvers, some of those kids had never touched the skin of a Black person? They would reach a hand out and brush it across my arm, as if it were an accident. That doesn't happen to me here. If a kid reaches out his hand to touch me, it's because he wants to be close to me. It's one of the reasons I love being in Africa. "

He paused and pushed his chair back from his desk and rubbed his eyes. Then he continued, "So they disrespected you. Is that it?"

"They disrespected all of us."

"Respect is important. But it's ancient history. You have to decide if you want to dig up all those skeletons. Once you start digging, there are probably plenty more."

"Mrs. Hart thinks there might be evidence of abuse in the files. Sexual relationships. The trustees want the files back because they're worried about what might be there."

"I wondered about some of those teachers. I wouldn't be surprised if something was going on. In those days we weren't as aware of it. Now we are."

"I sort of feel like the files really belong to each of us, whatever is in them, good or bad. But I can't find each student from our class and return his file. Most probably wouldn't even want them back. You don't seem too interested in yours."

"It's all long past, like an old injury. I don't want to dwell on it. If I got mad every time someone said or did something stupid, I'd be mad all the time. I don't have time for that. I used to tackle people to get it out of my system, but I'm too old for that."

"I guess I need to read more of the files and see what I find. I'm not so ready to forget what happened."

"All right. So you need more time. I think you're embarrassed and humiliated to remember what they did. You're feeling what we felt at Danvers when we were kids. It's brought that all back. Isn't that it?

You want Danvers to apologize?"

"I don't know. An apology would be good a start."

He perched on the edge of his desk and continued. "It'll never happen. No one's ever apologized for slavery. You know what I'm saying?"

"Maybe we could get to the bottom of everything. If we knew the truth, we could talk about it. Like what happened that night you went into Mr. Shangly's apartment and were drinking?"

"How'd you find out about that?"

"There was something about it in Dr. Hart's papers. Mrs. Hart gave it to me. It was a release form that said that all of you were drinking in Mr. Shangly's apartment. That he did something unprofessional. You never told me about this."

"Shangly gave us liquor and got caught. It was a mistake. End of story." Tim got up and paced around the room with his tea cup. He took a sip and said, "We had some creepy teachers."

"Oh yeah. I had Mr. Goodson for Latin. He made boys take off their shirts to display their physique. He said it was to teach us about Greek and Roman sculpture. It was so embarrassing. I heard they got rid of him."

"I knew about that. Those teachers were worse than embarrassing. Some of the guys on the football team warned me. I kept my distance. You couldn't trust any of them. They'd always be trying to get you to do something illegal. They'd try to frame you for something you didn't do, like Steven being with that girl. We all know that never happened."

I hesitated a moment and then said, "It wasn't made up. It was me with the girl."

"You? You were the one?" He looked incredulous.

"Yeah. Steven covered for me."

"I'll be damned! I knew it wasn't him. But I never would have suspected you, Thames. So you're as bad as the rest of us."

"She was Steven's friend, but she was with me that night. He covered for me. But she married him in the end."

"I'll be damned."

"I recently spoke with her. She told me Steven's pretty sick now with liver disease. I'm going to see him when I get back next week."

"I'm sorry to hear that. I actually liked the guy, even if he was full of shit most of the time. We all did what we had to do to survive. Did you know that he taught me to swim?"

"Swim? Why did he teach you to swim?"

"They had this requirement that you had to be able to swim across the pool to graduate. Remember? I didn't know how. I never told anyone about it – I was embarrassed. But I thought I could just do it if I moved my arms and legs fast enough. Maiser was laughing his head off while I was swallowing water during the test. That asshole would have let me drown."

"So what happened?"

"Steven saw me trying to teach myself the next week. He was on the swim team. He could tell I didn't know what I was doing. He made me put my head in the water and he held me up with his hands and taught me to breathe. And then he taught me how to swim. My own private lessons. It was our secret. I was an athlete and we were supposed to be good at everything. But where I grew up, Black kids didn't swim."

"Why not?"

He gave me a hard look. "We never went to pools." He sat back down behind his desk. "Tell Steven I'll be praying for him. He used to send me money for my foundation."

"Really? Did you ever talk to him?"

"Yeah. Every few years. Just small talk. But he never told me he was sick. We're not getting any younger. We can't take our health for granted. That's why I try to stay in shape. I still work out with the kids."

"Do you?"

He nodded. "Let me know if I can do anything for Steven. I'll give you my number."

"Okay, thanks."

I thought that maybe that was the end of our meeting, but Tim picked up a pen and tapped it on his desk. "You know, I could use a break. How about if I drive you to Tanzania? I got a Jeep that's running and we could take a little side trip on the way."

I laughed, surprised. "Are you sure? I was just going to take a bus."

"No. I'll take you. I have something I want to show you." Tim walked to the door and called for his secretary, telling her he needed to change his schedule. He had never been one to think too long about a decision in football or in bridge. Once set in motion, he was like a boulder tumbling down a gully, and now he was carrying me along.

19

Tim arrived at my hotel after dark. A hotel bellman in a red jacket and a security guard in blue-gray fatigues with a rifle stood admiring the black Jeep as I loaded my gear. Tim passed them some Kenyan shillings for protecting the vehicle while we were inside. He had changed into safari clothes – a tan jacket and green khakis – and wore black and silver glasses.

"Where are we going?" I asked.

"Hell, if I told you it would ruin the surprise."

We drove through the Nairobi night, as shadow figures hovered on streets and emerged from corrugated metal roofed huts that lined the roadway. Men without shirts, women in long, draped tubes of brightly colored cloth gazed and beckoned to us. The blurred swirls of movement were lively and menacing at the same time. We passed the bus station where traveling villagers with baskets of fruits and vegetables pushed through throngs waiting for something to come loose – a falling banana or a traveler's moment of hesitation that revealed vulnerability.

"Come, friend, and let me help you. I know a good hotel for you. Let me take your bag for you."

I was relieved I wasn't taking the bus.

We drove past street vendors with roasted chicken and ugali corn mush, past a club with loud music and a crowd of teenage boys and men dancing near the door. The women were mostly hidden, just tantalizingly visible through a window. Pretty soon we had reached the outskirts of the city and were heading into the country on a two-lane highway with mostly trucks and buses. Sometimes we could get up to 50 miles an hour; other times we'd have to wait for the right opportunity to pass a slow-moving truck. And then there were the potholes that jolted me from my reveries.

"Sorry, Thames!" called Tim after one particularly bad bump.

I thought I saw a giraffe in the headlights as we passed a heavily forested area. Was it a dream? We stopped for gas and I asked for the bathroom and was directed to the forest behind the station. Moments later, we were back on our way. Finally, we turned onto a dirt road, passed warning signs about animals, and stopped next to an acacia tree.

"Where are we?" I asked.

"We're going to take a rest here until the morning. If you got to piss be careful because there are hyenas. They can pull off your arm in one bite." We pushed the backs of our seats down almost flat and they became our beds. I didn't think I would be able to sleep like that, but with all my travel I must have been exhausted. I closed my eyes and covered my head in a piece of African fabric that Tim had in the Jeep. The first time I opened my eyes the blackness of the night was already lifting.

When the morning light revealed our location, I was surprised to find us parked in a grassy knoll near huge trees. Three giraffes were munching on leaves high up on the trees, and they seemed unconcerned about our vehicle. "So now can you tell me where we are?"

"We're going to be visiting a friend of mine. A chief of the Maasai. Do you know about the Maasai?"

"I've seen pictures of them with the beads and the holes in their ear lobes, and I guess wearing blankets and with spears. I suppose that has all changed by now?"

"Not as much as you might think."

We got back into the Jeep and drove on. I was just beginning to get hungry when the Jeep climbed a high bluff. I could see a small village of mud huts arranged in a circle down below.

Tim pointed and said, "I think that's it. If not, I guess we might get speared."

As we neared, I heard children calling out with high-pitched whistles to signal our arrival. There were a few other vehicles – mostly official looking – with game park insignias. A middle-aged African man in a gray t-shirt and khaki pants walked to our Jeep and slid his hand across Tim's hand, and then mine. He had an expansive grin in a narrow face, and a gold front tooth that glimmered in the sun.

"This here is Ole Kapalando," Tim said. "He's the head game warden of this park and chief of Serengeti." Then he introduced me: "This here is Thames, my *rafiki*."

"*Jambo, habari gani,*" said Kapalando. "You are welcome to my home. Please come for some food. '*Chakula ni uhai*', as we say in Swahili. Food is life."

"*Jambo,*" I answered.

"Kapalando is Maasai, but he has become more or less civilized," said Tim, laughing, and Kapalando laughed too as if it was something they had discussed before.

We followed him toward an enclosure of mud and stick huts.

"How did you meet?"

"Through his cousin, an international runner. He was a very talented and convincing guy. Unfortunately, he died a few years later, but I've been visiting Kapalando here in the game park every year since then. I've brought along people like you from time to time. Sometimes Kapalando and I go up in his plane and chase around poachers and he shows me how a real Maasai lives. Sometimes we go on a ceremonial hunt. It's different every time. That's why I brought you here – to show you the real Africa. We've forgotten what our ancestors knew, but it's still there in our genes. Instead of hunting animals we play football. Or cards. But here the people haven't forgotten: They know how to recognize danger, how to hunt, how to fight. What do you think? Are you up for it? Would you like to look for a lion, Thames?"

"I don't know," I said. "I've never hunted an animal before."

"Most of us are the animal that gets hunted, eh? Every month there would be a boy at Danvers who disappeared from our herd, expelled. And we got used to it, as if it was the natural course of life. We didn't shed a tear; we just felt grateful that we weren't the one in the lion's jaws."

I looked at him with a shock of cognition: he, too, had felt the same as I.

"Don't you want to know what it feels like to be the hunter? The Maasai still understand the ancient traditions."

I wondered: Would I run from the lion? Wasn't that how I had survived all of my life?

Kapalando ushered us through the door into his home, which was far larger than most of the other mud and stick huts that formed the enclosure. A woman holding a young child in her arms greeted us. She seemed much younger than Kapalando, perhaps in her mid-twenties, with short, cropped black hair and a round, kind face with large lips and stretched ear lobes.

"This is my wife, Amika," he said. "Our tradition requires that I offer her to you."

I had heard of the Maasai tradition of offering a wife to visitors. But to hear the words now, the way one might be offered tea, was shocking. I wondered if it would be insulting to refuse. I just shook her hand and smiled.

Tim studied me. "Well, what do you say? He's offering you his wife."

Her eyes peered at me curiously, as if she had never seen anything quite like me before. Perhaps sleeping with me would be like sampling an exotic food for her. But Kapalando explained what we were discussing and she began to laugh, then went to a corner of the room to retrieve some biscuits and eggs that had been cooking in a pan. Kapalando brought us milk tea.

When we finished eating, Tim and Kapalando conversed in Swahili. I understood only an occasional word. Several other children appeared, stared at me, and touched my skin. The kitchen was remarkably cool and comfortable. I found myself sinking into my seat as I sipped on my tea, wondering what Tim had planned for me.

20

When we finished eating, Kapalando asked me if I would like to accompany him and Tim in his airplane to look for poachers; perhaps we would see some animals along the way. I had no idea how a plane would take off and land on this African plain, but apparently there was a small airport not far away. As we walked into the glare of the sun, I heard voices calling out and whistling. *"Wapi na moto?"* or "Where is the fire?"

Then I noticed a circle of smoke rising up in the high grass about a mile away.

Kapalando's expression changed suddenly and he grabbed burlap bags and handed some to me and to Tim. "Come quickly," *"Haraka, haraka,"* he urged, and took off running.

I followed after Tim and Kapalando. We came to a large, open field where the leading edge of fire had advanced. I was gasping from the sprint and smoke. A group of Maasai boys and men were beating at the fire with burlap bags. I watched as they rushed into the burning grass and swatted down the flames with their hands and burlap bags and then rushed back out. It seemed like a hopeless task. There were not enough of us. We did not have enough equipment. Just burlap bags.

The tall, dry grass exploded into flames as the fire spread. I felt its searing heat. Smoke filled my lungs and I began to violently cough. Grass crackled as it burned and the dust and smoke obscured the village. Then the flames were suddenly all around me on both sides and I realized the impossibility of the situation. There was no way that we could do this.

The fire was encroaching on the village. I wanted to run as fast as I could, away from the fire swirling all around me, but my legs were frozen and I could not seem to move.

Tim noticed my confusion. "Come on, follow me!"

He grabbed my arm and pulled me forward. I watched as he swung his burlap bag madly at the burning grass. The flames disappeared momentarily before reappearing again.

"Come on, you got to fight it, smother it, kill it. Swing as hard as you can," he said.

I ran blindly forward, my eyes burning, and swung my burlap bag at the fire, harder than I had ever swung at anything.

"That's it!"

I rushed through the fire to a place where it was not yet burning and caught my breath. We were charging like bull fighters with bags instead of capes, challenging the flames to burn us as we attempted to deliver a death blow.

"*Wapi na moto?*" cried out the voices around me as they yelled out an exuberant and defiant challenge to the fire: "Where are you, fire?"

I ran through the smoke again, swinging my bag. It had seemed hopeless. But now there were more of us, maybe twenty. Shouting Swahili voices urged us on.

"That's it, harder, swing harder," yelled Tim as I beat at the burning grass.

I swung my bag with more conviction, and I could feel something welling up from deep inside of me. We would not lose this battle. We would be enough.

How long had we been going? Ten minutes, twenty, half an hour? Bodies jumping through the flames, the sound of the burlap on the ground swat, swat, swat. The voices crying out in Swahili. I looked around and miraculously the fire was abating, first in one corner and then another. How was it possible? *Wapi na moto?* we screamed. Our faces were covered with soot and our clothes were torn. My pants had burned at the cuffs. *Wapi na moto?* yelled Kapalando as he swatted out the last flame.

"It's okay, you can stop now," said Tim as he grabbed my arms that kept beating at the smoldering grass. I was in some kind of trance, swinging the bag back and forth like a metronome. I had not seen him come up behind me. But it was all over. We still had to patrol for sparks that might reignite the dry grass, but the fire was no longer burning.

"It wasn't possible, what we did," I gasped. "How did we?"

He shrugged. "We had to."

We stood there surveying the scene for a moment. It was now quiet with just a faint breeze rustling the grass. I could see the sweat on the black faces mixing with the smoke and ash. But what was most remarkable was the shared joy radiating from face to face as we realized what we had done. It was impossible for twenty men and boys to stop a fire with burlap bags, but somehow we had done it. We had saved the village.

I surveyed our little army. There was a boy of about ten in shorts and a t-shirt, with large eyes and high forehead, who pointed at me and whistled and covered his face in embarrassment. There was a man in a torn blue shirt with a scraggly beard whose face suddenly opened into a huge grin. About ten men wore traditional Maasai blankets while others wore shorts and nothing else. Their arms were all thin and muscular. Where had they come from? And almost as quickly, they began to disappear.

As he approached me now, Tim said, "You just killed the lion. You went to the beast inside the fire! How do you feel? You're a warrior."

"I'm exhausted," I said. "And in awe."

"Yeah, that's it." he said. "That's it exactly."

21

After we had assured ourselves that the fire was out and had assigned four boys to patrol and pour water on any live embers, we returned to the house. We were dirty, thirsty, and sweaty. I drank from the earthen pot and did not care how the water tasted. It was cool and liquid.

"We were so fortunate that you were here visiting when this fire came. I don't know if we could have stopped it without you," Kapalando said to me and Tim. "Now, if you like, we can walk to the river and wash ourselves."

We walked across the grass fields to a line of trees. Beyond them, I could hear the river. There were thick bushes and hanging vines along the short, steep descent down to the sandy bank. We found smooth gray rocks where we sat and took off our clothes. My shirt was covered in soot and dirt, and my pants were singed near the ankles. I had small blisters where the bottom of my pants had touched the skin. I began washing my ankles in the water. I hardly noticed Tim wading into the water until he floated out into the middle of the river.

I noticed how different my body was from the Maasai around me. It was not just the skin color. There was something about how our bones were connected and shapes of our heads and faces. All of the attention to body shape from the research project had made me acutely aware of differences in our bodies. And the photographs made me more conscious of being naked. But here there was no shame in our nakedness. Our bodies had been our weapons in the fight with the fire. Each one had a purpose and a beauty and we could take pride in them. I floated out into the cool river with Tim and the others, and found an eddy where I could stand and feel the water flowing through my limbs. The nerves of my skin tingled as they tried to make sense of the changes in temperature as the water flowed over them. Cool air drifted from the banks where the animals from the plain would come to drink. I felt like I had earned my place among them. I was one of them now. I stood serenely in the river, my chest rising slowly with each breath, until Tim came along and splashed water at me.

"Come on, stop pissing in the water," he said.

"I'm not. I was just thinking about how beautiful it is here. How peaceful."

"Yeah, well don't get carried away. There are crocodiles in this river and probably hippos. You'd make a nice meal for one of them."

I took one more deep breath, made my way back to the bank, and got dressed.

When we got back to his house, Kapalando showed me photos that he had taken of the animals around the village – elephants, giraffes, baboons, wildebeests, and a few lions. While Tim rested, I went out in Kapalando's truck with him to a place where he often came upon animals. We saw four giraffes munching on leaves, and then a wild buffalo and some elephants.

That night we had milk mixed with blood, which almost made my stomach turn. Several of the village elders came to sit and converse with us, but I could not understand them. We drank tea and prepared for bed. Kapalando's wife came over to me and looked down at the ground shyly. I explained to Kapalando that our custom was not to sleep with another man's wife and that I meant no disrespect.

He laughed and said he understood but that he had to make the offer. He apologized for not being able to take me to hunt a lion due to the unfortunate fire.

"No, it was my honor to be able to help," I said.

"Assante sana," he said, and he rubbed his palm across mine. As I lay down on a straw mat with a sheet and blanket and pillow, I recalled an ancient memory from when I was a young boy sleeping on a mat in

the Philippines. It was before I lived with the Thameses, where I usually slept in a bed. The image of the mat on the floor was insubstantial and as fleeting as the last wisps of smoke from the fire. I clutched my fingers, trying to hold it and smell it and see who was there beside me, but it was only a hand leading me forward into a deep, strange sleep.

22

In the morning we began our drive to the hospital in Tanzania, where I was supposed to meet with Dr. Tukutuba. Kapalando wanted us to stay one more day to rest and recover, but I felt the need to stay on schedule. As we drove off across the savannah, Tim pointed out some wildebeests far up on a hill and said, "Whenever I leave the Serengeti I feel that I am leaving a part of myself behind." We continued in silence through the grassland.

After musing about the previous day, I laughed. "I've never imagined I would run toward a fire, instead of away from it."

"We're brought up to fear fire and run from it. But sometimes you have to run toward it to stop it."

"Fear is there for a reason."

"If all of those men were too afraid to fight the fire with those bags, what do you think would have happened?"

"I guess the village would have burned down."

"Damn right. When I went out on the football field, my opponents wanted to take my head off. I had to make them think I was going to take their heads off. There was no room for fear. You had to believe in yourself and your team, know that you could do it."

We passed a watering hole where small animals were cautiously drinking. They looked like a kind of antelope or gazelle with gray and brown fur and a white and brown face. Giraffes stood in a cluster nearby, stripping leaves from acacia trees. I was surprised that these animals were living away from the game park, near the roads where cars and trucks passed by.

"Look, you can't show anyone that you're afraid of anything or they'll push you around like those animals at the watering hole; they'll chase you and attack you and eat you if you run. That's the way of the world: Eat or be eaten. It's just bad luck if you get born to eat grass and have to run away from the lions. But if that's your nature, I guess you have to accept it."

"Do you think it's my nature?" I asked.

"I think you're a fox. You're sly. You're always thinking and planning and plotting and scheming, but you keep it to yourself. That's how you were when we played cards together."

I smiled at the memory. Tim really had taken notice of me, then.

He continued, "When you jumped into the fire you probably saved my life because I would have kept going until I burned up, except that I was watching you and marveling at how you'd become such a fighter. You helped me regain my perspective and not get too crazy. There aren't too many people who I can say actually might have saved my life. But you're one of them."

"I'm glad you think I helped."

"You did, Thames. But now I'm lost, so help me by looking at the map. The hospital's in Arusha, which is not far from Kilimanjaro."

We stopped and chose our route. "I should be able to find the hospital, but first we got to cross the border over to Tanzania," Tim said. "You never know how things will go at the border crossing."

I nodded. "How far is it?"

"Oh, if we don't get a flat or run into a herd of elephants, we should make it in about four or five hours. But this is Africa and you never know. And I'm not joking about the elephants. They roam around and can show up without warning so don't be in any hurry."

We drove past small towns where women were decorated with red and white beads around their necks and carried large bags on their heads. Men and boys drove thin cattle in front of us, blocking the road. Tim seemed to enjoy watching the men rush about, prodding the animals with sticks, shouting and whistling as they attempted to move the beasts toward a water hole near a bridge.

"So do you have a woman?"

"No, I'm by myself, more or less."

"Well, I understand wanting to have your own space. I'm the same way. The men here have more than one wife. Did you know that?"

"No, but that was true in some of the tribes of the Philippines."

"I got a lady back in the States. And I got an ex-wife. But no kids. I don't need any of my own. I got plenty of kids in my program."

"You're probably helping raise more kids than most actual parents. Anyway there are about six billion people in the world now. Someone has to take care of what we got. That's what I'm doing."

We continued over rolling hills and climbed to higher elevation where the vegetation became more dense and green. At the border crossing, the guards seemed irritated that we had disturbed the soccer game they were listening to on the radio. They glanced briefly at our passports and stamped them and went back to the game.

We continued through Tanzania until we saw the sign for the Arusha Christian Hospital. Tim turned off the highway and followed a narrow dirt road to a large white building where a line of adults and children extended from a doorway to the dirt lot where we parked. Those in the back of the line stared at us, gesturing and laughing as we emerged from the Jeep and stretched.

Inside, I mentioned that we were there to see Dr. Tukutuba, and the clerk fetched a European nurse in a white and pink habit who extended her hand. She had light hair and a sincere smile that reminded me of my mother.

"Oh, you're the American doctor. I'm Sister Mary Elizabeth. Dr. Tukutuba is currently in the O.R., but I will tell him you are here. Would you like some tea?" Although she spoke good English I could tell that it was not her first language by her accent, which seemed to be German or Dutch.

"Yes, thank you. Tea would be wonderful. We've been driving for hours."

"Please come with me," she said, and led us into a small office with a picture of Mary and Jesus on the wall. The desk was overflowing with charts and loose papers and two simple wooden chairs accompanied it.

"It's important to drink enough fluids in this climate," she continued.

"We're always drinking tea here; it seems to keep us healthy. Well, I wish I could find you a more comfortable place to sit, but right now we have so many patients that they've filled up all of the rooms. Soon they'll have to go home and things will settle down. Just make yourselves comfortable while I get the tea."

"Thank you," I said, sinking down into one of the chairs. Tim remained standing for a moment and then sat behind the desk in the other.

We could hear the murmuring of Swahili out in the hall, amid crying babies and patients moaning in pain. After a few minutes, there was a commotion and the pitch of sounds changed. I heard loud cries for help and the patter of steps. We poked our heads into the hallway and learned that a woman was about to have a baby out on the road. Her husband had transported her in a wheelbarrow until the wheel broke. He smelled of dirt and blood and sweat, and looked desperate to get help. Two men followed him quickly out the door.

Sister Mary Elizabeth arrived with our tea and we told her what had occurred.

"Unfortunately these people wait until the last minute. They refuse to come in for prenatal care, and then they have obstructed labor and we lose the mother and the baby. By the time they get here it is too late."

"She's just out there. Maybe not far from here," I said

.

"Well, that is unfortunate. There is probably not much we can do. We have no ambulance. But I'll inform Dr. Tukutuba and we'll prepare the emergency OB tray."

I was surprised at the fatalistic attitude, but perhaps she was used to seeing these emergencies.

She took note of my expression.

"Would you like to assist Dr. Tukutuba in case there's a chance? He may need some help if they are able to get here in time," said Sister Mary Elizabeth.

"I'm an infectious disease doctor. I haven't delivered any babies or been in the O.R. lately, but I could try."

"Very well," she said, and she disappeared back into the hospital.

Outside the hospital, a crowd slowly moved forward like a huge centipede. There was a cloud of dust and the sound of yelling. Minute by minute, the voices got louder and differentiated into cries and shouts and moans. Tim and I ran out to see what we could do for the woman, but she was obscured by the arms of her helpers, which seemed to be attached to every part of her body. I could not even see her face until they finally lifted her onto a stretcher that the hospital had provided.

Sister Mary Elizabeth looked at the woman and said, "Come with me, Doctor."

I followed the stretcher through the door, past a hospital ward with twenty or thirty women lying on mats on the ground and then past another ward of men. We rushed into the operating room where an African doctor wearing a surgical mask nodded to me. "I am Tukutuba," he said. "You must be Dr. Thames. We may need to do a C-section."

"All right," I said, "but I haven't done one since medical school."

"No problem. You will just assist me." Dr. Tukutuba had a deep voice and relaxed, attentive brown eyes. His calm demeanor belied this critical situation.

The woman's eyes were closed as she grimaced and gasped in pain. Sweat dripped from her forehead. Her lips were pale and her abdomen was drenched in sweat and extended out from the rest of her thin body, almost tipping her off the stretcher.

Tukutuba examined her and shook his head. "Could be twins. I can hear a very faint heartbeat. Her blood pressure is barely palpable. We'll just do a crash section."

A nurse brought me a gown while another undressed the woman. I quickly slipped on my gloves. There was no time to scrub. Dr. Tukutuba poured antiseptic on the skin, sliced open the abdomen, and quickly exposed the uterus. In a few more seconds, the uterus was open and a baby's head appeared. Dr. Tukutuba handed the baby to the nurse as it began to cry.

"There is another one," he said. He pulled out the second baby and handed it to the other nurse. It was bluish black, crying weakly and struggling to breathe. "I think you should help resuscitate that baby," he said to me, as if this type of thing happened every day. "I can handle this. I think her pressure is coming up."

I nodded and went over to the nurse with the second baby. I suctioned blood and yellow-green meconium from the mouth and then squeezed a bag with a small mask to assist the baby's breathing. Although I was not used to caring for babies, I did what I could, just as I would if I had come upon a car wreck on a highway. I remembered that meconium babies sometimes needed to have a tube placed in the trachea and be put on a ventilator to help them breathe. I doubted there were any ventilators at this hospital. As I continued to help the baby breathe, Dr. Tukutuba leaned over to look.

"She's showing some distress, but I think she will be okay," he said. "Just keep at it while I sew up the mother. She's quite anemic and I can't afford to let her lose any more blood. Unfortunately, we have no blood here for transfusion."

The operating room suddenly felt chaotic and out of control. I looked back at the operating table and noticed that Sister Mary Elizabeth was assisting with the instruments and another African nurse was providing the anesthesia with a mask. I could smell the acrid blood and meconium and the sweat from the woman's body – odors so different from what I was used to in my daily life. In a few minutes, they wheeled the woman out of the operating room and Dr. Tukutuba took his mask off. He had dark chocolate skin and a small beard covering his lips and chin. His close-cropped hair receded at the front. He looked young, perhaps thirty, though I could not judge ages of Africans well.

"I can take over now. Thank you for your help. Usually they come too late. But once in a while we can save them. The sisters say it's the intervention of God. I am not so religious, but I still consider them miracles."

"I'm glad I could help. It's been a while since I've done this."

"Here in the bush we are just doing what we can. Your arrival was quite propitious. The Sisters would say that God must have wanted you to be here."

"Thank you. I see you're very busy now, but perhaps we can talk about your research study and the plant samples later."

"Oh, I can talk now. I think you will find my results quite interesting! Our prevention of HIV transmission in pregnant women is quite significant. I will show you in my notebooks. If I had more resources, I would have better data. But as you can see, we are a poor hospital and with so many needs. I hope that if you agree with my conclusions you might recommend me for a fellowship in the United States or Britain where I can continue my research. I will collect my notebook in the office in a minute, and you can see what I have done."

I nodded. Requests for support for training were very common. I usually made no commitments because I really had little influence. I also knew that every doctor we took away from Africa would mean fewer doctors for Africa, because that doctor might not return to the country where he was desperately needed. Many stayed in the United States or Britain where they could develop their careers and earn a hundred times more money.

However, I had been impressed at the ingenuity of this rural African doctor. If his data confirmed what I had seen in the initial letter, it would be an important advance.

I walked out of the operating room and removed my gown and gloves. I followed the nurses into the children's ward with the two babies. Tim and the father of the babies were there waiting for us. The father reeked of sweat and blood but beamed at us in gratitude.

"Twins," I said triumphantly as the nurses showed off the two babies. "The mother is fine too." A nurse translated what I said to the father and he grinned broadly and shook Tim's hand and hugged him.

The man said something to the nurse, and the nurse hesitated to translate it. "This man says he would like to name the two babies for you and your friend."

I smiled at Tim. One of the babies was a girl but I guessed it would not matter.

The nurse continued: "The man also said that he would like to give you one of the babies. He wants you to take a baby to America."

"What?" I exclaimed to Tim, thinking it was a joke. He did not answer. His eyes were fastened on the two babies. "Tim, what do you think?" I repeated.

"Unfortunately we can't save everyone or take them all to America," he said.

The nurse interrupted us. "What are your names?"

"Tim and Thames," said Tim.

"Tim and Tame?" the nurse asked. "These names sound the same. They will be Timo and Tema." She pronounced the words to the father who repeated them with the nurse, "Timo, na Tema."

As I was marveling that these babies would be starting their lives off with our names, Dr. Tukutuba came up beside me, carrying his notebook.

"Dr. Thames, I wonder if I could show you my research results now? I am not sure how much time I will have and I think you will be very surprised."

I looked at the handwritten notes. No one would give this type of report much credence. Yet the results were impressive. If they could be duplicated in a more controlled environment they might be important. "Do you think I could take your notebook with me when I go back to the United States? I'd like to show the results to a colleague who is more familiar with this research."

"That would be brilliant. I would be so honored for you to take my notebook with you. Is there a possibility that I could continue this work in an Infectious Disease Fellowship in the United States?"

"I can check with some of my friends when I return to the United States," I said. "There are some immigration issues, but I'll ask. Do you have the plants for me to take? I don't want to forget them."

"Oh, yes, I have several samples. This is a folk medicine, and the people here have been using it on wounds and burns. It is a fungus that grows on the dead branches of a tree from our area. Of course we remove it when they arrive and replace it with an antibiotic ointment. But perhaps there is something in it that will be of value to you. I have tried to study it, but we have no equipment. At least I can say that there were some patients that have been helped by it. Some of the diabetic patients with infected toes have been cured when other treatments failed."

He pulled out a paper bag and handed it to me. I smelled an

earthy, bitter odor somewhat like almonds. Inside the bag were pieces of bark, and a brown and green rubbery substance all wrapped carefully in plastic. I put a few pieces in my pocket and the rest in my backpack. I imagined the difficulty of talking this through customs, even with all of my special permits from the Centers for Disease Control.

After all of the excitement we were ready to relax, but Dr. Tuku-tuba wanted to show us the rest of the hospital. In the men's and women's wards, I was surprised to see families camped out on the floor, attending to sick relatives. Sometimes it was difficult to tell who the patient was. They all looked ill to me. Many were severely mal-nourished, but they waved to us as we walked by their beds or cots or floor spots.

"As you can see, we have too many patients. Not enough space. These people wait until they are very sick and then the problem has become difficult to cure. But the Sisters are always giving them hope. There is always hope. That is why I am hoping you can help me come to America to pursue my dreams."

That night we slept in the hospital in the guest room. Tim snored and kept me awake half the night. As I lay there in the dark, I won-dered if there was any chance at all that Tukutuba could find a posi-tion in a U.S. infectious diseases program. I had a friend from medical school who ran a program and I would be seeing him at our national meeting in Boston when I returned. So I would try. I imagined the life of a doctor in this place, with the Sisters and the limited options and suffering all around. Every day there would be a line out the door with more patients than you could see and a hospital so full of patients that they lay on the floor. It was like the animals on the African plain that died because they were a little too slow, or a little too sick, or they happened to be in the wrong place when the lions or hyenas came along.

God would have to figure largely into one's coping mechanisms.

In the morning we got dressed and had breakfast with Dr. Tukutuba. He had another notebook for me with more data that I put into my backpack. We loaded up the car and said goodbye to Sister Mary

Elizabeth and Tukutuba. Before we left, we wrote down our telephone numbers and said, *"Kwa heri,"* as if we would see them again, but knowing we probably would never be back. There already was a long line formed at the clinic door, and the heat was beginning to broil.

As Tim drove toward Nairobi, Sister Mary Elizabeth and Tukutuba waved to us from the hospital door. The line of patients shouted salutations and prayers to Allah or Jesus, and to us as if we were disciples, speeding off to perform miracles. And yet even as we brought modern medicines and techniques that seemed miraculous there was a paradox. I was carrying their folk remedies back with me in the hopes that they would be the source of our new miracles.

23

Tim decided to drive me directly to the airport since my plane would be taking off that evening. He was well aware of the potential complications that can get in the way of plans in Africa, particularly airplane flights: Strikes, storms, drunken taxi drivers, missing pilots. I tried to collect all my required documents – passport, ticket, cash for the departure tax, plus my carry-on baggage, files from the study, Dr. Tukutuba's notebooks, and the fungus on the tree limb. Tim had become quiet, even morose.

"Hey, Tim," I said. "Thanks for all this driving. Is there anything I can do for you when I get to the States? "

"Yeah," he said. "See if you can stir up some interest in the foundation. If you run into our bridge club guys, tell them to send donations. We need money. Now that you know what we're all about, you can explain it to them."

"I'm planning to try to see Steven when I get to Boston. I'll mention it to him if he's not too sick."

"And don't forget how we put out the fire. Get yourself a burlap bag and hang it up in your office to remind yourself. Remember what it felt like to jump through fire. You looked so much younger jumping through fire than at the beginning of the trip, when you were worrying about those old photographs and reports."

I nodded and started to shake his hand, but he held it up above his head. I hesitated for a moment before slapping his hand in a loud high five.

When I arrived in Boston after a stop in London and 25 hours of flights, I was exhausted. It was the same kind of depletion I remembered from my first flight to Boston as a nervous 15-year-old boy from the Philippines, forty years earlier. I was so different from that boy whose name had been written on a cardboard placard carried by a woman in a long red coat. And yet, I still felt the same thrill of excitement, uncertainty, and possibility about walking out into a new place, not knowing exactly what I would see or who I would meet.

But the fear that had accompanied and even heightened the excitement was gone.

I collected my bags and took the taxi through the tunnel to Boston, resting my eyes. When I opened them, I was in front of the hotel and people were waiting for me to exit the cab so they could take it.

Even though my conference had already started, I decided to take a nap. Jet lag had finally caught up with me. I did not even undress or unpack. The most I could do was flip off my shoes before I settled into the coolness of the sheets and blanket. I settled my head upon the pillow and felt my back finally begin to stretch out from the prolonged crouching position in the airplane seat, though my ears continued to buzz from the airplane engine vibrations.

My mind skipped oddly from Africa to Boston to the Philippines. People spoke to me in different languages, but I could only understand fragments of their sentences. *"Jambo, Mzungu, unapenda kulala?"* They asked in Swahili if I wanted to sleep. *"As sa ka padalung?"* They asked where I was going in Cebuano, my Philippine mother tongue.

As sa ka padalung, where are you going, was a greeting that people used when they met on the street or along a path. Why did they ask where you were going? In the United States it would be considered rude to ask. *None of your business* might be the answer. But not so in the Philippines: We wanted to know where our neighbors were going lest they encounter some difficulty, evil spirits, witches, devils, animals, or *barang.* We would always offer to accompany them if they were traveling alone.

Where are you going? It was a question I asked myself when I got on the plane that first time, and again when I arrived at Danvers.

Where are you going? Because I had no claim to this life and no path forward.

Where are you going? Because fires and ghosts were following.

Where are you going? Because I had run after a girl and lost her.

I awoke from my nap, still foggy-headed. I took a shower and dressed and walked down to the conference registration desk. As I was registering, one of my friends, Eugene Brown from University of Utah, noticed me and came up to shake my hand. He was a Division Head at the medical school and had published several papers about Mormons and AIDS education. This was apparently a touchy subject because the Mormon Church did not want to acknowledge the existence of AIDS in their community since it also implied homosexual behavior and drug use. His research had gotten him into some difficulty with the hospital administration due to the loss of certain donors.

"Hey there, Robert. I heard you were off to Africa."

"Hi, Gene," I said. "I just got back today."

"You look like shit."

"I haven't had much sleep. How's the conference?"

"Oh, the usual. Everyone is prancing about, trying to get a few moments with the big boys. There have been a few good papers presented on AIDS prevention in Africa. And lots of discussion about those other viruses, Ebola and Marburg."

"You know, when I was there I ran into a doctor from Tanzania who has been using one of the antivirals to prevent HIV transmission from mother to baby, and it looks like it actually works well. Unfortunately, his data is not controlled so someone will need to get some funding and repeat the study."

"Really? I'm looking for someone. He's Black, isn't he?"

I looked at him quizzically. "The doctor? Very much so."

"We need a minority on our faculty. I want those blond-haired Mormons to get a little wake-up call. They think the whole world looks like them so they ignore anything that doesn't fit their religious principles. They cannot imagine that their children could use drugs or have sex before marriage or be homosexual. So of course, why would they need any education about any of that to prevent AIDS, since it will never happen? I am so sick of it. What's his name?"

"Tukutuba, Joseph Tukutuba, I think that was it. I had it all written down but I seem to have left my notebook in my room. It was a long flight and my head is a bit clouded."

"Tukutuba. That sounds pretty African."

"He's from Tanzania. He speaks good English."

"Actually I'd like him to look and sound as African as possible. I don't want someone who's black on the outside and white on the inside. That's all they want to hire at the University. They need to see what a real African is like." I shuddered at the blatant racism and arrogance but bit my tongue lest I antagonize this possible contact for Tukutuba.

"I'm sure he would love to hear from you."

"Thanks, Robert. I'd be interested in looking at his study and any data you could share and how to reach him. It would help me with the recruitment. And even if I don't take him, it'll help with the affirmative action people."

"Okay," I said. "I guess I'm going to catch a few sessions." I waved at him, passed the security guard at the entry to the conference, and showed him my badge. He nodded absently.

As I was looking for an empty seat, a bald Asian man in a gray suit approached me. "Dr. Thames?"

I tried to place his face. I had seen him somewhere. "Yes?"

He pointed to the door, indicating that he wished to speak privately with me. I walked back out to the foyer.

"I am Jose Comodoy, from the University of the Philippines. I was hoping I might find you here. We met once before at the annual meeting in Bangkok two years ago. Do you remember?"

"Yes, yes, now I do. I'm sorry. I'm somewhat tired from a long trip."

"The last time we spoke, I mentioned that we were developing a Visiting Professorship in infectious diseases and we were hoping that you might consider it when we had the funding. Now we have received a grant from Pfizer, and I would like to offer this position to you for your consideration. You are our first choice. I have already received the approval from the rector."

"Thank you, Dr. Comodoy. That is very considerate of you. I love the Philippines. I was born there." I felt warm childhood memories flooding in and my face became flushed, but at the same time I detected a creeping anxiety over losing my American identity if I returned to the Philippines.

"Yes, I remember. You are from Cebu?"

"Yes, Cebu City."

"We are in Manila, the big city. We would be most excited to have you."

"Thank you. I would love to talk more with you later. I am exhausted from the trip. Probably you're tired from your travels as well? But this is very interesting and welcome news. Perhaps you have a card? I'll call you."

He quickly retrieved a card from his wallet and handed it to me.

"It is a one year appointment, Dr. Thames, but renewable for another year. And we have a travel budget. We would prefer a Filipino with international experience. As I have said, you are our first choice. However, we have a deadline, so please do not wait too long before calling."

"Thank you, Dr. Comodoy. I will contact you very soon." I gave him one of my cards and we shook hands and said goodbye. I went back into the lecture hall and sat down in an aisle seat. I tried to concentrate on the lecture, but my head was spinning.

This job offer that had fallen from the sky – unexpected and welcome – proved that I was still a relevant player in the international infectious disease world. The visiting professorship could keep me in circulation while I considered other options. I wondered how it would feel to be a Filipino in the Philippines where everyone looked more like me. I would have to think about it. I had been through other budget crises before that seemed to get solved at the last minute. Nothing was certain.

After a few minutes of listening to the speakers discuss new theories of antibiotic resistance, I realized my mind was racing too much for me to be able to sit still and listen. My feet moved absently, twitching, telling me I needed to walk.

24

I began walking along a narrow street outside. A fifty-year-old woman with red hair and a large cyst on her forehead shuffled by with a sign that read, "Jesus is the Answer. What is the Question?"

"What cha lookin' at?" she demanded.

"Just looking at your sign."

"It's not my sign. The man on the corner gave it to me for good luck. I could use some luck. Do you have a cigarette?"

"No, I don't smoke."

"Shit. No one smokes anymore."

"I guess not."

"Well, I do, when I can get one. Do you have a dollar?"

"The whole dollar?" I laughed. "Usually people ask for change."

"You can't buy nothing with change anymore."

I reached into my pocket, pulled out my wallet and gave her a dollar.

"Thanks," she said, as she put the bill into her pocket. "Now you get to ask me any question, and I'll give you the answer."

I paused to consider my question. "Okay. Where am I going?"

"How the hell should I know?" she said and shuffled on down the street.

Sometimes your feet discover a trail hidden from consciousness, like the half-covered track of previous cross country skiers buried in the snow. The track only becomes apparent with each step forward.

Each correct step feels right, and each wrong step meets resistance, irregularity, and stumbling. I allowed my feet to follow the sidewalk away from the hotel and down an alley, past a park, along an old cemetery, to a park named after a war hero, John Kelley Jr. My feet felt sore in the heels and ankles as I passed a bus stop and noticed people waiting for the bus: an African-American woman with a shopping bag, a Latino man with short hair and a little mustache carrying a backpack, a tall, red-haired high school student listening to music with ear phones and chewing gum. I was tempted to stop and ask them where I was and how I could get back to my hotel, but instead, I continued to let my feet lead me. It was as if Sarah was running ahead of me as we returned from our lap around the park, and I knew now where I was going. Down one more street and on to Gardener Street, to the house with the light above the door at the top of the stairs. I wondered if I should just stand there and wait, as if someone would notice and come out to greet me, but my feet continued up the stairs and my hand knocked on the door.

25

Awoman with a wrinkled, worried face and short gray hair opened the door a crack. It was not Sarah. I hesitated awkwardly, unsure of what I should say. The woman's willingness to wait for me to speak was fading like the sunlight and so I finally blurted out his name: "Steven Thompson. I'm a friend from out of town. Is this Steven Thompson's house?"

"Yes," said the woman, now hidden behind the door. "Mr. Thompson is not accepting visitors."

"I'm an old friend from high school, a very old friend … a doctor," I added, suddenly hoping the promise of a visit from a doctor would pry the door open. I waited as the woman considered her options. Finally, she opened the door.

"Come in."

I noticed boxes of medical supplies, the smell of antiseptic, and an odor of something familiar from my days on the internal medicine wards – blood. It was a smell you could not forget, perhaps imprinted in our brains genetically for millennia, so that we would pursue it when it indicated fresh food, and flee if it indicated danger. Movies will never capture the true impact of blood until they add that smell to the visual experience. I looked around for the source and then I saw the bed that had been brought down into the living room and the form of a body swathed in a light blue blanket. There was not enough light for me to make out the face, but I knew it was Steven by the expression on the woman's face.

"Mr. Thompson is not well. Perhaps you are aware of this. I'm Mrs. Ippoletti, one of the visiting nurses caring for him. We have not been allowing visitors, but since you are a doctor.... What kind of doctor are you?"

"I'm an infectious disease doctor," I said.

She nodded. "Mrs. Thompson will be back soon. Perhaps you can speak with her. Mr. Thompson has not been speaking today."

"Yes, Sarah called me. Do you mind if I see him?"

"Of course not, please come this way." She escorted me in to the living room where Steven lay. "I think he's sleeping, but I can't always tell."

At first I didn't recognize him. The shades were drawn, and in the shadows of blankets and pillows his body looked just like another pillow sticking out of the sheets and covers. But when I finally recognized him, I shuddered. Gone was the softness of youth, replaced by the mask of impending death. His face was gaunt and skeletal with an orange sheen, like a ripening pumpkin. Dilated blood vessels created red splotches on his forehead and cheeks. His eyes gazed out vacantly, making random horizontal oscillations. As they passed over my face they stopped and focused for a moment before continuing. His abdomen extended out from his narrow chest like a giant beach ball full of air.

"Steven," I said, "It's me, Robert. Robert Thames from Danvers."

His eyes opened wide as if he were seeing a ghost. His voice responded in stages as he mustered the effort to form words. I strained to understand the sounds escaping from his lips, just air at first, and then beginnings of words.

"....Rrrrrr....bbbb.....rrrrr........ttttt?"

"Hello, Steven," I said. "I'm sorry it's been so long."

His eyes grew more alive and his mouth attempted a smile. His lips were dry and cracked.

"Would you like some water?" I asked.

"Wwww......aaaaa.....tttttt........rrrrrrr.......uuuuuu......doing here?" he asked in a high-pitched tone, speeding up his delivery at the end, as if he had just awakened from a deep sleep.

Mrs. Ippolitto brought a glass of water, but he shook his head and turned his lips away.

"No…I can do it myself," he said, now with increasing cadence and clarity. He took the glass with a shaky white hand and began to clear his throat as he swallowed.

As I watched him drink and struggle, I was reminded of my days as an internal medicine resident, when I had cared for many patients who looked like Steven. Often they would go in and out of consciousness, experiencing moments of clarity followed by coma-like lapses, due to fluctuations in the absorption of protein in the stomach and intestines. The rapidity of the mental change often surprised me. Liver failure was the only illness that seemed to have such dramatic changes in mental clarity.

"About… time," he enunciated clearly, with a tinge of anger.

Perhaps the water had lubricated his throat, or perhaps it was the waxing and waning of hepatic encephalopathy. His face brightened and he seemed to have woken up from his nearly-comatose state.

"Steven, I had no idea you were so sick! I came as soon as I could. I meant to call you earlier. I'm sorry."

"Sorry for what?"

"Sorry for not … being a better friend." There had been several times that I had almost visited him. There were the telephone calls when I knew he was there listening but would not speak. There was the memory of our awkward relationship at Danvers and later, in college, when I visited him and Sarah. It had been confusing, and our lives had gone in different directions.

Mrs. Ippolitto interrupted our conversation. "I'll be out in the kitchen if you need me." She turned and walked out through the hall and disappeared into the kitchen.

"Worthless bitch," Steven muttered. "She sleeps more than I do, and I'm supposed to be dying." He shook his head, opened and closed his eyes, and then pointed a bony finger at me. "Can you touch it?"

"Touch what?" I asked.

"My finger. Can you touch it?"

"Sure, yes, I can touch it."

I touched his finger. It felt like a piece of a dead tree branch, dry and cool and cracking. I wondered if this was some kind of game, or perhaps a manifestation of his encephalopathy. Sometimes patients are not sure what is a part of their body and what is a hallucination, and I wanted to reassure him.

"What does it feel like?" he asked.

"I don't know," I said. "A finger, I guess."

"Not very descriptive, Doctor. Does it feel like a crayon, or piece of chalk, or a carrot?"

"I don't know. Not a carrot. It feels kind of dry."

"It's orange like a carrot. But not a carrot. Chalk? Is it chalk?"

"Yes, maybe orange chalk."

Steven continued to throw questions at me like darts: "But you cannot write with it on a blackboard. So it's not chalk."

"No, it's not chalk," I admitted, feeling uncomfortable.

"But imagine it is chalk, because I can move my finger and write letters in the air."

He demonstrated by moving his finger in a large circle. "That was an 'O.' It will always be an 'O' floating in space. When you write with chalk on a blackboard, you can erase it."

"Steven, I don't understand."

"If we were like chalk, we would write our life stories on a blackboard, and bit by bit the chalk would disappear as the story got longer and longer. And then we would die and along comes someone else to erase the story. Did you come here to erase it?"

"No, I just want to talk to you."

"Well, you can't erase it because I've written everything with my finger and it will be floating in space. If I point my finger at you I can make you disappear."

"No, I don't think so."

"Too bad." Steven let his head fall back on the pillow. "No…that's not true. I wouldn't want you to disappear. I've been waiting for you."

"You have?"

"Yes."

"Steven, I just came here to talk to you. I heard you were sick. Sarah called me. I was thinking about when I first met you when we were standing in line for those photographs."

"The naked ones?" He smiled and his eyes seemed to brighten for a moment.

"Yes, do you remember them?"

"I remember what you looked like. I remember everything from that day. You looked sad. Why were you sad, Robert?"

"I wasn't sad. I was afraid and embarrassed. I was ashamed for people to see me."

"What people?"

"Anyone. You."

"I enjoyed looking at you."

"I didn't enjoy it. I didn't understand why we had to have our pictures taken without our clothes."

"We were cute then. So were our pictures." He smiled.

"That's not the point. It was a study. A crazy study. Dr. Hart recently sent me the files and the photos. I want to talk to you about it. I looked at a bunch of the files – Mark, Richard, Tim, you, and me. In fact, I just visited Tim."

"Tim Washington? I want to see him. I want to see them all," he said. "I have dreams about them and our card games. I loved them all. I even have dreams about being one of the cards, the Jack of Diamonds. That's who I am in my dream. Not a bad card. And I have dreams about you."

"I guess we dream a lot of silly things when we get sick," I said.

"These dreams aren't silly. They're more real than most of my life. You have to find them – Tim and Mark and Richard. I need to see them. I have something to tell them, about what happened, about what we did. Something important."

"Can you tell me?"

"I'll tell you when everyone's here. You have to bring them here."

"I haven't seen Richard or Mark for years. I only just saw Tim in Africa."

"Tim's in Africa? He's gone back? I knew he would return to Africa. You have to bring him back here and tell him it's okay. He doesn't have to go back to Africa just because he's Black. It doesn't matter about your skin color. Look at mine. I'm yellow. But I'm not Chinese. You have to find them all. I have to see them now, before it is too late. We need to talk."

"Okay, Steven. I'll try."

"You have to try. I'm too sick to go anywhere. I get so tired. I just fall asleep. They say it's encephalopathy. My brain is swollen. I'm glad you came here. Let me see you."

I walked closer.

"Now turn sideways, like you did in those pictures." I turned and stood there quietly as his eyes moved over me. Then he frowned. "I can't really tell if you have changed with all your clothes on. If you could just take off your shirt, that would help."

"My shirt? You want me to take it off?"

"Yes."

I considered whether his request was just the disordered thoughts of a diseased mind. I wondered if he even remembered from minute to minute what he said.

"I'm not going to take off my shirt."

"I won't be here much longer. It's the least you could do. The last request of a dying man."

I took a deep breath and waited to see if he would lapse into coma, and spare me the indignity. But he didn't.

I unbuttoned my shirt. Perhaps it was because of the guilt stored up over the years.

"I don't do this for just anyone," I tried to joke. When my shirt was off, Steven stared at me. "How's that?" I asked.

He frowned again and laid his head back against his pillow.

"I thought that would help, but I think I need you to take off your pants. Your chest has grown larger, and now your arms have more muscles. Your face has lines on your forehead and your eyes are sunken down like rocks in mud. I can't tell about your legs. You seem to have gained weight in your stomach, but it's difficult to know for sure."

"Yes, I've gained weight. We all have. My eyes just look tired, because I had a long flight from Africa. I couldn't sleep."

"Your pants, now."

"What?"

"Your pants. Take them off."

"I'm not taking my pants off. What if the nurse came in? What would she think?"

"She won't come in. Anyway, fuck her," he growled.

"Why do you want me to take my pants off?"

"You owe this to me," he said. After a brief pause he added, "You're seeing me like this. Why can't I see you without your shirt and pants? It's only fair."

"Steven, we're not children playing a poker game. I just wanted to visit with you, and I'm sorry that you're so sick and I didn't visit you before."

"When I'm in pain, I remember that poker game. It helps me survive. It was one of the best moments of my life. Did you know that? It's what I think about to distract me from feeling sorry for myself. If you take your pants off, I won't ask for anything else."

"Are you sure?"

"Yes, just this one small thing. I want to remember you as you are now. No one will ever know."

I took off my shoes and unhooked my belt and pulled my pants down over my ankles.

"Let me see," he said.

I stood a few feet away and he stared. At first I felt like that boy again, with the photographer telling me where to stand and when to turn. But then I realized that there were just the two of us, and for the first time he seemed to be relaxed and happy.

"Could you come closer?"

I moved next to him. I could hear him inhale deeply, as if he were trying to take a deep breath. He touched my chest and ran his hand down to my stomach.

"Mmm. It's just as I remembered, like sweet milk." He inhaled again. "I used to try to breathe you in when I was near you. I thought I could hold you inside of me if I could just inhale and stop breathing. I wanted you that much." Then he began to speak again, softly, "Why does your skin smell like milk?"

"I don't know. I didn't know that it did," I took a step back. I realized that in my efforts to be compassionate and cooperative I was encouraging Steven's imagination and delusions. Why was I cooperating with this bizarre inquisition? But I felt powerless to stop it.

"It always smelled like milk. Why?"

"Maybe because I drink a lot of milk. The food you eat can affect how you smell."

"Yes, I remember the smell of your skin. It has not changed. It was different from mine. You were different from the rest of us. But why do you like to drink milk?"

"I have no idea. I guess it tastes good. I don't know. Maybe my mother didn't breast feed me enough. Who knows?"

"Why didn't she?"

"These are crazy questions. Well, you know. I told you. She was sick. She had tuberculosis. She couldn't take care of me. That was why I got adopted by the Thameses. That was why I ended up at Danvers, and why I'm here today."

"But why are you here today?"

"Well, I meant… why I'm here in the United States and not a clerk or farmer in the Philippines. But I'm here with you today because I wanted to see you. I wanted to know what happened to you, to see what you looked like."

"What do you think of my body?"

I looked at Steven's swollen stomach and legs and the yellow tint of his skin. "It looks like you're sick."

"Why do you think I'm sick?"

"I think you must know. I can imagine it probably has something to do with alcohol or drugs."

"Yes for the alcohol. What drugs?"

"I wouldn't know. The most common are heroin, cocaine maybe. Okay, I'm getting cold standing here. I need to put my clothes back on. This has gone on long enough."

"Not yet. I need to look at you."

"Are you in pain?" I asked.

"What do you think?"

"I think you are."

He rolled his eyes back and took a long gasping breath. "Did you know that I used to follow you?"

I stared at him, uncomprehending.

"I would wait for you. Usually outside the hospital. At night. I would follow you. But you never noticed me. One time you looked right at me and didn't recognize me. I would finally end up at a bar and find someone who reminded me of you. Why didn't you notice me?"

"I don't know. Probably it was too dark. I had work to do. I had to study. You should have said something."

Now, as I thought about it, I recalled sometimes seeing someone in the shadows at night after I left the hospital. I would think it was someone waiting for me, someone I knew, but then the person would move off into the shadows. I had almost called out to him several times. Now I wondered if I knew but did not want to acknowledge Steven's presence.

"What should I have said?" he asked.

"Anything. Just to let me know you were there."

"Did you want me to be there?" he asked.

"I don't know, Steven. Maybe we could have talked. Maybe we wouldn't have had to meet like this so many years later. Maybe we could have fixed things."

"What things?"

"Why do you want me to stand here without my clothes? I'm trying to be kind, and you're trying to punish me. You know what I am talking about! We could have fixed things between you and me and Sarah, and what happened that night."

"What happened that night?"

"Steven. You were there. You know what happened. Why didn't you tell them it was me?"

"Why would I?"

"I was the one with Sarah that night. Did you want everyone to think it was you?"

"Yes. I wanted it to be me and her and you. I wanted us to be together. But I didn't want them to hurt you. I would never hurt you. Even when Maiser kept asking me who else was there, I wouldn't tell him. Even when he said that I wasn't the right type to be with a girl, that it must have been someone else, I wouldn't tell him. Even when they sent me for counseling, I never mentioned you. It was to protect you."

"I'm sorry," I said.

"Those nights when I followed you, I felt bad for leaving Sarah alone. I wanted to stop. I still wanted all of us to be together. But it was like a constant thirst and I just couldn't resist it except when I drank alcohol or took drugs. And that's what I did," he said.

"It must be terrible."

"You could cure me. You're a doctor."

"Not that kind of doctor."

He laughed gruffly. "Did you know I once saved a man? He was choking and I grabbed him around the chest and squeezed him and he could breathe again. I saved his life. It was the best thing I've ever done, and the one time I have held a man and just squeezed him without thinking about myself or you."

"Steven, I'm sorry. I do care about you. But I don't have the same feelings for you that you have for me."

"I wish you could just grab me like that man and squeeze me and I would be cured."

"I know. I can't."

"Then I have another favor to ask you."

"What is it? I already have all my clothes off."

"I know how you feel about Sarah."

"What do you know?"

"I know you talked to her on the telephone. Even though you promised you wouldn't."

"I just called to check on her, but then once we started to talk we couldn't stop."

"I know that you loved her, that you still love her."

I didn't respond. I stared at a spot on the ground, hoping this moment of humiliation would pass like the others.

"They've recommended hospice for me. It was my fault for drinking and taking drugs. But when you're young, you never imagine this. You go to bars and parties. You meet people, girls and boys who want to have fun, and you party together. You wake up in the morning next to someone you've never seen before. You go to your law office unshaven, with a splitting headache and a puncture over a vein in your arm that you have to cover with a long-sleeve shirt. Now my liver is shot and I'm spitting up blood. Even now I'm swallowing it so that you won't have to see it." He paused for a moment and spit blood into a plastic bowl. "Is it red?"

"Yes," I said. "This all must have been tough on Sarah. How could you do that to her?"

"I know. I once offered to share Sarah with you, but you didn't know how to share. Now I don't care anymore. I don't want her to be alone."

"I don't think that she – "

"I'm only asking that you look out for her. I don't want her to be alone. She'll have enough money. There's the Thompson trust money from my parents and there's the house, which will be hers."

"Steven, we're not the same as we once were."

"Help her if she needs it. Can you promise me that? She has friends, but no one like you."

I nodded. "Okay."

"Do you promise?"

"Steven, I'll try."

"You won't tell Sarah that I asked you?"

"Not if that's what you want."

"She doesn't want your pity. She'll refuse it."

"I know."

Steven rested back against his pillows and let his eyes close, as if he had just released a heavy burden. After a moment he continued, "Robert, there are times when I fade into deep sleep. I'm partly awake and partly asleep and I have dreams. But I can think about certain people and certain places as I am dreaming and it makes me feel better."

"That's good."

"It's called a hepatic coma. It's a lot like taking certain drugs – like Quaaludes or OxyContin. I've taken them all. The only difference is that with the drugs, you know when they'll be coming on, and that in a few hours it will be over and you'll return to your normal state. But now I never know. I might not ever come back."

"That must be stressful."

"It's not so bad. Anyway, when I feel it coming on… what makes me feel good and safe… is how it was when we were kids. I wish we could be kids again, that we could play cards and drink wine and eat spaghetti to-gether. I keep thinking about us playing cards, and I see the kings and aces and different cards turning up. It wouldn't matter if I won. And I think of Tim and Mark and Richard, all of us together like a big family of brothers. But I've also been thinking of something else. Something that was wrong. Something we did that was wrong."

"What?"

"I wish I could make it disappear, like an old hand of cards. I want to fold, but the bets are too high."

"What do you mean?"

"Could we play cards now?"

"Steven, I don't have any clothing left. I would have nothing to bet."

"You can get dressed now. Get the cards, and I'll show you my hand."

"Okay," I said reluctantly. I was exhausted from Steven's manipulations but I felt that we were coming to something important. I pulled on my pants and tied my shoes and, finally, buttoned my shirt and tucked it into my pants so that I looked put together. I found Mrs. Ippolitto out in the kitchen. "He wants to play cards," I said to her. "Do you have any?"

"Cards?" She looked at me curiously. She opened drawers in the kitchen and pulled out a pack. "I think they're all there."

I walked back into the living room with the cards and two cups of tea, but he was dozing. I watched him for a while and called out softly, "Steven...?"

He did not awaken. I moved to a chair and sat and watched him breathe for a while. The sounds escaped from his mouth like an intermittent wind, blocked by lips that seemed glued together until they would suddenly loosen and allow a rush of air to escape with an audible "Puh." I felt myself drifting into a hypnotic half sleep. Perhaps it was the time change and all the travel. I let my eyes close for a moment. When I opened them, a woman was bending down, staring at my face. I recognized the eyes, but the hair was no longer brown. Streaks of gray coursed through the long hair.

"Robert?" The wrinkles of the forehead and eyes animated her face as she squinted at me.

"Hi, Sarah," I said, sitting up. The pack of cards spilled onto the floor.

26

Sarah still had the thin runner's body that I remembered, but now there was stiffness in her legs and back as she straightened up after helping me gather the cards.

"I came to visit Steven," I explained. "I should have let you know, but I was in Boston for a meeting and it kind of happened spontaneously."

"Well, communication never was your strength."

"I'm sorry," I said, a flood of feelings washing over me.

She smiled tightly. "A little warning would have been nice, but he's been mentioning your name over the past few days, so I guess he willed you here."

"I meant to visit you both so many times…"

She put the last of the cards into the box and closed the lid. "And?"

"I thought you didn't want to see me again."

"I think our memories might be different: You were the one who wouldn't call back when I left messages for you. Even last year…"

"Last year? I have no recollection of that."

She shook her head. "It doesn't matter. Steven needs you, and now you're here."

"But how are you, Sarah?"

She exhaled deeply, rubbing her ears and the back of her neck. I noticed the wrinkles behind her ears, and silver earrings with an etching of Yin and Yang. "It's strange how I used to think about changing the world. Now I think about changing bandages and sheets."

She set the pack of cards on the side table. "Were you actually playing with him?"

"Trying. He wants me to invite the old bridge group here."

"Yes, he told me the same thing. But I wouldn't take it too seriously. Lately, he's been going back into the past in his dreams, as if he could fix things. He doesn't know what he's saying."

"Like what?"

She stared at me intently, eyes tearing up a bit. "Steven and I loved each other, but it hasn't been easy. We drifted into a pattern, and it wasn't always a good one. Sometimes I wonder whether there might have been something different for us. We were so innocent and foolish when we were kids. Now everything is so serious."

Steven began to make sounds that were barely intelligible. "Hey diddle diddle…. the cat and fiddle…. the cow jumped over the moon…. Hey diddle diddle…. the cat and the fiddle…. Who wants to diddle, I'm in the middle of a diddle…..." He began to move his arms and legs as if he were trying to climb out of bed.

"Robert, could you help me? I need to tie him down or he'll climb out of bed and end up on the floor."

I grabbed his arms and she attached rolled up bandages that served as restraints. We secured his arms away from his body as he began to flail. "Get his legs," she said.

I held his ankle but he pulled loose and kicked me in the nose. I grabbed at it again and his other foot kicked my ear.

"Watch out!" she said.

Sarah had his other leg and was pulling it down straight and attaching it to the bed frame. As I held his leg against my chest, my head rested against her shoulder and chest; our bodies formed a V at the foot of the bed. I sat there, immobile, letting our bodies connect. She did not move for five, ten, thirty seconds. Blood was trickling from my nose. I could feel the sweat dripping from her neck. Steven was splayed out completely, his limbs at the 10, 2, 4 and 8 positions of a clock face.

"Are you okay?" she finally asked, stepping away from the bed.

"Yes, sure."

"He got you pretty good," she said. "You're bleeding." She rustled around in her purse for a tissue and held it out to me.

"It'll stop if I hold pressure," I said. I pressed my fingers across my nostrils. The bruise on my face from Steven's kick was throbbing. "He's still pretty powerful!"

"Tell me about it."

Suddenly I felt fatigued again. I balled up the bloodied tissue and put it in my pocket.

"I just got in from Africa. I should probably head back to my hotel…"

"Do you want any ice?"

"No, I'll be fine." If there's anything I can do for you, here's my number." I handed her a business card.

She accepted it, but looked deflated. Perhaps that's what made me think of an excuse to visit the house again. "What do you think about my contacting Tim and Mark and Richard to come by for that bridge game?"

She smiled. "I'm not sure he's up for bridge, but if you want to call them, I suppose it couldn't hurt. You were his best friends." She reached into her purse for her business card. "Let me know when they want to come. I'll make it work. Don't wait too long."

We hugged at the door. She held me against her body longer than I imagined possible. With each breath, I felt the passage of a decade: ten, twenty, thirty years. Finally, she loosened her grasp and exhaled deeply.

"It's been so long since I've hugged anyone like this," she said. "It feels good."

"For me too," I said. "I wish we'd had more time."

She tilted her head and looked at me strangely.

"I won't be far away if you need me," I said. "I'm going to set up a visit with Mark over the next few days. He's in Connecticut. "

"Thanks. Sometimes I could use a friendly voice."

She gave me a small kiss on the cheek, and I walked down the steps into the rain. The water on my face was comforting, like cleansing the dirt out of a wound. I walked toward the park where I had once followed Sarah on our run.

As sa ka padalong. Where are you going and who will be your companion?

I had been her companion then. Our legs had been so strong and limber.

A taxi passed by me, and then another. I began counting them.

Every destination has an element of time and space, I thought. My travel to Africa, the visit to Steven and Sarah, the places I studied and worked, the individual moments that expanded and contracted as we clutched them to our chest through the accelerating passage of time. Our lives were now rushing toward their conclusions.

A third taxi passed, and then a fourth. My face was now soaked in rain, but I began to wonder when the fifth cab would come, and if there would be a sixth. If I stuck out my hand, I might never get my answer.

"As sa ka padalang? Where are you going, sir?"

A yellow cab had stopped in front of me. Perhaps the cabbie recognized something in my face or body that was familiar. He was a small, brown-skinned man like me, with short, straight black hair, a Filipino in a blue jacket, who saw me standing alone in the rain.

"Where are you going, sir?" he repeated.

"Back," I said. "Back, please."

"O, O, sigi," he said in our language, "I will take you back, sir."

Book 3

27

When I returned home, there was a message on the telephone from a number in New York I did not recognize. It was from Tillman Hobson of the Danvers Board of Directors, asking me to call as soon as possible. I called mostly out of curiosity. A secretary answered and I gave her my name and waited. A few minutes later, a man with a deep, affable voice came on the line.

"Hello, Robert, this is Tillman Hobson from the Danvers Board of Trustees."

"Yes."

"How are you doing?"

"Fine."

"Great. That's great. I'm not sure if we've met. I'm the Board president."

"No, I don't think I've met you."

"That's too bad. I try to meet as many of our alumni as I can. Danvers really changed my life, as it probably did yours. A Danvers education is a rare and wonderful experience. I'm sure you would agree."

"Yes, it definitely changed my life. I was from the Philippines. I had no idea what a prep school was when I came to Danvers, though my dad had gone there."

"Well then, I'm sure you would agree that we want to make such opportunities available for other boys and girls too. You were probably there before Danvers went co-ed. They have girls now."

"Yes, I've been there for a few visits over the years."

"Great. Great. Nothing like a visit to reconnect with the place. I understand that you were very close to Dr. Hart and his family."

"He was a close friend of my dad's. When I got to Danvers, the Harts looked after me."

"Dr. Hart will be missed. We're naming the new infirmary after him. I will never forget how he took care of my knee when I injured it skiing. He was a great general practitioner. They don't make them like that anymore."

"No, doctors are all becoming specialists these days."

"You're also a doctor. Is that right?"

"Yes, infectious diseases."

"I have great respect for the medical profession. But let me get to the point: I called because we recently became aware of a research study that Dr. Hart had been conducting. This study involved boys from three of our classes back in the 60s. Several Ivy League colleges participated, and we were one of the sites for younger students. Without going into the details, I was wondering if Dr. Hart ever mentioned this study to you."

I hesitated for a moment, considering my options.

If I told him I had the files, I could put an end to all the distraction. Someone would come to my house and load them into a truck. I would never have to think about them again.

But at the moment, I still held all of the cards.

"Could you tell me more about the study?" I asked. "It's not really ringing a bell."

"That's just it – we don't know much. We had no idea the study existed until Dr. Hart attempted to sequester the files in our restricted library collection. When we discussed the matter with him, just prior to his death, he said that he no longer had the files and refused to elaborate. One of our former faculty members, Dean Maiser, thought the data had all been sent to Harvard years ago, when the research was completed.

But now we understand that there may be several boxes of confidential files at large."

"Dean Maiser must be a hundred years old," I said.

"Not quite. He's a tough old goat. He's hunched from arthritis, and nearly blind, but his mind is sharp. He remembers the study and the files. Without him we would have no leads at all."

"But why is it so important to retrieve them?" I asked.

"These are private research files and the property of Danvers. If any of the material became public, it could be a great embarrassment to the students involved. It also could harm our trust with our current students and their families. Any release of information would be a violation of research ethics and a liability for Danvers vis à vis potential law suits. It would be a criminal matter for anyone who participated in removal of the files. So you can understand that we are leaving no stone unturned in trying to recover these files."

"Does this have to do with the photos taken of us? They made us take off our clothes. Strip naked."

"We're trying to verify those details. I've heard rumors of such photographs, though we cannot confirm them without the files. Obviously they would be of great concern."

"Well, I can confirm to you that I had photographs taken of me and watched as my classmates were photographed as well."

"Then you do understand our concern."

"Yes."

"Your name came up as someone who had a personal connection to Dr. Hart and might know something about these files. If you have any information, or know anyone else who does, we would be very appreciative. Also, please keep this information confidential. We don't want any publicity while we are trying to verify the facts."

"Sure," I said. "If I can think of anything I'll let you know."

"Thank you. And perhaps we can meet at one of our alumni gatherings in Washington. Or even better, come to our Big Game weekend up at Danvers."

"Yes, I'll try to do that. Thanks for calling."

I sat in silence for some time after the call. I had lied again to someone powerful from Danvers, some forty years after lying to Dean Maiser about Sarah and Steven. At first I experienced some of the same feelings of guilt and anxiety that I had at Danvers as a powerless student. But then I realized that I had just as much a right to my file as anyone. Danvers didn't own me, my images, or anything written about my potential as a young man. I had the files and knew what they contained. Hobson's threats and intimidations were empty; I knew that he was bluffing.

It was time to be patient, keep my cards hidden, and wait for my partners to move with me. But I could not wait too long. The clock was ticking.

28

I decided to call Mark Harrison right away. Mark never hesitated to give advice. He also might know where to find Richard Burris. As one of our most active alumni, Mark kept up with all of our classmates, even those who never gave money or wrote entries for the alumni magazine. I usually spoke to him during the annual Danvers fundraisers. He would call and ask about my job and family and tell me about his, and eventually he would get down to business and ask me for a contribution for Danvers, and I would agree.

I called information for Hartford, Connecticut, and then let the operator connect me.

"What a pleasant surprise!" he exclaimed after I'd introduced myself. "I'm usually the one shaking you down for those annual donations. I suppose you're returning the favor."

"I'm not asking for money, but I do need some favors."

"Didn't they teach you to never ask for more than one favor at a time?"

"Sorry. I'm not used to this kind of thing. It's just that…remember Steven Thompson from Danvers? He's very sick, and he'd love for our card group to get together and visit. He wants one last game of bridge." I explained about Steven's liver disease and the immediacy of the situation.

"Of course I'm willing!" he responded. "This sounds serious. One last game. I suppose we all have our wish list. That wouldn't be at the

top of mine. I think I would want one final meal at Le Meurice in Paris…
but you just tell me the day."

"I will. You're the first player I've called."

"Steven was a bit of an odd duck, but weren't we all in those days?"
he mused. "He used to come over to my room with his stash of *Playboys*
and I had mine. We'd enjoy some 'aesthetic moments' together admiring
the art work, so to speak, smoke a joint, and make a trade or two. I think
he's a lawyer, business law, and it all started with those *Playboy* negoti-
ations."

"That sounds about right," I laughed.

"I never could figure out that mess with the girl at Danvers. We all
envied him over that. She was quite a beauty. I heard he ended up mar-
rying her."

"Yes, he did. Her name is Sarah."

"Yes, that's right. Pretty girl, a little wild and political, a Jane Fonda
type – Black Panthers and SDS, wasn't she? Radical chic. I saw them in
college. Well, sorry to hear he's so ill. And what was the other favor?"

"I'd like to come by and talk about some research files from our
Danvers days. They were supposed to be part of a medical research
project. I thought that maybe you could help me."

"Well, certainly. I'm on our hospital board here at Saint Francis, so
I'm very interested in medical research. You do international medical research, isn't that right? Is this some kind of medical study about Danvers
students? Is it a vaccine study?"

"Not exactly. But I think you'll find it interesting."

"Sure, whatever I can do to help. *Non sibi.* Isn't that it? Why don't
you join us for dinner on Saturday? Is anyone going to be with you? I
can't remember, are you married?"

"No, I'm still single. Probably just me unless I can talk one of my
many girlfriends into joining me," I laughed.

"That's the spirit. Never too late. Some of the boys are on their third
marriages by now. Not me. I'm still with my first love. No need to switch
horses in mid-stream. I'll tell my wife to plan for two guests, and if you're
by yourself, we'll have left-overs, which never seem to be a problem in
my house."

He gave me his address, and I asked him the whereabouts of Richard Burris.

"Oh, he's an enigma. He works in Los Alamos, New Mexico, at some kind of secret research lab. I've tried to reach him several times, but he has an unlisted number, and if you call his office, they just take your name and number and ask a bunch of questions. He never calls back."

"I see," I said, disappointed. How was I going to play bridge without my old partner?

"But you know what?" Mark said cheerfully. "I read about him in the papers recently. I think he just had a book come out and is giving lectures all over the country. So maybe you can go to one of them or contact him through his publisher."

It was one p.m. when I finally hung up with Mark. I decided it was time to check in with my team. I had a group of microbiologists and biochemists who were eagerly awaiting my specimens from Africa. I had put one box of fungus in my suitcase and another in the backpack. I hoped everything was still safe and viable after the long transport.

As I walked past the panhandlers at the Dupont Circle Metro station, I gave them each a quarter and they barely grunted at me. I read the Walt Whitman phrase that encircled the Metro escalator: "*The hurt and wounded I pacify with soothing hand, I sit by the restless all the dark night – some are so young; some suffer so much – I recall the experiences sweet and sad.*"

When you cared for someone who was suffering, there was sweetness and sadness and a kind of intimacy. I remembered it from my days on the medicine wards when I would watch someone fading away, and now it reminded me of Steven. I squeezed on to the Red Line to Metro Center and stood between two young women who were reading magazines as they held on to the handrail. They were so absorbed in what they were reading that they did not notice me observing them – the eye shadow and the lipstick, the softness of youthful skin, the dangly silver earrings. I was thinking of the Walt Whitman line, "some are so young... sweet and sad" as I walked to my office.

"Hey, Doc," said the security guard, Ralph, as I displayed my ID badge.

I put the specimen through the metal detector and he handed it back to me.

"You're good to go, Doc. I don't never want to touch none of that stuff in your bags. If the metal detector don't buzz, we're cool."

Ralph had once checked my specimen bag after a trip to Asia and found a particularly foul-smelling fungus that almost made him retch.

I handed my specimens to the receptionist, and she called Curtis from the lab to pick them up. Then I walked into my office. My pictures of Mount Apo, ringed in clouds, on Mindanao Island, stood guard over the office. I had taken it with my dad's Kodak camera more than fifty years ago. A few family photos and some old graduation pictures lined my desk. All my diplomas, licenses, and board certifications filled one wall. An award for global research contributions from the International Infectious Diseases Society on a wooden plaque leaned against old textbooks on one of my shelves. It was the net sum of my life, the minimum facts for an obituary.

On my desk were several travel vouchers requiring my signature and a report I had written that needed to be reviewed and signed. I turned on my computer, plugged in the passwords, and settled down to work.

A few minutes later, Mr. Grundel knocked on my door. "Robert. Welcome back."

"Thanks." I glanced up and then back at my computer to make it clear I was occupied with work.

"When you have some time, I'd like to go over a few things," he said. "We have some paperwork to fill out, a standard release. But I want you to know that I'm working hard to keep everyone funded. That includes you. If only we had a few glimmers of something on the horizon. Something to tell to our friends in the Senate. Do you think you might have found anything in Africa?"

"I met an interesting guy in Tanzania. He has some promising research. And I brought back some new specimens."

"Good. Very good. That's what I was hoping to hear. Come by my office when you have a chance. I want to hear all about the trip. I want you to know that I'm in your corner. I'm just doing my job, covering all the bases."

"Sure," I said. "As soon as I finish this memo I'll try and get there."

I looked back at my computer until he walked out. I had no intention of stopping by his office. There were many more important things to do.

I had been thinking about my other research project, the files. There were a few new facts that had recently been dropped into my lap like the ripe fruit of the durian tree. As a scientist, I understood that new facts were a gift, but it came with risk and responsibility. Was I prepared to follow the trail, wherever it might lead? There was the mention of my biological father in the file. Who was he? I had a name – Berenson – age, and known place of death. It might be possible to locate a relative. All of my reading through files of my classmates had whetted my appetite for more information about my own history. With all of the databases on the Internet and the trained librarians who assisted me with my research, it might be possible to find something.

The other research related to the letter to Dr. Hart from William Sheldon. There was the name of Dr. Thomas Hutchinson on the signature line. I wondered what I might be able to find about Sheldon and Hutchinson. While I knew that Sheldon had died long ago, Hutchinson might still be alive. There also might be information about Dr. Hart's research project that had come from the data collected from the other schools.

I began with Sheldon because I thought he would be the easiest to find and his name might be linked to Hutchinson. I found the Sheldon pages and entries on the web. His theories continued to be used in current sports physiology to help with selection of outstanding athletes who could lead a team. His book, *The Atlas of Men: A Guide for Somatotyping the Adult Male at All Ages*, was described in detail. I went online to our library and found that we had a copy of the book in our archives.

Then I decided to see what I might find under Berenson. I entered the name and the Philippines and World War II. There were a lot of Berensons. Several in Boston. Thomas Berenson was a lawyer who had died three years ago. His son had written a nice obituary that effectively ruled him out as a relative. Alfred Berenson sold photos and music videos of weddings. He had been born in Chicago and likely was unrelated to me. And there was an optometrist named Donald Berenson who was practicing near Boston in a city called Chelsea. He was about the age my father would have been, and had been born in Boston. I looked at his picture and felt a pang of recognition. Then I found an obscure article in a newspaper. It was a scanned article from the Chelsea Record about Donald Berenson receiving an award for civic leadership. In a short description of family history, there was mention of a brother who died in the Philippines during World War II. As an experienced researcher, I knew that this might be a coincidence, but decided I would make an appointment with his office to have my eyes examined when I visited Steven in Boston. It was a possibility – not quite a probability – but worth a visit. I hadn't had my eyes checked for many years, so at the very least I could cross that off my "to do" list.

Thomas Hutchinson was not difficult to find, either. There was a Dr. Thomas Hutchinson at the Harvard Peabody Museum who specialized in physical anthropology. He had written an article about the history of physical measurement in anthropology. In his article were references to William Sheldon and somatotypes. He seemed a likely candidate for the colleague who had been working with Sheldon on Dr. Hart's research study. The museum was in Cambridge, so I might be able to fit in a visit. If Dr. Hutchinson still worked there, he would be quite old. Even if he were originally involved in the research project, how much would he remember?

I walked out to the elevator and rode it to the third floor library. There were medical journals displayed on the wall in bookcases, and there were stacks of books farther down the corridor. Chairs and desks with reading lamps lined one wall. Computers sat on two of the desks. I seemed to be the only person in the library except for our librarian, Evelyn, who greeted me and asked if there was anything she could do to help. Evelyn was not only a research librarian; she was also an expert detective who loved to help on other types of searches.

"I have a rather odd request. I'm looking for an old book called *The Atlas of Men,* by William Sheldon," I said. "And if you have time, I'm looking for information on two people: An optometrist in Chelsea named Donald Berenson and an anthropologist at Harvard named Thomas Hutchinson. Anything you might find on either of them would be very helpful."

"Oh certainly, Dr. Thames. I always expect something unusual from you. I think the last time you wanted me to find a book about some kind of fungus that grew on tropical fruit. Let me see what I can do." She got on her computer and smiled. "Your book is in the special collection. I'll be right back with it." A few minutes later I was sitting at my desk thumbing through the book while Evelyn researched Donald Berenson and Thomas Hutchinson.

I read through the introductory chapter where Sheldon described the purpose of the somatotype process: "The somatotype is therefore a groping for a reflection in man of the orderly continuum of nature and in a more specific way it is also an attempt to identify the music of one's own particular dance in life."

Later he said, "We define the somatotype more formally as a trajectory or pathway through which the living organism will travel under standard conditions of nutrition and in the absence of grossly disturbing pathology."

There followed pages and pages of photographs similar to those in my files but with the genitals obscured by photographic alterations. Every possible somatotype appeared at different ages in three poses, front, back, and side. In addition to the photographs, Sheldon had provided a short summary of characteristics of the somatotype, relating it to an insect or animal that seemed to possess similar attributes. Some individuals were wasps; others, like Mark Harrison, were elephants.

I turned the pages to my somatotype 3-3-4.

Cottontail rabbits. Quiet sensitive, introverted little herbivores who mind their own business and by doing so generally manage to replenish their population as fast as the carnivores can eat it up… rather unremarkable, moderately frail little fellows who seem never to be very well-fed or well-loved, or even much attended to…Many do well at academics or some type of artistic pursuit. A generous proportion breaks down mentally.

So there it was – my somatotype. I was a bunny, not a fox or a lion, as Tim had suggested. But then I checked again. What if my first number 3 had been a 2? And my last number 4 had been a 5? What if I was really a 235? Then I did become a fox. What if they had miscalculated and instead of a rabbit being eaten by the carnivores, I was a fox, sly and defiant as Tim had suggested?

I gave the book back to Evelyn. "Thanks. I found what I wanted."

"Here's a print-out of those two names you wanted me to research," she said, handing me an envelope with printouts on Donald Berenson and Thomas Hutchinson. I thanked her and tucked the printouts under my arm.

Back in my office, Curtis from the lab came by to verify a few issues about my specimens, and we discussed what studies to do on them and the general lack of promising new materials over the past six months. "We're due for something big," he said. Perhaps he could tell I was distracted, because he left my office without the usual chitchat about the poor condition of the local baseball and football teams and how it reflected the poor morale of our government in Washington.

I decided I might as well sign the release for Mr. Grundel. I walked over to his office and knocked. The door swung slowly open and revealed an empty desk with several papers on it. I walked over and saw the one with my name on it. I read through the summary of my service to government and the key phrases, "outstanding physician scientist," and "renowned international researcher." One of our project managers described me as a "committed advocate for the developing world." Another lauded my discoveries as "having the potential to save thousands of lives." I had published 76 articles. My thirty years of government service were summarized in two pages, along with my days of sick leave and vacation. There was also a place for any disciplinary actions, which Mr. Grundel had marked "none." I acknowledged the accuracy of the summary, looked at the form one final time, and signed it. Then I left before Mr. Grundel could return.

29

As I drove out of Washington on Saturday, I found myself wondering exactly why this trip all the way to Connecticut was necessary. It was going to be at least five hours, depending upon the traffic up I-95. What did I hope to accomplish? Mark had always been a strong Danvers supporter, leading fund raising campaigns and making calls to alumni. Perhaps I wanted to shake him up and create some doubt in his mind about Danvers. Perhaps I wanted to get another perspective. I had heard from Tim and Steven. Neither had felt that he fit in at Danvers. But Mark was a class officer and the son of an alumnus. He had supported Danvers since graduation and seemed to believe in its view of the world. What would he think about being classified as an "elephant" in the Danvers research study?

As I was driving, my cell phone buzzed. It was Sarah.

"Hi," I said. "Is everything okay?"

"Yes. He's the same."

"I'm in the car, driving to Mark's."

Her voice seemed to tremble as she spoke. "Sorry to bother you."

"It's no bother at all. I can drive and talk. Are you okay?"

"Yes. No. It's just so hard. Sometimes I wish I could just get away for a day."

"You could meet me in Connecticut. You could have dinner with me at Mark's."

"I don't think I could just leave Steven. He's so fragile."

"What about Mrs. Ippolitto. Can't she take care of him?"

"I don't know if I can handle Mark Harrison, either."

I laughed. "I could meet you for coffee after dinner."

"Huh? Some wild rendezvous in the middle of Connecticut?"

"No, just a little breather. A break. It might be a nice change of pace."

"Robert, I expect logic and common sense from you. Not crazy ideas."

"Well, okay, tell me what I can do. What happened today?"

"Well, I washed and shaved Steven, and then washed the sheets. And then he vomited on them so I changed them again and changed his pajamas. Then I tried to get him to drink some juice. Do you want to hear any more?"

"I get the picture," I said. "It doesn't seem like Mrs. Ippolitto is helping very much."

"No, she paces herself. But I did get an interesting call from a man named Tillman Hobson from the Danvers Board of Directors. Do you know him?"

"He called me too. He thinks I may have Dr. Hart's files and he wants them back."

"Those guys haven't changed, have they? He wanted to know if he could visit. He seemed to know that Steven was ill. He's the last person Steven would want to see. Then he wanted to know if I had heard anything about some missing research files. Those Danvers guys are always worried about their reputations. That was what I remember when Steven nearly got expelled for being with me. All they could talk about was the school's reputation."

"I was with you," I said.

"I know. But you know what I mean."

"Yes, I remember."

"Anyway, all they cared about was how it would look – the Danvers reputation. They didn't care about me or Steven. We were kids. I was traumatized for two years after that, probably longer. My parents sent me to a psychiatrist. I was afraid of relationships for the next three years. Did you know that?"

"No. We never talked about it."

"No, we didn't. Did you ever wonder how I felt?"

"Yes."

"But you never talked to me. You never asked me about how I was coping."

"I'm sorry."

"And now you want me to have a rendezvous with you in Connecticut?"

"I'm sorry. I shouldn't have suggested the idea. It wasn't appropriate, considering the situation."

There was a long pause and then she sighed. "It's all water under the bridge, as they say."

"That's an expression I never could understand – water under the bridge. Doesn't water always flow under a bridge?"

"Oh it doesn't matter. It's just an expression. Probably about someone who dropped something valuable into the water flowing under a bridge. It means you can't change the past and you have to move on."

"I see."

She was quiet for a few seconds and then said, "Maybe it would be good for me to get out of the house. I'll call you later if Mrs. Ippolitto can stay late tonight."

After the phone went silent, I thought about her call. Why had she called me? Why had I invited her to come to Mark's house? What was wrong with me? Even though I was driving past cities, over bridges, past forests, and behind trucks and cars of all types, I hardly noticed them.

30

The sun was setting as I pulled into Mark Harrison's driveway and parked. A large black lab ran to my car and began barking, jumping, and scratching at the door. A portly man strolled behind him, slouching forward as he moved, his striped shirt straining against an obese belly. He had a ruddy face, thick neck, and lips that stretched broadly.

"Now Blackie, you be nice to our visitor. He's one of us." He thrust a hand at me as I stepped out of my car. "Hi Robert, so nice to see you."

I wondered if he noticed the shocked look on my face: So many of my friends had gotten gray or put on a few pounds, but Mark's transformation was more extreme. He had always been rather large, but now he was enormous. His scalp retained only a few areas of gray and brown hair on the top and sides of his head. I grabbed his hand and noticed it was fleshy and strong.

"Hi, Mark."

"Come in. Don't mind the dog. He's really quite friendly, as you can see by the way he's licking your hand."

"Thanks. I like dogs," I assured him.

"Now that we're empty nesters, my wife insisted on a replacement for our children. Dogs are certainly less expensive, but they still need constant attention. I can't remember – do you have any kids?"

"No," I said.

Mark shrugged. "It's never too late. One of my partners just had a baby with his new wife, and he's in his late sixties. Of course, she's only

35. But, you know, you still look like you could pass for a Danvers student – except for the gray hair. Well, come in, come in."

He ushered me up the path and into the big white colonial where he introduced me to his wife, Ann, a large woman with a checkered apron around her waist.

"So glad to meet you," she said. "I was just basting the chicken. I hope you like chicken." The house had absorbed the smell of the chicken, fat, thyme, and onions roasting.

"Yes. It smells delicious."

"Dinner in half an hour? I'll let you two catch up."

"Thank you," I said.

Mark led us into a large, comfortable living room with a surfeit of pictures. Everywhere I looked, there were faces beaming back at me, from Mark and Ann at their wedding, to portraits of their children at different stages of growth – childhood to adulthood. There were so many pictures I could not tell how many children they had actually raised. One photo perched on the top of a piano featured Mark as Class President of Danvers in his red Danvers sweater. I walked over to examine it. He stood in the center, surrounded by the other class officers standing behind him in a row.

"That was a few years and a few pounds ago," said Mark, "but who's counting? And I've earned each one of them," he laughed. "Now, you don't look like you've gained much weight at all."

"No, not much," I said. "About 20 pounds since Danvers."

"Well most of us white guys don't seem to hold up as well as you Asian guys. We're paying for those teenage beach parties with trips to the dermatologists. But I have noticed that you Asians seem to age with less wear and tear. Maybe it's the sushi."

"I think it may be the genetics, with a little more melanin to protect the skin."

"Yeah, well, everything has changed; it's easier to buy sushi than to get a burger here in Connecticut. Imagine that! Even at Danvers they have all these students from Korea, Japan, India, even Africa. You were one of the early ones, but now they've taken over almost half the class. They have an Asian salad bar in the cafeteria!"

"Wow," I said, both as an expression of surprise at Mark's blatant racial biases and at the significant changes that had occurred in the make-up of the student body since my days at Danvers.

"You would feel right at home at Danvers now," he continued. "Well, I guess it's just the way of the world. Hell, we'll all be working for the Chinese in a few years. Like it or not, they're the best students. But they still have to learn the rules of business and society where just being smart will not get you to the top. You need the social intelligence to become a leader. We want Danvers to continue to be the incubator for the future leaders, and we want them to identify with our values of community, honesty, loyalty, and giving back to the school and society. We've been hosting some of them here at the house over the holidays when they can't get back to their home countries. We had a nice African girl here last year. *Non sibi* – not for the self. That's what they taught us at Danvers. Robert, you worked hard, harder than most of us white guys. And you deserve what you've gotten."

"I was always afraid of flunking out. If I hadn't worked hard, I would've failed. It wasn't easy," I said.

"That's how it was for all of us. Of course it wasn't easy, particularly if you weren't quick on your toes and couldn't make things up like moi. People had to prove themselves and learn how to talk in a group, make a joke at the right time, be a gentleman, and sometimes defend ideas and dish back the insults. We learned about leadership, character, and etiquette too. I hear about it from the students who stay with us even now. They're wonderful. But they don't play those Saturday night bridge games like we did, and that's too bad; you need to learn how to bluff too. That's what card games teach you. Sometimes you get dealt a bad hand, but you still have to play it to win. So what the hell happened to Thompson?"

"Liver failure. It's pretty bad. He's all yellow and swollen."

"Sounds awful. Well, we're careful, never more than two glasses of wine with dinner. You only have one liver. He always seemed rather thin and fragile. You two were pretty close, as I recall," he said.

"Yes, we were, but then we sort of lost contact after graduation."

"I try to keep up with our classmates through the annual giving fund.

I like to make the calls and catch up. Thompson donated most years."

"So you've been talking to him?"

"We had lunch in Boston a few times. He's an interesting guy, lots of volunteer work, but he never let on about his illness. I'll usually find out about weddings and grandkids. But they don't always tell you when they're sick. Sometimes I don't find out until the obituary shows up. People are funny about that kind of thing."

"I didn't know until recently either."

"So he wants to have us all come up and play a few hands of bridge? I've heard of stranger requests. I'm a little out of practice, but I'm sure it will come back to me. As you know, I never strictly followed the rules, anyway."

"I'm not sure how much actual card playing we'll do," I said. "Steven is very sick. I'm a little worried about the stress of having us all there at once. How do you think we should plan it?"

"Usually I'd say to bring some good vino and beer and some French bread and cheese; have a little party. But I'm out of my league on this one – you're the doctor. Anyway, he wouldn't have asked if he didn't want us. Let's play it by ear, the way I'd bid on cards, huh?"

"Right," I laughed. "I hope we can get everyone together. I wish I'd thought about doing this sooner. I'm still trying to find Richard Burris. Thanks for your suggestions. I think I'll be able to get Tim to come. I just saw him in Africa."

His eyes widened theatrically. "You saw Tim Washington in Africa? That's amazing! The guy's a legend. I always watched him on television. He sent several quarterbacks to the locker room with concussions. "

"Yeah, he's pretty much the same as when we were at Danvers."

"I wish I could look the way I did back then," said Mark.

"That reminds me: Do you remember those photographs that they took of us after we arrived at Danvers? We had to line up at the Art Building and – "

"Strip buck naked. Sure as hell I remember that! Now if I had those pictures, I could probably leverage more donations to the alumni fund," he laughed.

His laugh was infectious; I found myself laughing too.

"We could even open a web site and post them for laggards who don't contribute to the school," he added.

"Do you know what they were for?" I asked.

"They probably needed to see if we had any low hanging fruit, if you know what I mean. I'm lucky to even find my low hanging fruit anymore."

I shook my head. "It was for a long-term research study. They did measurements of our bodies to see if they could predict our personalities and leadership potential."

"What? I'll be damned! That should have worked in my favor. My body was probably closer to Winston Churchill's than anyone else's. I should have been Prime Minister of England!"

I laughed along with him, but pretty soon he stopped and cocked his head at me. "How did you find this out?"

Something about his tone made me hesitate.

"Dr. Hart. He had the files with the pictures and other information he'd been collecting about us since we graduated." I inserted a small deviation from the truth. "He sent them to a storage facility just before he moved to a retirement home. But he sent me a few to see if I might be interested in continuing his work. One of them was yours." I indicated my satchel on the floor. "I brought it here for you."

Mark rubbed his head and took a deep breath. "Well, I think this is a good time for a drink. What would you like?"

"I don't know…iced tea or a lemonade."

"Lemonade? Do you want some rum or gin in it? I'm going to have a Scotch on the rocks before I look at this thing!"

Mark went off to get drinks and I pulled out the file and glanced at his photo again. The expression on his face was of extreme concentration, as if he were considering a bank merger.

When he returned, I handed him the file and he studied it.

"Jeez, this is surreal, like walking into a time machine. I look at the picture and I start thinking about my dorm room and the Beatles!"

After a moment, he stared at me. "So if this was a study, what were they measuring? I mean, they should have had a fluffer to get us up to size. You know what I mean?"

"What's a fluffer?"

"Thames, you obviously have not been watching enough porn. Let's just say it has to do with what makes X-rated movies distinct from R. Fluffers are sort of specialists who help the performers get ready to perform."

"Sort of like athletic trainers in the locker room?"

"Exactly, but they aren't massaging arms! So what do these numbers mean?"

"It has to do with how much muscle or fat or nervous tissues you had. The theory has been pretty much disproven, but it was a way to classify bodies based upon how much of each type of tissue you had."

"God, I never noticed how wide my neck was. My head just sort of melts into my neck like ice cream melting into the cone. And then my shoulders and chest are the ice cream dripping out of the cone. And my gut is sticking out even though I was trying to hold it in. That's the one thing I remember: trying so hard to hold my stomach in I could barely breathe. I think I'd like a re-do."

"Huh?"

"The picture is not very complimentary. In my mind, I looked so much better." Mark sat down heavily in an armchair. "Do you mind if I scan through this now?"

"No, please, take your time." I walked around the room perusing more photographs.

Finally, he cleared his voice. "This says that I am an endomorph. It describes the characteristics of endomorphs over here in the margin – 'jovial, emotional, lazy, and outgoing.' They call me an elephant. But I've never thought of myself that way. I've always felt like this body I have is sort of a costume. Underneath, I'm a normal-sized person. I feel like someone gave me a backpack to carry around, and I keep hoping that they will let me take it off. So if I move a little slowly it's because of the back pack, not because of my personality. Do you get it?"

I nodded, wondering if he was upset. It was hard to tell.

"And all the joking and stories I tell, I do that because people expect it; I know I'm pretty good at it. But I don't think any of that has to do with my body shape. I've done pretty well for myself – vice president of two banks, several boards of directors."

"I agree, it seems like a strange theory and it doesn't fit everyone. So you didn't know that Dr. Hart was conducting this research?"

"Hell no! I always thought the photos were for posture analysis."

"Dr. Hart collected on-going information about each of us over the years. He worked on it his whole life. None of us were informed, or consented to this research. Don't you think someone needs to take responsibility for that?"

"Dr. Hart should, but he's dead."

"But the school sanctioned it. Don't you think that, at the very least, Danvers should admit what it did was wrong and apologize?"

"It would lead to lawsuits and bad publicity for the school. What would be the point?"

"It would be the truth. It would show that even Danvers can make mistakes and take responsibility for them. Maybe some students were affected for the rest of their lives."

"Like PTSD? I don't buy it. People are always looking for excuses for their failures. They want someone to blame."

"The classification idea, based upon body type or skin color or class background, is like eugenics – deplorable. The deans at Danvers were trying to mold us into their ideal, and those photos and the measurements are the proof. People like you and me were never going to fit, so we perceived that there was something wrong with us."

He shook his head. "What good does it do to go and create a scene about something that happened more than forty years ago?"

"There's more. Have you heard about some of the sexual abuse between teachers and students at other prep schools?"

"I've read about it. I think it happened at Saint Paul's."

"It also happened at Danvers, and they never did anything about it."

"Well that was the policy forty years ago. I'm not saying it was right, but those teachers are all dead."

"But the students aren't."

He nodded slowly. "So you've thought it out. What do you want from me?"

"I don't know. That's why I'm here. To get your advice."

He opened the file again. "You know, it's strange. When I look at this picture I can remember how I felt in those days. I thought I would be a U.S. senator. My uncle was a congressman and my family had connections; their friends were active in politics. I tried to show the other boys that I could be a leader. Maybe I wasn't good at sports, but I'll never forget when I got elected Class President. It was the happiest moment of my life."

I smiled. He shut the folder and handed it back to me.

"But the world has changed. They don't want someone like me, someone who respects tradition and decorum. No, they're looking for athletes and actors and people without principles who can make up facts as they go along. And they're looking for diversity – that's the new code word and we all know what that means. I don't mean to complain, but I can't even get elected to the Danvers Board of Directors."

I was surprised to hear this; I would have guessed he'd be a shoo-in.

"Maybe you could use this research project to your advantage. You could contact the Board and help them find out where Dr. Hart hid the files. You might even get invited to join the Board if you helped. They need more minorities on the Board. I've heard it myself from none other than Tillman Hobson himself. Anyway, all this talk about our bodies is making me hungry. I think it's time for us to eat!"

We joined Ann in the dining room and ate chicken baked in a cream sauce with potatoes and spinach. I found myself thinking that I would gain weight too if the food was always so good. We had a lively conversation about local politics, and after dinner they offered me coffee, dessert, and a room in their home to spend the night.

"No, thanks," I declined. "I'll need to be getting back."

After I said my goodbye to Ann, Mark walked me out to the car. I had to move slowly to adjust to his pace.

"Robert, you can count on me for this event with Thompson. I can help with the logistics, like hiring a nurse if we need to do that. I might even find some old *Playboys* to cheer him up. I've realized as I've gotten older that we need to take care of each other and the school. It's our legacy and the way people will remember us."

He stopped me in the driveway and touched my arm. "But this file thing worries me. It feels like trouble. We don't want someone poking through our lives. You never know what they will find. You need to call Hobson and help him find those other files. *Non sibi*, remember that. It's not about you. It's all of us."

"I'll try," I said.

"I'm glad that you understand. Remember, we're all family." He hesitated for a second and then said, "Overall, we haven't done too badly for ourselves, have we?"

"What?" I said.

"You and I. Not too bad for Danvers boys. "

"No, not too bad. Your house and family are beautiful. . You've done well." As I congratulated Mark for his successes I had to pause and think about it. Was I proud to be accepted as one of the boys? Would I want to be a minority representative to the Board as he suggested?

Mark smiled and put his thick arm around me in a short, vise-like squeeze cutting short my doubts.

Then he called for his dog and headed back to the house.

31

As I was driving away, my cell phone began to vibrate. It was Sarah. "Hello," I said, a little breathlessly. "Hi, Robert. Are you finished with your visit?"

"Yes, perfect timing. I'm just leaving Mark's house."

"Are you still interested in a rendezvous?"

"Absolutely. Where would you like to meet?"

"There's a nice Hilton just off of highway 91, as it becomes 291 outside of Springfield. I've been there a couple of times."

"A hotel?"

"It's only about an hour away from you, and it will only take me a little more to get there this time of night. We could get coffee in the restaurant and you could probably stay there overnight."

"Great. Thanks. I should be able to find it."

"I'm going to leave now, so keep talking while I get into the car. Tell me what you and Mark discussed. I'm curious."

"Not much. We talked a lot about Danvers and how it's changed, and how he's measured up in life compared to the rest of our class."

"Steven did that too, of course. Constantly. What about you?"

"I don't know. I do my job. I want to do it well. I'd like to think that I have discovered something useful that has saved lives. I don't really compare it to other people at Danvers."

"But you still want their approval, right? Danvers set the bar, and you all lined up to jump over it. Look at where it got Steven. I don't know what they did to him, but it was not good."

"What do you mean?"

"All his life he's been hiding. I used to think it was me. That he was afraid of me. That I pushed him too much, wanted too much from him. But now I think it was that prep school." Her voice had an edge. "All of you have scars. What did they do to you?"

I didn't respond, wondering what Steven had told her.

"I guess I should calm down and concentrate on my driving before I run into someone," she said. "I'll call you when I get close."

"Okay, see you soon."

As I drove, I thought about what she'd said. Even though I hadn't fit the mold of a typical Danvers boy, I now carried the brand. If I harmed Danvers, I injured myself.

The Hilton was easy to find. My head was still buzzing with the vibrations of the engine when I parked. What would I say to Sarah? Why had she arranged to meet me at a hotel? What if she changed her mind?

I sat in the car for a while, trying to quiet my thoughts. Then my phone rang.

"Hello?"

"Where are you?" she asked nervously.

"I just arrived. I'm in the parking lot."

"I'm waiting for you in the coffee shop." She sounded unsure of herself.

"I'll be right there."

The cool air revived and steadied me. The parking lot had rows of cars and vans lined up just like the banks of coconut palms in the Philippines. For a moment I felt displaced, confused about how to navigate past the barriers of walls. I circled around and found the path to the hotel lobby, which was already adorned with Thanksgiving decorations and an early Christmas tree. A bored bellman nodded to me.

"Coffee shop?" I asked.

He pointed to the right, past the registration desk and through an alcove.

Sarah was sitting at one of the window tables, wearing a long, tan raincoat. A platinum blond waitress in a blue and white uniform looked up as I passed.

"We'll be closing in fifteen minutes," she said.

"Really?" I asked, looking at my watch, surprised. "Could I get a quick tea?"

"Cream and sugar?"

"Sure. That would be fine."

Sarah stood up as I approached. I gave her a clumsy kiss on the cheek, and she pulled me tightly against her. I could hear her muffled cries into my coat.

"Oh Robert…. It's been so hard. I feel like I'm going crazy!"

"I know," I said, patting her back.

The waitress set down a cup of tea and a bill. "No rush," she said. "Take your time."

Sarah wiped her eyes and stepped back, laughing. "I'm sorry. I didn't mean to sob right off the bat."

"It's okay. That's why I'm here."

"I should have checked the hours," she said. "They're closing soon."

"Don't worry about it. We'll go somewhere else."

I sat across from her at our booth. We were the only people in the coffee shop. The bright lights accentuated the deep circles around her eyes. Her hair was pulled back tightly from her gaunt face, with long streaks of gray. Her lips looked pale and dry and could have benefited from some lipstick.

"Robert, I'm sorry. I need someone to talk to. I've never watched someone die before."

"I know how terrible it is. I'm sorry. How is he?"

"In and out of consciousness. Some days are better than others. His breathing is noisy and rough, and sometimes I think he's choking – he seems to stop breathing for a few seconds – I really don't know what to do. He seems to be holding on for some reason."

"He doesn't want to go to the hospital?"

She shook her head firmly. "I know he's suffering, but he refuses. I think he has something he wants to say. Maybe when you and the others come up, he'll tell you."

"You think it's something like a deathbed confession?"

I regretted my statement as soon as I said it. There was no reason to anticipate something sordid, and yet my last visit with Steven had left me feeling exposed and humiliated.

"Oh, I doubt that. Probably some dream he's been having. He wakes up with these half-finished visions every day."

"Is Mrs. Ippolitto helping?"

"Yes, and another woman who comes mostly at night. A nice Russian babushka. I don't know what I would do without them. But most of what Steven needs is from me. He wants love, and I'm doing my best, but I was never very good at that. I give him what I can but there's nothing left. "

"It's not your fault." I paused and then added, "I'm concerned about you."

The waitress came by and offered a refill for Sarah, but she declined. I looked at the clock. Our time was quickly expiring.

"Robert," Sarah said. "This may seem strange, but could you get a room here?"

"A room?"

"Are you planning to drive back to Washington at this hour?"

"No, probably not."

"I'd like to talk a little longer, and, to be completely honest, I want you to hold me."

"Hold you?"

"Yes, just for a little while."

I took another sip of my tea and said, "I'll be right back."

I walked over to the registration desk where a young Asian woman was at a computer, and asked for a room.

"King or Double, sir?"

"King."

"Do you have any luggage?"

"Luggage? No." I gave the woman my credit card, got the room key, and walked back to Sarah, who was paying for our drinks at the cashier's.

"I'll get that," I offered.

"No, it's all taken care of." She smiled and took my arm.

We rode up in the elevator to the sixth floor and walked quietly to room 626. As I slipped in the key, opened the door, and turned on the light I felt a mix of trepidation, curiosity and excitement. I'm not sure what I expected – music, candles, or the echoes of that barking dog from that night at Danvers. A blinding overhead light revealed a king-sized bed that filled most of the room. The crisp bed sheets and blanket were pulled back at the top, and a small table and chair sat next to a television. I stood there awkwardly looking at the room for a moment, and then sat down on the bed. Sarah walked past me, took off her raincoat, and threw it on the chair.

"Robert, I want you to do something else for me."

"What would you like me to do?"

"I want you to shut off the lights and take off your clothes and get into bed. I want you to hold me. Just hold me. That's all. Can you do that?"

"Yes," I said. I hoped that she wouldn't feel me trembling.

I shut off the lights. I unbuttoned my shirt and pants, took off my underwear, and slipped under the sheets. I felt Sarah next to me, and then she moved closer, and her arms wound around me, pulling me closer until our bodies were touching all the way from our feet to our shoulders. Her skin felt cool and smooth against mine.

She laid her head on my chest and I felt one breast and the scar where the other one had been taken several years prior. I inhaled her as she lay against me, her scent and her sweat. And gradually I felt her melting herself into me. I felt her thoughts filling my brain like a massive transfusion of blood as she lay against me. What I felt was immense and overwhelming. This was not sex. Was it love? Or some primordial place where life began and ended? It was a place I had not ever visited, except perhaps for a moment on the grass at Danvers after we had made love and lay in each other's arms, floating above the trees, buildings, and houses, and now she'd brought me there again. Our bodies exposed to each other, touching in their nakedness, the parts old and new, healthy and diseased, one continuity of skin and blood and sinew and thought moving and pulsating in a rhythm of primitive music. I could feel her chest rising and falling with each breath, her heart beating against mine.

I held her like that for five minutes, ten minutes, an hour. It did not matter. I would have held her like that all night. Too soon it was over and I was back in my own body, my own skin separating me slowly, painfully from Sarah's, like an adhesive bandage from a wound. As she moved away from me, I could feel the space between us growing cold.

"I'm going to leave now," she whispered.

"Okay."

I listened to her dressing and then, when she was at the door, she said, "You know, he was in love with you."

"I know."

I wanted to ask her what had just happened, what she felt, what it meant. When would I see her again? I wanted to ask her why she had to go, and why now? But the door opened and then closed behind her.

I lay in the bed for a while and then got up and looked out the window at the stars. I asked myself why there is so much emptiness and blackness between each star in the sky.

Then I watched the lights of her car blink on and the beams make a circle in the parking lot before heading out toward the highway.

32

The next day I drove back to Washington, through the traffic and the endless towns and bigger cities, but I barely noticed any of them. My mind was racing.

As I walked up the steps to my apartment, I felt twinges of a headache and some flashing lights in my eyes. Sometimes this was the first sign of a migraine. They appeared rarely, usually if I did not get enough sleep. I began to yawn. Perhaps it was just eyestrain from the drive and staring into the sun. I preoccupied myself with mail and cleaning the floor and the sink. The boxes of files stood guard in my hallway, impeding my movement and disturbing the harmony of my home.

But the more my mind churned, the worse my headache grew. I tried to take a nap, but I couldn't sleep. My pounding head indicated a serious migraine developing, the type that could take away my ability to talk or think clearly. A neurologist had once described them as "stroke mimics," which meant they could look just like a stroke with weak limbs and speech problems, but I would eventually return to normal. If I took a medication before the symptoms developed, I could often stop the migraine, but now it seemed too late. I sat up and my stomach twisted into a knot; I almost vomited. I fumbled for a pill and dropped it on the floor.

Sometimes if it didn't get better I needed to go to the emergency room for intravenous medication. Sometimes I would become disoriented and wander like a sleepwalker. Sometimes I would forget names or even my address and phone number. Now I felt compelled to walk, as if by walking I could prevent the migraine from overtaking me.

The next thing I knew, I was out in the street without any money or keys. I felt as if I were being transported through space against my will. I was wearing my t-shirt and tan pants without a belt; they hung down on my hips. I gazed longingly at a jacket on a homeless man pushing a shopping cart. He must have recognized the look because he hurried past me. I wanted to ask him for directions, but I had no idea where I was going or what I would do, and he was already too far away. My head pounded like a snare drum, interrupting every rational thought before I could form a cogent question.

I tried to think who I might call if I could find a phone, someone who would take me to an E.R. for an injection of Compazine or morphine, but every name I tried to remember slipped out of my mind. If I could just find my way home, maybe I could close my eyes and go to sleep, and with time it might pass, but I was too disoriented.

I just started walking toward Dupont Circle, past the Victorian homes and the laundry shops that stayed open late for downtown lawyers and office workers. Everything looked familiar, but my house had disappeared among ones that looked just like it. I walked down New Hampshire to M Street and over to the Fairmont. People were walking past with little name tags. A man with a black mustache and slicked-back hair dropped his name tag onto the sidewalk as he reached for his wallet. I picked it up, intending to return it to him, but he was off in a cab before I could form words.

"Michael Rivas, Ph.D." read the tag. I clipped it onto my shirt and walked through the door of the hotel.

"Sir, are you looking for the lecture?" asked the bellman. I nodded. "It's downstairs one floor, on your left." He was a tall, very dark man with a British accent.

I walked down the stairs and found a couch, lay down, closed my eyes for a few seconds, and woke up an hour later with a hotel security guard shaking my shoulder, asking if I was okay. I sat up and blinked a few times, amazed that my headache had partly diminished. I nodded to him and walked into the foyer. There was a sign advertising the lecture. The first speaker was Richard Burris, touted as "a leading theoretical physicist" and author of a new book, *Falling into and out of Black Holes*. I tried to steady myself, feeling like I might have just entered one: What were the chances that I would find Richard Burris in Washington, D.C., at precisely this time, and in this strange manner? That was something that only a scientist like Richard might be able to explain.

I grabbed a glass of lemonade and a plate full of bread sticks and took a seat in the large conference room. Richard Burris – it certainly looked like him behind a tangle of unruly beard – sat at the front of the room, eating shrimp and drinking a glass of red wine. As he ate, bits of bread became entangled in his beard, creating an embarrassing spectacle. Eventually a man in a tuxedo brought a napkin to him and whispered in his ear. He calmly wiped his beard clean, as if it was the most natural thing in the world to do.

A woman in a light blue suit walked to the podium and quieted the crowd before introducing the two guest speakers. "I know we're all going to enjoy this debate between two of our most outstanding theoretical physicists. Dr. Burris has a new book that he will be signing after the lecture, but don't let that sway you too much: Both of these speakers have written and thought deeply about today's subject. Please give them your full attention. The food will still be here when they're done. Why don't we start with Professor Burris?"

Richard got up and paced at the podium, peering at his opposition, a small bald man with thick black-rimmed glasses. I'm not sure that I could have identified Richard on the street without some notice, but now I could recognize him in his lanky form, nervous twitching, and incessant pacing. He had, after all, been my bridge partner and I had looked across the table at him for hundreds of hours.

"Thank you," he said.

I wondered if he would be able to speak in an intelligible manner in front of a crowd. I waited with some anxiety, recalling his speaking problems at Danvers.

"Uncertainty is a basic principle, built into the impossibility of measuring anything with absolute accuracy." He spoke in a voice that I had never heard before. Gone was his flood of disconnected words, replaced by a smooth current of language and ideas.

"Is it due to the limitations of tools of measurement, or is it a basic characteristic of matter, light, and energy? In fact, matter can be transformed into heat and energy, as we all know from watching meteors. Uncertainty is just one way of accepting the transitory and shifting nature of the universe. But you don't have to look out into space for confirmation. Open your eyes wide. Now just close them. Press on your eyeballs. What do you see? Is it nothing? What is nothing? Now consider emotions like anger or fear or love, or principles like truth or excellence. Could you quantify any of them with certainty? In science, we use measurement to approximate truth, but we realize that it is not truth. It is an approximation and we describe our methods of measurement so that others can replicate our work and make even better approximations of what we are trying to describe. But we always must recognize the uncertainty of our measurement."

How had he learned to change his speech cadence and tone so completely?

Richard went on to describe equations and experiments for those who needed scientific proof. I did not understand what he was saying, but I found myself lulled into a trance as I listened to his voice and closed my eyes. I wondered if the uncertainty principle could explain the trajectory of my life. Was I like the gyroscope that spins happily on its axis, never doubting its stability, until it slows, begins to wobble wildly, and crashes into the surface?

The Stanford professor who followed Richard was much smaller and more compact in build. His eyes became animated as he described classical mechanics, his glasses flying off his face as he gestured, demonstrating the effects of gravity when they fell to the ground in front of him. He put up a good fight, reminding us that when we threw a ball into the air, we had a pretty good idea where it would land. All we needed to do was watch a baseball game to find the proof. We did not need complete certainty. We just needed a high enough probability. Perfection was not necessary. Certainty was not necessary in the real world. We could adjust our position. That was the nature of learning and what made human beings the most successful creatures on earth.

When the speakers were finished, Richard was surrounded by a ring of physicists, journalists, lawyers, and students discussing one equation or another. I joined the circle. He looked at me, and then my name tag and said, "Yes, Dr. Rivas?"

"Hello, Richard," I said. "I'm not Dr. Rivas. It's me, Robert Thames. I found this name tag on the street, but it got me into the lecture."

Richard looked around, somewhat alarmed. The others gawked at me. Perhaps they worried that I might be dangerous, someone planning a violent act.

I tried to reassure them. "I was your bridge partner at Danvers, remember?"

"Robert Thames? From Danvers? Why yes, just as I was saying, 'we can never be too certain about anything.' Even a name tag can be wrong. Robert, it is indeed you. What are you doing here?"

He excused himself from the circle and ushered me into a corner where we could talk.

"Actually I found you by accident, but I was looking for you," I said. "That probably doesn't make sense, but it's true. Do you remember our classmate, Steven Thompson?"

He squinted, as if summoning an image. "He sat next to you when we played cards. I sometimes wondered if he was giving you signals about the other hands."

"Yes," I laughed, "that Steven."

He nodded. "He wasn't very good at cards. I thought it was concentration. But he was actually quite capable of concentrating. He spent an entire night on the physics building roof with me, taking notes of different stars' brightness. He never dozed off."

"I didn't know that."

"I think he was more interested in you than our card game, if I may be totally frank. Of course, we couldn't discuss such things in those days."

I decided to let that one pass. "Unfortunately, he's very sick and can't discuss much of anything these days. He's dying of liver disease."

"Oh…I'm so sorry to hear that." Richard looked genuinely saddened.

"He'd like all of us who played cards together to visit him and play a few hands. It's sort of his last wish. That's why I needed to find you.

He said those card games were the happiest time of his life."

"How odd. Why would those be his happiest moments?"

"Perhaps he admired our skills or conversation. But it doesn't matter, does it? Mark Harrison and Tim Washington will be coming, and we'd love to have you as well."

"I'm on a schedule for my book tour. I'll be going to Atlanta and New York and Philadelphia and then Boston."

"He lives in Boston."

"I suppose I could come after my reading and lecture. I'll be there in a few weeks, actually, ten days to be precise." He jotted down a cell phone number and handed me his card. The room was emptying, so we walked out into the hallway together. "What are you doing here in Washington, Robert?"

"I live here. I'm a doctor working in international health and infectious diseases."

We found an alcove in the hallway with a small table with two chairs. Richard draped his lanky frame over one of them. Two young women walked by and complimented him on his presentation.

"Thank you, nice of you to notice," he said, lifting his head toward the women like some kind of religious offering.

The women stood there for another moment staring at him in awe and then moved on down the hall.

"Now that was something that never happened to me at Danvers," he said.

"Well, we didn't have any girls there, except for the dances."

"I have so many young female admirers now. Who would have guessed? In high school they all went for the athletes. The rest of us were left to our own devices. I worried that I might be gay, particularly after an experience with Steven that night on the roof of the physics building."

I looked at him in surprise. "You and Steven?"

"Not much of anything really," he said. "I've always found looking at stars an erotic experience. I suppose he did too. I can laugh about it now. Imagine the energy of the big bang that created the universe. It's the ultimate orgasm. I was grateful that someone else felt the way I did.

After that night I only went out looking at stars with young women. Anyway, how about you?"

"I'm fine. Not married and no kids. I travel a lot. I've been pretty much out of touch with anyone from Danvers for the last thirty or forty years, until now. But recently some strange things have been happening." I told him about Dr. Hart's passing and the old files and photographs that showed up at my door.

"Are you referring to those posture photographs? I wonder how I ever passed that. I have the worst posture, and it's only gotten worse with age. I swim a few times a week, but you know, when you sit hunched over in front of a computer for eight hours a day, what can you expect?"

"They weren't exactly posture photographs. They were measuring all kinds of things like the length of your arms and legs compared to your chest, the distance between your eyes, even your genitals. They were trying to classify us into somatotypes. Have you heard of that?"

"That theory was totally discredited. I once attended a museum exhibit in Chicago about it. There were statues and photographs from the '30s that were meant to prove that white men were the ultimate evolution of the human race. No one questioned scientists at that time. Now we laugh about it. It's another example of the adage that 'if you can measure something, it must be important.'" He smiled. "But they were not measuring what was important."

"Dr. Hart wanted me to complete his research and publish the results. There are life histories, photographs, somatotype measurements, and even disciplinary letters in the files. What do you think of that kind of data?"

Richard rubbed his head as he sometimes did when contemplating a difficult bridge bid. Then he raised his hands as if in surrender. "In spite of my diatribe against measurement, in support of uncertainty, I do believe in the scientific method. Measurement is the only way to test a hypothesis, but you have to base your hypothesis upon valid scientific theory. I doubt there is any valid theory about body measurement, except perhaps if you are trying to select sumo wrestlers or jockeys. And even then there will be other important factors like motivation and training."

"So Dr. Hart was wasting his time?"

"I doubt he really understood the goals of the research. I think this research was the last gasp of the eugenics crowd, attempting to protect humanity against the Blacks, Jews, and Asians who were beating them at their own intellectual or physical games. If a body type could be elevated and worshiped for its purity and excellence, then they might beat back the people like you, who were breaking down the doors of Danvers and Harvard demanding to have an equal chance. They needed to make sure the ideal body type was a white, upper class male. And if they could link the body type to an idealized personality type – for example, the All American Man – then voila, you have it, a rationale for certain admissions policies for colleges or graduate schools. You have the excuse for maintaining the status quo of the white male elite. But it didn't hold up. You should see my lab now – full of Asians and Indians. I think most of the faculty at Danvers understood that was happening even then."

"So what kept this theory going for so many years?"

"Racism, power, fear. The usual tools of a hierarchy. We had plenty of that at Danvers, but it was submerged. The writers and main characters in the novels we read were white males. So were the great contributors to philosophy, sociology, history, and art. That was the prevailing view of excellence at school, and academia at large."

Richard waved at two men in suits who were down the hall calling to him. "I'm sorry, but my colleagues are waiting for me. Would you like to join us?"

"Thank you, but I'm getting over a migraine. I need to go home." I felt a sudden wave of exhaustion. "One other thing before you go. Do you remember a night when Dean Maiser caught all of you drinking?"

He looked abashed. "Unfortunately, I had several drinks that night. I was not accustomed to alcohol. I remember that Mrs. Shangly looked quite beautiful. That's all I remember, except that Dr. Hart and Dean Maiser made me sign a paper saying I wouldn't drink again. "

There were now two women with the two men waiting for him. We stood up.

"It's amazing that I found you here," I said.

"Yes, it is."

He shook my hand and then gave me a quick hug. "Please call. You have my card."

"Yes, I'll send you the details about Steven. Make sure to practice your bridge."

As he walked back down the hall, Richard's friends emitted a small cheer. I thought about how his life had followed a path that was not surprising but not exactly predictable either. I only knew a small fragment about him, based upon how his mind worked in a bridge game. The chance meeting in a hotel in the midst of a migraine attack seemed unlikely, but, as he had said, "Improbable events might happen if you wait long enough."

Or perhaps it was *barang*, swirling and driving us together for its own purpose.

33

I walked over to the hotel desk and asked to use the phone. "Certainly, Dr. Rivas," said the clerk, noticing my name tag. "If you can give me the number I'll call for you."

I smiled at the thought of my new identity, so easily assumed with a name tag in a hotel. The clerks and bellmen at hotels probably had their own ways of classifying the people who came to them with requests and problems to be solved.

I struggled to remember the phone number, then reached into my pockets, vaguely remembering I still had Sarah's card. I handed it to the clerk and he dialed it for me, then handed me the receiver.

"Hello?" Sarah answered.

"Hi, it's Robert."

"Are you okay? Your voice sounds strange."

"I'm having a migraine and got a little disoriented. Sometimes my words get a bit garbled. But I wanted to tell you that I found Richard Burris, here in Washington at a hotel. Isn't that the strangest coincidence? I was just walking around and found him here giving a talk."

"That's amazing!"

"I think he'll be able to come to play cards and see Steven. He has a book tour and will be in Boston. Everyone will be there."

"That's wonderful. I'm glad you found him."

"Yes, now I just need to reach Tim and find out when he can come back and then coordinate everyone. It should be about ten days. Will that work?"

"I'll make it work," she said.

"Richard looks almost the same as he did when we were in high school except for his beard and some gray hair. No more garbled words. Now it's the ideas that are difficult to understand."

"I'm changing Steven's sheets right now so I can't really talk," she explained. "I have to get back to him."

"Sorry. You should do that."

"Are you going to be able to get home?"

"Yes. I just wanted to tell you about Burris. It seemed like such a coincidence."

"Great luck, I guess."

I wanted to tell her that it was more than just luck. There had to be some force driving us together now, just as it had once driven us apart. We would be coming from all over the world. I wanted her to understand the magnitude of what was about to happen. I also wanted to tell her I'd been thinking about her, but she said, "Talk to you soon," and hung up.

I returned the telephone to the clerk, noticing flashing lights across her face. The lobby was making me dizzy. I needed to get outside and into the air.

I left the Fairmont and began walking up toward Dupont Circle. The homeless man and woman who panhandled every day at the Metro entrance were there with their plastic cups. Just seeing them was reassuring, reminding me that the world had not changed in spite of my night's improbable adventure. Seeing Richard Burris again had not generated a chain reaction that altered the universe.

I walked past them and around the Circle, veering down my street past the bookstore and barber shop. I had left the front door open. I glanced around to see if anyone had come in and robbed my house, but everything seemed in place. The files were in the boxes; the furniture was where I left it. So why did my life now feel so different?

I locked the door and flopped down on my bed to a display of fireworks in my brain; bursts of light and darkness that reminded me of the Fourth of July. As the darkness gradually encroached, I imagined the boy in the photograph with different name tags – Rivas, Berenson, Thames.

The boy was like a chameleon, blending into different backgrounds as he walked across the ceiling and walls. I lay there watching him for hours until I finally fell into a deep, cleansing sleep.

34

The next day, I woke up and tried to piece together everything that had happened during my migraine. Had I really met Richard Burris at the Fairmont hotel? I checked my pocket and found the card he had given me. I decided I should try to contact Tim Washington, since his trip to Boston would be the most difficult to coordinate. I called his foundation office in Boston and explained why I needed to talk with him, and minutes later he was on the telephone.

"Tim?" I said. "Where are you?"

"Right where you left me, more or less," he said. "In Nairobi."

"I just called a Boston number."

"We have a special international connection. What's up?"

I explained about visiting Steven and his final request to play bridge. I mentioned that I'd dined with Mark, and had found Richard Burris at an auspicious lecture at the Fairmont in D.C.

"Do you think you might be able to fly over to meet with us in ten days? I know it's not easy, but he idolizes you."

There was a silence on the other end of the line. I waited for several seconds before inquiring, "Tim? Are you still there?"

"Yeah, I'm thinking." He hesitated again. "I don't think I always treated Thompson very well. I'm always telling the boys that the team is what makes the individual strong. We were once a team, and even if the bonds have weakened, we can try and be a team again. I should see him before it's too late."

"So you'll join us? In ten days?"

"Yeah, you can count on it."

And that was how it happened; that's how we picked the day. I was so euphoric after the phone call that I made an appointment with Dr. Berenson for an eye exam. I had no idea if he was actually my uncle, but I had this feeling that when we stood in the same room and our eyes met, we would recognize each other.

I also contacted the Peabody Museum to make an appointment with Dr. Hutchinson to find out what he remembered about Sheldon's research and the history of the Danvers files. It was time to conclude my investigation of the research project, and I thought that Dr. Hutchinson would have the answers I needed to finish my quest.

I walked around the house a few times. The musty smell of old paper and cardboard made me sneeze. I opened a box and pulled out a file at random. Thomas Pratt stood in front of me, a blond fifteen-year-old from Pennsylvania. I had known him as a soccer player, an outgoing, friendly guy always surrounded by other boys joking and laughing. I remembered the picture of him in the yearbook wearing a leather motorcycle jacket and a cigarette hanging out of his mouth, James Dean style. His file followed him over the years and told a deeper, darker story of depression and divorce, failure in business, success in a computer company with a write up about the fastest growing new companies, a picture of him with that same smile, thinning hair and wrinkles around his eyes. His story ended with a sudden disappearance, speculation about drugs, financial problems, bankruptcy. Suicide was suspected; murder was possible. His body measurements were unremarkable, almost equal contributions of ecto, meso and endomorphic tissue types 4, 3, 3, a good balance. What had happened to him? Deep in his file was an envelope with a letter. I opened it. The letter was from Dean Maiser to his parents.

Dear Mr. and Mrs. Pratt.

It has come to my attention that your son Thomas has violated school policy. We do not allow drugs. Thomas has admitted to smoking marijuana, and we have placed him on internal probation. This letter in his file is confidential and will only be disclosed if there are further violations at which point he will be expelled from Danvers.

Sincerely,

Dean Maiser

I wondered why the letter would be in the research file. Perhaps Dr. Hart had included it to demonstrate the continuity between Thomas Pratt as a student and his later problems. Buried further in the file was a handwritten note from Dr. Hart in an envelope. "Confidential: Thomas Pratt described homosexual relationships with faculty members (Goodson, others) during our counseling session. I referred him to Reverend Davis and our consulting psychiatrist, Dr. McNair. Dean Maiser informed. Not the first complaint against Goodson."

So here was some of what Mrs. Hart had hinted at. I wondered if these experiences had led to the mental health problems, the drug abuse, and the suicide. Why had nothing been done about it?

I moved on to another file – Paul Berger, staring out at me with a smirk, as if he knew a secret. Paul had been a writer for the newspaper, and we had both gone to medical school. He had joined the faculty at Tufts Medical School and become a critical care specialist. Then he became the vice president of a pharmaceutical company. He married a woman from Sweden and they had two children. And then there was a clipping about an investigation by the government about dangerous side effects of a drug that killed seventy people. His company knew about the risks, but hid their research findings. He pled guilty to a felony and went to jail for one year with a fine of four million dollars. He lost his medical license. Paul had the lanky frame of an ectomorph, somewhat resembling Richard Burris but with more muscle. The somatotype analysis predicted his high academic attainments, an anxious, suspicious nature, and a tendency toward solitary pursuits like reading, music, and art.

Were his decisions and choices within his control? Or was it just bad luck?

I read about Jeremiah "Jay" White, who graduated from Danvers and ultimately entered Harvard Law School. I vaguely knew him through Tim at Danvers because he was one of the few African-American students. His father had been a preacher and Jeremiah was very religious. Jeremiah became sick with lupus at Harvard and the disease destroyed his kidneys and eventually his brain. At the time, the treatments were not very effective and he had serious side effects. I remembered hearing about Jay's illness when I was a resident, and how he had a particularly aggressive form of the disease, unresponsive to any therapy.

I wondered if things might have been different if he had not been African-American, if maybe there were new treatments that a White patient would have gotten. It was not anything anyone said, but I sometimes sensed that they might have tried harder if he had not been Black, that the doctors all accepted his fate too easily. The file contained his obituary with a brief note from Dr. Hart confirming the end of the follow-up. I scanned the picture of Jay, looking for signs of his impending demise. Did he have a sense of his own mortality? Did he sense that he would not have the opportunity to experience a full life? His eyes were downcast and his face somewhat emotionless and vacant. But there was the slightest hint of a smile in his lips and mouth, as if he was thinking of a joke but unwilling to share it. He slouched forward making himself look bigger and rounder like a bear. He had a high endomorphy score of 6 and an ectomorphy score of 2 and mesomorphy score of 2. Was that a potentially lethal combination?

There was Kevin O'Shea, the runner who had set records for the mile and half-mile. His mesomorphic body and square jaw suggested he would be a leader, and he had in fact become the vice president of a running shoe company in Oregon, and later a congressman. He was a 3-5-3 on his somatotype, almost perfect balance. Kevin had that ability to remember names and make you feel special just by his smiling at you. It did not seem to matter that he was academically near the bottom of the class. We all wanted to be Kevin when he was in a crowd. In his posture picture, his chest thrust forward, suggesting he was proud of his body. I could imagine the Danvers teachers passing his picture around as proof of the Sheldon theory.

My fingers rubbed the old sheets of paper as I turned the pages of the files. I remembered that when I was a young boy, I would take the fibers of the leaves from the abaca plants that grew by our home and twist them into patterns and forms. I could create animals and houses and even families with parents and children. I would play with them when I was alone and I would become absorbed in this world. I incorporated ants and beetles and pebbles and rain. Now I strained to remember how I had once done it, how I had given life to fibers and pebbles and taught them to speak and travel to imagined lands. I felt my fingers rubbing the paper as they had once done with the abaca, and I closed my eyes and tried to coax an image of each boy from the file.

The telephone rang. I automatically reached for it.

"Hello, this is Tukutuba. Is this Dr. Thames?"

"Yes, how are you?"

"Very well. I am so sorry to disturb you. But I am here in Dar es Salaam and have a good telephone. I wanted to see if there was any possibility for me."

"I don't understand. What possibility?"

"I am asking about the Infectious Diseases Fellowship. I am hoping to be able to come to the United States."

"Ah yes… Well, I have spoken to one of my friends from Utah. I told him about you. He's looking for a fellow or junior faculty member. But these things take time. "

"Oh, thank you so much. I love Utah! It is in the United States?"

"Yes, it is in the west near Arizona and Colorado."

"Oh, yes, I love Arizona and Colorado. I would love to go to Utah. I love Utah. Please tell him that I will come as soon as I can arrange transport."

"No, don't make any plans yet. It's just a possibility," I said.

"I understand. Thank you so much. I have been praying to God for this. This is the happiest day I am alive. Thank you, Dr. Thames. You are a messenger from God. I will call you again soon. Goodbye. *Salamat.*"

"Goodbye," I said.

Before I could process the conversation the telephone rang again. It was Tillman Hobson from Danvers Board of Directors. He was not as happy as Dr. Tukutuba.

"I hope I'm not disturbing you. You may remember that we talked about Dr. Hart's research files."

"Yes."

"I've heard that you have some of those research files. Is this true?"

"Dr. Hart sent me a few files, just to elucidate what type of information is in them. I believe he wanted me to take over his study. But then he died. I never did find out where the rest of the files were."

"Well, I would certainly expect the return of any files in your possession. We are very concerned that the files and their confidential information could fall into the wrong hands. Our first priority is the protection of confidential material of our former students. Wouldn't you agree?"

"I agree."

"Then I'm sure you will understand that we need those files back to Danvers immediately where we can review them and assure their protection. You can send them to the library, and we'll secure them in a locked room. We will, of course, reimburse you for any expenses, including any time you have spent on the files. As for the remaining files, we certainly would like your cooperation in locating them."

"My only hesitation in sending the files to Danvers is that none of us who participated in the research ever consented to be studied. If I sent them to you, I would be recognizing that you have a right to possess them, when in fact, I think they belong to each participant."

"I understand. This entire episode is confusing. But I must insist that you return the files. There is considerable liability for the school, and for you. Our lawyers have already analyzed the issues and prepared motions to a judge clarifying our authority for this material. They will seek a court order if necessary. Would you like me to send you their memo?"

"No. First, I'm going to discuss the files with the men – formerly boys – who were the unwitting subjects of the research."

"These were students who were supervised under the principal of *in loco parentis*. The Danvers faculty had the latitude to make decisions about issues such as research. I discussed this issue in detail with Dean Maiser. The study had all of the appropriate approvals and protocols. His concern is that the files contain confidential material that goes beyond the initial research."

"I can imagine his concern and desire for confidentiality," I said, "particularly if there were incidents of sexual relationships between students and teachers that were never reported, as has happened at other prep schools."

"There's nothing of the sort! That would be a very serious matter and would need to be investigated. All the more reason for you to return whatever material you have. If you have specific information or evidence, I will make sure it reaches the proper authorities. Perhaps you would like to talk with Dean Maiser yourself? I believe you would be impressed with his recall of details and policy."

"No, thank you."

"I understand your concerns and your reticence. This is all quite troubling. I can assure you that the current Board of Directors had no knowledge of the research or any other inappropriate activities and does not condone the methods that were used at that time. The expectations about research and supervision were very different years ago. This is a very delicate situation, and we want to work with you to find a resolution. All of us are volunteers on the Board. We depend on alumni like you to assist Danvers. Will you work with us?"

"I'll get back with you after I discuss it with the subjects of the files I have."

He gave me two telephone numbers to call him back. "We want to work with you to find a resolution," he said again. I hung up the phone.

I walked out of the house down the street. At the Metro, I gave a homeless man a dollar from my wallet and he folded it into his palm hungrily. I tried to imagine what it must be like to be homeless in Washington D.C. and live on the sporadic donations of people like me.

The escalator was broken so I had to walk down the metal steps, past people dragging suitcases or hobbling on crutches. I pushed into a crowded Metro car and got compressed against a young Asian woman in a short skirt and a Black woman in a white coat wearing a name tag for a nursing conference. The Metro car threw me against both women and then against a metal pole and then the door. I could smell shampoo and the various perfumes and soaps that covered their skin as I bounced between them. I could smell the sweat from the jogger who stood against a door in his shorts and t-shirt.

We stopped and several people struggled to get off the car before we started again, but there was not enough room or enough time, and so the doors closed. I could not help but think of Tukutuba, who desperately wanted this life, and the doors that kept opening and closing, giving him only a brief glimpse of his destination before it flew past.

At my stop, the crowd surged forward out of the car, carrying me with them through the turnstile and up the escalator. I walked the two blocks to my office, and Maralee, a large African-American security guard, recognized me and greeted me warmly.

"Hey, Dr. Thames. Been away for a while?"

"Yes, I just got back from Africa."

"Oh my, I'd like to go to Africa some day before I die," she said. "Maybe you can pack me away in your backpack next time – if I can just lose those fifteen pounds that I'm working on." She smiled at me and signed me in.

In the office, I made all the mandatory visits to my colleagues and checked on my specimens with the laboratory technicians. There were one or two samples that seemed to have possible antibiotic properties and everyone seemed very excited. "This could be the one, Doc," said our research lab analyst.

I checked my mail and my appointments. I made airline reservations for my trip to Boston, and blocked out two days on my schedule for the trip.

At a meeting later in the day, I passed around Dr. Tukutuba's notebook about his HIV experiment, and one of my colleagues who specialized in AIDS examined it, frowned at the cover and the handwritten notes, and declared that the results were "interesting, but probably not valid or publishable."

I nodded as I imagined the effort that had gone into that notebook, the dreams it represented, the distance it had traveled, and how quickly its message had been dismissed.

35

I t was not easy to get to Boston to visit Steven. My early morning flight was delayed because of a thunderstorm. I sat in the airport, imagining the conversations we would have as we tried to create a sense of normalcy in a room with a death bed and a card table.

Would we vacillate between the profound and mundane, like the occasional flashes of lightning illuminating the rows and rows of empty airplanes?

When I arrived at Steven's house, Sarah met me at the door.

"How is he?" I asked.

"Not good," she said. "He's been sleeping most of the day. I'm not sure he'll recognize any of you. It may be a wasted visit."

"Maybe he'll perk up once we're all together."

Sarah was quiet for a few seconds, and then she said, "I guess anything's possible. I need to go out to the pharmacy at some point to pick up a prescription, so I may have to leave you with him."

"It's not as if you're leaving him with strangers."

Sarah sighed and buried her face in her hands for a moment before managing a weak smile. "Mark's already here."

She led me into the living room where Steven lay sleeping in his hospital bed. His breathing was irregular – increasingly rapid breaths followed by a long pause – and then the cycle started again. His lips looked dry and cracked and his hair was matted against the pillow. He smelled of salt and sweat and rot.

There was a card table set up next to the bed with four folding wooden chairs. On the table were two decks of cards, a pad of paper, and a pencil. Mark sat in a straight-back chair watching Steven, afraid to get too close. He looked relieved to see me.

We only had a moment to say hello before we heard Tim's deep voice in the entryway with Sarah. He wore a long overcoat and looked much more like a businessman than in Africa.

"Hey, Thames," he said, shaking my hand. He greeted Mark, grabbed a chair, and sat down. "I just flew in a few hours ago. I'm whipped."

Richard Burris was the last to arrive. He gazed around as if he were doing a security scan. I suppose it was just his natural curiosity, but it seemed odd that he examined paintings on the wall and sculptures on pedestals before he took note of Steven.

Sarah served us tea in the dining room, and then we went back into the living room where Steven rested. He lay with eyes closed and his mouth half open, as if the work of breathing was his sole purpose. His face was a deep mustard color, and his abdomen protruded out from under his sheets.

"What's actually happening with Steven?" Richard asked.

"His liver's not working anymore," said Sarah. "He goes in and out of awareness. Have you ever heard of a hepatic coma?"

Richard shook his head.

"It produces hallucinations. He doesn't know what's real, or if he's dreaming or remembering or making something up. They're difficult to witness. You should prepare yourselves." She paused for a few seconds, just observing her husband. "He may be able to hear you but not respond. He may wake up and be completely lucid. I suggest you just go ahead and play cards. That's what he wanted."

Richard Burris sat opposite me, as he had when we were bridge partners. Tim and Mark were on my right and left sides. I began to shuffle the cards. Then I dealt them.

The hand motions felt natural and the faces looked familiar, but everything felt off-kilter. Mark shifted in his chair, apparently quite uncomfortable.

"Don't you think we should say something to him? We're here because he invited us. Shouldn't we try and wake him up?"

"It would be fine if you to want try," said Sarah.

Mark got up and moved closer to Steven. "Hey, Thompson," he said. "Steven, wake up and talk to your Danvers buddies. We came here for a card game. We need you."

Steven did not respond. Mark looked crestfallen, so I walked over to the bed.

"Hi, Steven, it's Robert. I'm here with some of your friends – Tim, Mark, and Richard. Can you hear me?"

Steven's labored breathing continued, each breath making a horrible gurgling noise. I watched him for a minute, feeling helpless. I had convinced everyone to make the trip, and now it might be for nothing. I sat back down.

"Let's play bridge," I said in a voice louder than I expected. I felt self-conscious, maybe on Steven's behalf, so I suddenly asked the group, "Hey, if you could pick your favorite type of hand what would it be?"

I didn't address my question to anyone in particular, but Richard responded immediately.

"I like symmetry," he said. "I love to get all four aces. I don't care about the other cards. Four aces provide an anchor for the underlying chaos. You have a definite winner in each suit, and it limits the damage that can be done."

"I like lots of picture cards – kings and queens," Mark said. "It makes for a colorful hand, a full court of lords and ladies. It presents lots of possibilities for your partner, and I feel a certain kinship with the picture cards that's absent with pure numbers." He hesitated for a second and then added, "I always feel happy when I get that type of hand."

"I like lots of cards in one suit, particularly hearts. I'm not sure why," I said. "If I can get eight hearts and include a picture in the suit, I know I can open with a three bid and shut down everyone else."

"I'm with Thames," said Tim, "except I like the spades. Nice black spades. And you know that spades are higher than the other suits." He laughed and we all joined him.

Steven coughed and opened his eyes. We all looked at him in astonishment.

"Who are you?" he asked in a raspy voice.

"It's me, Robert," I said, "and Richard and Mark and Tim. We're all here. Remember you asked me to get them here to play cards? We just dealt out the first hand."

"Where are my clothes?" he asked, frantically reaching out.

Sarah heard him and rushed into the room. "Here's some water, Steven." She offered him a green plastic cup with a built-in straw. He sipped at it, choked, and then swallowed. "He needs to drink," she explained to no one in particular.

"I can help with that," I said, and coaxed the cup from her. The silence, punctuated by the swallows, created an eerie, uncoordinated rhythm that sounded like the last beats of a song at the end of a concert.

"Steven," I said, "do you remember what we used to sing when we were playing cards?" Mark and Tim raised their eyebrows as I started the first chords of "Satisfaction" – the Rolling Stones' version.

Tim began drumming the card table. "I can't get no….no…no…no satisfaction…" We all sang, embracing the strangeness of the moment.

At first Steven held his hands against his ears, but at the end he smiled and clapped. "That was pitiful. Just pitiful," he said. "I could feel every beat against my liver. No more singing or you'll crack my spleen to pieces."

We all laughed, and his eyes lit up. I was shocked by his sudden clarity. We all were. It was as if he had returned to us as a teenager again, at least in spirit.

"Since you tortured me with that song I think I have a right to know: What gives you satisfaction? Each one of you… the first idea that crosses your mind." Steven pointed to Tim.

"Sex," said Tim.

We all chortled.

"I'm just being honest!"

"No surprise," said Steven with a smile. Then he pointed to Richard.

"Solving an elegant physics problem, one that no one had been able to solve before, and writing it up for a journal and then seeing the idea published."

"Whew, no competition for that one," said Mark. Steven pointed at him.

"Me? I love good food, paired with good wine and friends. Actually, an entire five course meal with wine at a five-star restaurant in Paris."

"For me, today, it's water," said Steven. "I'm so thirsty…"

I held the cup up to him again. His lips and throat quivered as he drank. He wiped his mouth with the back of his hand and then pointed at me. "And you, my friend?"

"I haven't thought about it," I said. "But… I guess I'd say surprises. I've always liked surprises – opening packages, envelopes, getting off an airplane in a new place."

I looked at Sarah. "How about you?"

"Oh God, just getting through another day without a crisis!" She seemed lost in thought for a few seconds and then said, "It used to be running. And speaking of running, I need to run off to the pharmacy. Steven has a new prescription I have to pick up." She put on her coat. "You boys make yourselves at home. I'll be back in half an hour. I have my cell phone."

"Goodbye, my love," Steven said, blowing her a kiss.

She blew one back from the door. "See you soon."

We turned to look at Steven. His face was gaunt. He had not shaved for several days and had patches of gray stubble along his jaw. Dried blood was caked around his lips. He had a small white basin for spitting and there was evidence of more blood in the basin. As he looked up at me the whites of his eyes glowed deep yellow. "Robert," he said.

"Yes?"

"There's something I want to say."

Mark, Tim, and Richard put down their cards, as if choreographed.

Steven took a long sip of water. "First, thank you for coming here. I know I'm a mess. I smell bad. I frighten myself when I look in the mirror." He paused and took a breath. I noticed how the air whistled through his lips as he breathed. "My thoughts are often very confused."

"Maybe we should just play cards," I said. "You don't have to speak.

We can play a hand together. Would you like that?"

I picked up my cards and showed them to him. I don't know why I tried to stop him from talking. He reached over and grabbed my cards. His fingers trembled as he held them and I tried to steady his hand.

"One club," he whispered, and I nodded and repeated the bid louder.

"One diamond," said Mark.

"One no trump," said Richard.

"Pass," said Tim.

Round and round went the bidding until finally we ended in three no trump. Richard would be playing the hand. I took the cards from Steven when he drifted off, his head rolling back on his pillow. Richard moved over to the bed to talk with him.

"Steven, my wife and I chant Buddhist meditations to help calm ourselves when we feel frightened or confused. It might help you. It's simple. You just say, 'O My A.'"

"O My A," Steven whispered. "O My A."

"It gives us strength to face whatever comes our way." Richard said. "I hope it will bring you peace."

Steven opened his eyes. "We could have protected them, the other boys. But we lied." Tears began to roll down his cheeks.

I looked at the others; they exchanged uneasy glances.

Steven struggled to sit up, "You know what I'm talking about."

"He may be hallucinating," I whispered to Tim, but he didn't answer.

Mark got up and went over to Steven. "We had to lie. It was a matter of survival."

Tim joined Mark on the bed next to Steven. "It's all in the past, man. Let it go."

Steven stared at him blankly. "I've been lying in this bed so long. I go over it and over it, and I know I can change how I remember the past, but that's not what I want. You have to help me now." He reached out and Tim took his hand.

"Steven, there's no point in going back. We can't change what happened," said Tim.

"If we don't care about the truth, we're as bad as them," Steven said with quiet authority.

"Who?" I asked, looking from one man to the other.

Tim got up and went to the window. "You're talking about the Shanglys?"

"You know I am," Steven said.

Tim looked back at him. "I've been thinking about this for a long time. I haven't wanted to talk about it, but it was my fault. That's the truth. I've had to live with it." He paused and turned back to the window. "When Mrs. Shangly invited us into the apartment, I knew we shouldn't go. She was drunk. I knew it was trouble. I sorely regret it."

"She had the hots for you, Tim. We all knew that." Mark looked at the others for confirmation. "She always came by the card room and gave Tim neck rubs, remember?"

Richard nodded. I couldn't, for the life of me, remember. All of us liked Mrs. Shangly.

"But when she gave us wine, I knew we should leave," Tim said. "Only no, I had to stay there and drink more. I spent years getting beat up on the fields of that hard-ass, white boys' school, and I was longing for the softness of a woman's touch. When we started to dance, it felt so good. It was everything I wanted…"

"What happened?" I blurted, unable to control myself.

Tim shook his head. "Steven was upstairs with Mr. Shangly, and the others were in the kitchen. Mrs. Shangly and I were alone. And then her heel caught in the rug and she pulled me and I tripped. We fell onto the floor. I didn't want to fall on her, so I angled to the side and – "

Mark interrupted "He whacked his head on the coffee table. I saw what happened. I heard it crack. I thought he had a concussion 'cause he seemed so confused, just lying there…"

"Hell, I got my head hit harder than that at practice every day. No, I wanted to stay down. I didn't want to move. I could have, but I didn't. I liked having her there next to me, her lips hovering near my face." He smiled at the memory. "I just kind of – played dead for a while."

Mark pushed himself away from the bed as if he were pushing away the memory. "I never should have called Dr. Hart. I just got scared."

"Are you sure that's all it was?" Tim teased.

Mark flushed pink. "What do you mean?"

"Mark was jealous," cackled Steven.

"Well maybe a little," said Mark. "But I was also worried; there was blood all over the place!"

"What did Dr. Hart do?" I asked, trying to get back to the story.

Tim shrugged. "He brought Maiser; that woke me up alright."

Richard finally spoke: "Maiser took Tim into to the kitchen and accused him of sexual assault."

"I thought it was all over," said Tim. "My whole career in college and football. Maybe even some jail time."

"But it wasn't true," said Richard. "It wasn't assault."

"You think that mattered to Maiser? I was lying on the floor with a woman – a faculty member, someone's wife, a White woman – and we'd been drinking. I was big and Black and there was blood all over. It was unseemly. That's what mattered to Maiser."

Steven's eyes were closed, but I could tell he was listening intently. Tim looked at us. "When he accused me of a sexual assault, I told him that I knew what a 'sexual assault' was because it was going on at Danvers between our teachers and us students. That stopped him for a second. You remember?"

Mark and Richard nodded in accord.

"That's when I told him about Mr. Goodson and Mr. Cheadle," whispered Steven. "I busted right into the kitchen and told him what Mr. Goodson had done to me."

"And he told you that Mr. Shangly was the one." said Tim. "That asshole was after Shangly."

"Where was Shangly?" I asked.

"In the bathroom, cleaning up his wife," Mark said.

Steven moaned loudly; we all looked at him. "I felt like I was suffocating. I couldn't breathe. I agreed it was Mr. Shangly. We all did. I just can't figure out why."

"Because Mr. Shangly gave us wine," said Mark. He looked at me. "Shangly had taken Steven upstairs to his bedroom. Who knew what he was doing up there? Maiser was so convinced."

"It was the only logical solution," said Richard.

"He was just showing me some masks from New Guinea," Steven

said. "Mr. Shangly never did anything to me. It was Mr. Goodson. He was the one. And Cheadle. And I didn't make that up. I told Maiser. Didn't I, Tim?"

Tim was rubbing his forehead as if he had a bad headache. "You did, Steven," he answered in a subdued voice. "But he wasn't interested in the truth."

We all sat looking at the table, unsure of how to respond.

"The truth is that I knew what was going on," said Tim. "I saw Mr. Cheadle in the showers after a practice. He hung around there gawking at us. Then one night I was getting dressed, and I saw Ian McKee – you know, the wide receiver on the team – carrying on with him. It made me sick. I turned around and ran and never told anyone. I was afraid of getting involved. So maybe I had it all coming to me, what happened."

I wanted to say something comforting, but all I could come up with was, "You were only sixteen, Tim. We were just kids."

We looked at Steven. He seemed to have slipped back into sleep. Richard shuffled and dealt the cards and we played a hand, following suit, watching the eyes and movements of our partners, taking comfort in the routine, the rhythm and the strategy of the game, and waiting for someone to say something. But nobody did.

Then I heard a knock at the door and thought that Sarah had forgotten her keys. But when I opened it, there were two men staring at me from under their maroon Danvers caps. One looked like a marine with strong shoulders, blue eyes, and a square jaw. The other was very old and frail, stooped over and supported by the first. The marine introduced himself.

"I'm Tillman Hobson," he said and reached for my hand.

Steel blue eyes cut into me; excessively white teeth flashed a confident, predatory smile.

"Robert Thames," I answered, feeling confused. Had Sarah invited them? I stepped aside to let them in, marveling that she'd want them here at this time.

"Good to meet you in person, Dr. Thames," he said. "We've talked on the phone. This is Dean Maiser." I scrutinized the face of his companion – the most feared man at Danvers. Even in advanced age, his nearness caused me an involuntary shudder.

"We're visiting with Steven," I said. "If you're here to see Sarah, she'll be back in a few minutes. Steven is ill."

"No, we're here to see you," said Hobson. "All of you. It will only take a moment of your time." He stepped past me, into the living room. Tim, Mark, and Richard rose from their chairs as Dean Maiser rumbled toward them.

"How did you know we'd all be here?" I demanded.

"Word travels fast. Mr. Harrison mentioned it to one of our board members. The board member became concerned and called me. I contacted Mr. Harrison, who informed me of the gathering."

"Mark?" I said in disbelief. "Why would you do that?"

"I didn't know they were coming here," he said throwing up his hands. "He said he wanted to send a card to Steven."

"This is not a good time to talk," I said, indicating Steven's bed.

"Dean Maiser and I want to express our support for what you're doing here today. It's through solidarity with each other that we become strong," said Hobson. "By coming together today, you exemplify the finest Danvers traditions."

He sounded like he was reading a speech. I glanced at Tim, who looked angry.

Hobson continued: "Excuse us for our interruption, but we understand that some research files have surfaced that are of a very personal nature. We apologize for any embarrassment or confusion they may have caused. Dean Maiser can explain the history of the files and answer any questions you may have about them. When he finishes, we'd like your cooperation in returning the files to Danvers for safe keeping."

Tim glared at Hobson. "This is not the time or place for this discussion. As you can see, Steven is very sick. We're all very upset. You both need to leave. Now."

Maiser took a step forward and began to speak. "I'm an old man. I never know from day-to-day whether I'll wake up in the morning, and if my mind will be clear. Mr. Thompson is not the only one who is ill. That is why this conversation cannot wait. All I ask is that you give me a few moments. I would not have come here if I did not believe that what I have to say was of the utmost importance."

We stood silently, tacitly agreeing to give Maiser his chance to speak. Tim, our undisputed leader, folded his broad arms across his chest, cocking his head to the side.

Maiser didn't waste a moment. He moved to the center of room, as if addressing a gathering of new freshmen students.

"When we agreed to participate in the study – as partners with Harvard and Yale and other colleges – we committed to sending all of our research material to Harvard at the end of five years. Our role was very limited. Dr. Hart assured us that he had submitted the files to the study directors. It now appears that he took it upon himself to retain a copy of the files and continue the research without any knowledge or consent of the Danvers Board or the school. When Mr. Hobson and I confronted Dr. Hart about the files last month, he became very agitated. He admitted that he had continued the research secretly, and we had a very uncomfortable confrontation with him."

"And then he died," I added.

Maiser shot me a dirty look and continued. "He had a heart attack shortly after we left. Perhaps he was consumed with remorse at his poor judgment – "

I interrupted Maiser. "I don't think Dr. Hart was trying to do the research in a deceptive, secretive way. The other researchers had abandoned the project. He continued because it was in his nature not to give up."

"We will never know why he behaved in such an irresponsible fashion, but I believe his guilt led to his death. We were as shocked and disturbed as you are. And that is why we need to have the files returned to Danvers so that we can perform a full investigation. Some of the information in the files may be confidential." He paused for effect. "There are possible allegations of misconduct and abuse in the files. Dr. Hart should have reported any incriminating information to me and the local authorities. But Danvers had nothing to do with any of it."

"That's a lie," I said. "Danvers had everything to do with it. You knew about the abuse."

Steven's eyes were open now, keenly focused on Maiser. I could hear him clear the phlegm from his throat. I brought him the cup of water, but he pushed it aside.

"I told you… I told you about Goodson and Cheadle…"

"You told me about Mr. Shangly," said Maiser, gently remonstrating Steven. "That was in the document you signed. We did a complete investigation,"

"No…" objected Steven. "You pressured me into that."

"Mr. Cheadle was an outstanding teacher and coach. No one ever complained about him. Mr. Goodson left for a better position. I was protecting you boys from Shangly and his wife. They were dangerous alcoholics and…'swingers' I guess they say nowadays. And child molesters."

"You weren't protecting us," I said, expressing the rage that had been simmering inside me for so long. "You let teachers embarrass us and abuse us. We were stripped naked and photographed like lab specimens. How do you think it made us feel?" I heard the volume of my voice rise. "How do you think it feels to find out that we were part of a study we never consented to? That our teachers were gaping at our nude pictures and laughing? What about the boys who were molested?" I felt my fist ball up. "You have no right to the files or the photographs. I have all of them, and one thing is for sure: They're not going back to Danvers."

Tim caught my eye; it took me back to that fire we had fought together in Africa.

"Damn straight," he said. "Now it's time for you to leave."

He put his hand on Dean Maiser's shoulders to direct him to the door.

"Take your hands off me!" yelled Maiser. "Where is your respect? We made decisions for each of you and molded you into successful adults the best we could. Colleges and businesses knew what they could expect from a Danvers boy. But none of you measured up. *That's* the truth. I should have expelled all of you when I had the chance. None of you were good enough to be Danvers boys. And now you want to ruin the reputation of the school and the futures of students who had nothing to do with this."

"Is this about money? Is that what you want?" Hobson implored us.

"It's not about money," Mark said, clenching his jaw.

"Then what?" demanded Maiser. "Why would any Danvers student damage an institution that has done so much for them?"

"Look at me," said Steven. His voice was surprisingly strong. "See what it did for me? I never recovered from what happened there. Goodson and Cheadle started with backrubs and progressed to blow jobs. I suffered my whole life from the shame of what they made of me. I helped them. And now I'm dying from it."

"That's a hallucination of a disturbed mind!" spat Maiser.

"It's the truth. And there were other boys."

"There were no other boys," said Maiser, shaking his head at Hobson.

"Paul Camillo, David Johnson, Eric Howard, Steven Macon. Phillip Knifer." Steven was almost yelling. His eyes were wild and his face was twitching.

"Impossible. Phillip Knifer was on our Board."

"The swimmer, Richard Lewis, the wrestler, Ian McKee, the track star, Kevin O'Shea. Mr. Goodson had our files. He got them from Cheadle and you. There were twelve of us. He showed me all their pictures. I was there when he raped Kevin O'Shea."

"What?" gasped Hobson.

"He said it was more exciting if I … participated. At first Kevin went along. He liked to show off his body and Mr. Goodson gave us wine and admired every muscle on Kevin's body like a sculpture. He massaged him and so did I. But then Kevin wanted to stop. But Mr. Goodson kept going. I was there. I saw it all. And you gave Kevin's files to Goodson. You knew."

"He requested those files to assist him in his tutoring. He was tutoring Kevin O'Shea. These are lies, pure lies!" Maiser yelled.

He pushed the card table aside to get to Steven, but I blocked his way.

Steven's eyes looked frantic, like a wild bird trapped in a room. Everyone stared.

"It's the truth," he said. "I want Danvers to admit what happened. I want an apology to each boy." He began to retch and cough, spewing droplets of blood.

"Get out of here," I said to Maiser. I actually pushed him toward the front door.

Mr. Hobson said, "I'm sorry, very sorry. I... I didn't know!" and followed him out. As I closed the door behind them, I heard Steven retching again: one long, loud sickening sound after another.

When I reentered his room, Steven sat up straight. His eyes rolled back and his body shook. Then he began to vomit a river of blood – deep maroon blood at first and then more cherry colored. I reached over for the white basin, but the blood quickly filled the basin and began to drip onto the sheet. There were clots of blood like pieces of raspberries and cherries. Mark ran into the kitchen and returned with a large bowl and Steven filled the bowl with more blood.

"Call 911," I said. I tried to hold him as the blood spouted from his mouth. Tim brought a metal soup pot from the kitchen, and the blood made loud pings as it struck the bottom.

Sarah walked into the room a few minutes later. "Oh my God! Has anyone called 911?"   Richard nodded. He was standing against the wall, white as a sheet. Steven was making some kind of gurgling sound.

"What?" I asked him. "What are you saying?"

"O My A. O My A," Steven said. "O my A."

"O My A," echoed Richard. "O My A."

By the time the paramedics arrived, Steven had filled the soup pot and Richard brought another ceramic bowl with scenes from Italy painted on the outside – gondolas on the water and churches by stone bridges. We helped the paramedics move Steven onto a stretcher. He was still vomiting blood when they rolled him out the door.

Tim and I accompanied Sarah to the hospital. Mark was in the bathroom, feeling queasy, and Richard was cleaning up.

"He didn't want to go to the hospital," said Sarah as Tim drove her car like we were on the highways of Tanzania, "but what am I supposed to do?"

Steven survived the night. He was in the intensive care unit and they would not let us visit. They gave him twenty units of blood and by morning the bleeding stopped. Sarah sat with us in the waiting room. Her eyes were red and swollen and her mouth hung open listlessly. She let

Tim hold her, and then me. She was numb and distant. Her hands were cool against my neck, and I could hear her short rapid breaths. "Robert," she said.

"Yes."

"What happened last night while I was gone?"

"Maiser and Hobson showed up," I said, and I explained in detail about the files.

"Steven told everyone about the sexual abuse he suffered at Danvers. He named the teachers – and the students who were molested. I think that was why Steven wanted to get us together. He wanted us to do something about it before it was too late. I think the naked photographs – the body measurements and classification scheme – were part of the abuse, and we all experienced it. Steven never imagined that Maiser would be there, and when he saw him, it all came out. In blood."

Sarah listened quietly. "I always suspected there was abuse. Steven would wake up in the middle of the night screaming that there was a man chasing him. I thought that maybe it was Maiser, but Steven could never see the face in his dream..."

Tim and I decided to donate blood that morning to compensate for some of the blood that Steven had required. We went to the Red Cross and the technician stuck a needle into our arms. We lay on stretchers across from each other. I watched the blood flow through the tubing – the same, deep, maroon-colored, venous blood from each of our arms – on its way to the collecting bottle, and I imagined it eventually finding its way to Steven.

36

They made me rest after I gave the blood; I must have drifted off for an hour or two. When they woke me up, I looked around. Tim was gone. I felt refreshed from my nap and called Dr. Hutchinson to see if he were available for a short visit.

"I don't get many people who are interested in that work anymore. Are you in Boston?"

"Yes. I could be at your office in a half hour."

"Well, I like your style! Come on down."

"You're at the Peabody Museum, right?"

"Yes. Down in the basement with all the old bones and fossils."

The building was red brick, with large stone arches featuring a banner for an exhibition of Mayan pottery. At the front desk I asked for Dr. Hutchinson. The gray-haired docent paged through her directory and finally asked, "Are you sure about the name? I can't find him listed."

"He told me he was in the basement."

"Well in that case you can take the elevator; it's a separate program." She pointed to the elevator and smiled pleasantly to indicate that our conversation was finished.

The elevator was like an old-fashioned bank vault with a black and gold interior and slow thick doors. It seemed to fall in slow motion to the basement, and then opened onto a long, dark corridor. There was a glass door at the very end with a sign that read "No Entry." I pushed against it, but it did not budge. I was about to go back upstairs when a young woman emerged from the women's bathroom on the right. She was about twenty-five years old, tall and thin, with the ease and enthusiasm of a graduate student.

"Can I help you?" she asked with a wide smile that accentuated her narrow lips.

"Yes, I'm here to meet with Dr. Hutchinson. He's expecting me. I'm Dr. Thames."

"Well, you're in luck. I'm going right past his office right now."

She used her key card on the door and we started down a long hallway with bookcases on either side, filled with small boxes and stacks of paper. On the tables between the bookcases were piles of bones or fossils with various labels attached. When she indicated an office with a closed metal door, I knocked lightly. After a few seconds, a thin man in a rumpled black suit opened the door. He appeared to be over 80 years old, with a curved back and disheveled gray hair that hung down over his thick glasses.

"Dr. Hutchinson?" I asked. I reached out my hand; his fingers were weak and bony. "I'm Dr. Thames. I'm here to talk with you about somatotype research."

He squinted in my direction. His eyes showed just the slightest hint of life now and his mouth and cheeks began to contort into some semblance of a smile. "And you are…?"

"Dr. Robert Thames."

"Oh yes, you said that."

"I understand that you've done research on body types and how they predict behavior."

"I'm a physical anthropologist. I study bones and human tools, food, waste and habitation. The study of body type was a fad at one time. We don't do that anymore. But it's become a bit of a hobby for me. I worked with Dr. William Sheldon years ago when I was a graduate student. That was the golden age of the 'somatotype,' as they called it. We had research grants from the government. But people lost interest. Now, with the availability of genetic analysis, we'd be able to test out some of his theories in ways that were never possible previously. But nobody approves anymore." He grimaced. "It's not 'P.C.'"

"Well, I'd like to talk with you about some research material that has come into my possession," I said. I told him about Dr. Hart's files.

"I heard that younger students were involved in the study, but I never saw the material." He looked at me carefully. "I'd love to see what you have."

"Unfortunately, I didn't bring them with me."

"Pity, I'm sure they would have value – historic value at least. Sheldon used certain techniques in his photography and in his measurements. I would recognize the technique. But I can't say what their actual scientific value would be without seeing them."

"I was wondering… Do you think any of the site researchers might have continued the study to the present, even after the funding ran out?"

"That would be highly unusual. But curiosity is powerful motivation."

"How could they have done this research without any consent from the subjects? These were children – young teenagers."

Dr. Hutchinson rubbed his ears. "When they began this research, the rules were quite different. We got the consent from the schools and the government. People trusted institutions, and they trusted science and scientists. After all, it was science that had produced antibiotics that cured pneumonia, and it was science that produced the nuclear bomb that ended the war." He pushed a stack of papers back and sat on top of his desk. "Do you know much about dog breeds?"

"A little."

"Dogs are bred for certain characteristics – herding, fishing, hunting, protection. The profile of the breed has to do with physical characteristics, but there are also associated behavioral characteristics. The ideal for each breed has the desired physical and behavioral characteristics. For each breed there's a concept of excellence. Dog breeders try to identify characteristics that are the ideal for a breed. When a dog has these characteristics, he can be a champion. Does this make sense?"

"Yes, I think so. As applied to dogs," I said.

"Dr. Sheldon believed that humans were endowed with certain physical characteristics that made them fit for leadership, while other characteristics might predict criminal behavior. The photographs allowed categorization of human attributes, just as you would measure the distance from a dog's neck to its tail, or the curve of its spine, or the length of the snout. The idea was to use the measurements to identify people with certain personality characteristics that would predict future leadership and other talents that could be nurtured through education."

"Was there any real scientific evidence for the use of these measurements?"

"Well, again, you have to understand the historical context. This was all before the discovery of the human genome. Back then, scientists wanted to utilize the scientific method. They could measure physical characteristics and follow their subjects over time. They used the tools that were available to them and they developed theories based upon their observations of animals."

"But why nude photographs? Couldn't they have done their measurements with clothing?"

"Sheldon had his protocols. They made sense at the time. What if there was a correlation with testosterone or estrogen in the behaviors? Wouldn't you want measurable evidence of these hormonal effects in the sexual characteristics of the subjects? I suspect this was the thinking that led to such decisions. I'm not defending it. I'm simply providing a possible explanation."

"Did anyone ever mention sexual abuse at the schools where they did the research? Any misuse of the photographs?" I asked.

"No. That would have been a violation of ethics. We monitored those kinds of things carefully, but of course each site had its own monitors who were responsible for protecting the materials. To my knowledge, there were never any reports of that kind."

"Thanks, Dr. Hutchinson." And then I impulsively asked, "What would you suggest that I do with the files that I have?"

"I'm sure the museum would be interested. You could send me the entire set. I have several graduate students who could look them over." His eyes glistened expectantly.

"I'll think about it."

"Actually, there's an anthropologist, semi-retired like me, who might be interested in talking with you. He's been looking at the Sheldon research. He's in a building just a few blocks away. Would you like me to see if he's in?"

"Sure, okay." I listened as he punched in a phone number. There was a brief conversation. Then he wrote down an address and an office number and handed it to me. Then he walked me to the elevator and shook my hand.

"We don't get many visitors and even fewer who are interested in somatotype. I suppose you were a 3, 3, 4," said Dr. Hutchinson.

I stared at him, surprised.

"Your somatotype. A 3, 3, 4. A rabbit. It's a good somatotype for a scientist or a doctor." He winked. "That was mine, too,"

As the elevator door closed, I said, "Actually, I think I'm a fox."

I walked out of the Peabody Museum and down the street to a stop light, crossed, and turned right to the Anthropology Department Annex. I was looking for Room 221. I knocked and waited. The man who answered had a gray beard and a gaunt face. His clothes were rumpled and stained. He ushered me into a small, dank office filled with files and papers on the desk. He stretched out his hand to shake mine, and I got a strange feeling. It hit me in the pit of my stomach.

"I'm Professor Shangly," he said.

"Mr. Shangly?" I was astounded. "Mr. Shangly?" I searched his face for the person I knew so many years ago. "It's me, Robert Thames, from Danvers."

His face brightened and now I recognized the expression on his face.

"I was in your dormitory. Benson Hall. We played bridge outside of your apartment."

"Yes, now I remember you. You're from the Philippines."

He indicated I take a seat and sat down next to me. "You know, after we left Danvers, I got my Ph.D. in anthropology. I wrote a paper about *barang*. Sorcery, insects, black magic. Powerful stuff. Do you remember that we talked about *barang*?"

"Yes."

"Plenty of *barang* around Danvers," he said with a laugh.

"Yes, and you got swept up in it."

And then I told him everything – about Dr. Hart sending me the files, and the horrible events at Steven's bedside, and Maiser's efforts to cover it all up. He listened attentively to my chaotic summary of the events of the past month, nodding firmly several times.

Then he said, "When Dr. Hart asked me to assist him, I thought the research would be part of an update of Sheldon's book, with more information about a group of highly intelligent and ambitious boys. I had my doubts, but for someone with an interest in anthropology, the opportunity was irresistible." He shook his head. "Only later did I realize that there was a dark side, a very disturbing dark side."

"What do you mean?"

"There were a few teachers who had an unhealthy fascination with you boys. They were attracted to the beauty and vitality and youth of their students. They wanted to get close to it. Most of them respected the rules, but Dr. Hart's study and the photographs upset the equilibrium. Dr. Hart tried to protect the materials, but there was an informal advisory group that would discuss certain aspects of the study and request files. At first it seemed to be a legitimate interest in science, but… it wasn't."

"Did you know about the sexual abuse?"

"I wondered. I heard rumors. I never had any evidence. But I knew about other kinds of abuse. Maiser targeted certain boys, rooted them out. I suppose the culture was always intolerant of differences, but the files and the photos gave him leverage. Sometimes the faculty response was subtle. I would hear of nicknames or acerbic humor. Sometimes it became more overt, a culling of the herd through rumor and innuendo. Maiser would find something in a boy's room – a book, a bottle of wine, a naked pin-up – and before we knew it, the boy was gone from the school."

I nodded, recalling that an inordinate amount of boys had been expelled or withdrawn from Danvers during our time there.

"And there were certain boys that became a fascination, who were both attractive and repulsive to the men. Steven Thompson was one of them. It was his androgynous appearance, like a young David Bowie, that elicited those contradictory reactions. Tim Washington was another. They were fascinated by his musculature and his raw power, and frightened by his blackness. I believe you were another one."

"Me?" I was shocked.

"Yes. They could not understand how you succeeded; how someone who they thought looked like a dishwasher or gardener could get better grades than an upper-class boy from Boston. Maiser wanted to rid the school of those who did not fit his ideals. I tried to protect as many of you as I could. Maiser hated my wife and me. We were insurgents. So he got rid of us."

"It must've been terrible. Why didn't you fight it?"

"We were at fault, discredited. We'd given alcohol to students. And my wife... was a bit too friendly to some of you. I agree it was unprofessional and inappropriate."

Dr. Shangly stared out the window for a few moments and then asked, "You know, you could use the research files to expose and disprove all of the old assumptions and show how Danvers and other schools exploited the students."

"I'm not sure what I'll do, but I definitely won't return them to Danvers."

"I'm glad that you survived Danvers and the *barang* that was all around us," he said.

Before I left, he showed me a picture of Mrs. Shangly. She had died four years earlier. She was sitting on a huge rock overlooking a canyon. Her hair was white and her eyes were opened wide, gazing out at the clouds the way I remembered.

37

I drove across the Mystic River Bridge and got off at the first exit. What was it that I really wanted from this old man? A moment when we would look into each other's eyes and I would feel something that I had never felt before? And what would I do then?

Chelsea was an industrial port city with oil tanks and old brick factories and small stores that dotted the narrow streets. While Boston seemed to have been influenced by its closeness to Harvard, Chelsea could have been influenced by successive waves of immigrants – the Irish and Jews, the Italians and Polish, and later the Puerto Ricans. Chelsea had the look of an old industrial city, all of its wealth and vitality suctioned out, leaving just an empty hull.

Dr. Berenson's office was part of a three story building with offices on the first floor. Next door were a pharmacy and a small grocery. Inside the office were two threadbare sofas and three chairs with embroidered flowers. The receptionist, a woman of the same style and vintage as the furniture, gently chided me for being late.

"Sorry," I said, "traffic."

She asked no questions about why someone from Washington, D.C. might want to see an optometrist in Chelsea, Massachusetts. She gave me a form to fill out and told me to sit down and the doctor would be with me in a moment. I quickly filled it out, wondering if Dr. Berenson might somehow recognize me by my name. Under "purpose of visit," I wrote "blurry vision."

As I waited, I scanned the office for family pictures, but there were none. A Red Sox pennant hung on one wall and a Boston Celtics World Champions 1960 pennant hung on another. Finally, a gray-haired man wearing a tan lab coat shuffled out and shook my hand. He had bushy eyebrows and curly greased hair combed over his balding scalp. The dominant feature in his face was a long narrow nose protruding out beyond tired blue eyes. He wore thick, black-rimmed glasses.

"Last one of the day, Annie," he announced to the receptionist wearily.

He looked at me once and then again, as if he had seen me before.

"So, Dr. Thames, from Washington, D.C. You've traveled a long way for an eye examination. Did you lose your glasses at a meeting?"

"No," I said. "I just thought it was time."

"No time like the present," he said cheerfully. "Come in, come in."

We proceeded into the examination room. Dr. Berenson darkened the room except for an eye chart. He placed lenses on my face and asked me to read letters as he changed the lenses. I squinted to make out the letters through the blur and guessed when I was not sure. He would ask, "Better or worse?" as he changed the lenses.

"Better."

"Better or worse?"

"Worse."

"Better or worse?"

"Better."

Finally, he sat back and turned on the lights.

"Well, Dr. Thames, you have unusual eyes. One is nearsighted and the other is farsighted. You'll probably never need glasses, because your right eye can be used for reading, and your left eye for distance. Your only problem is that if you try to sight a rifle, you will probably look at the target through your left eye while lining it up with your right. Have you ever tried that?"

"Yes," I said. "I thought I was doing something wrong."

"Well, now you know. I suppose that one new fact is worth something."

"Yes, it is." I paused for a moment, considering how to proceed.

"Dr. Berenson, I'm here for another reason besides the eye checkup."

"You certainly don't look like you intend to rob me."

I smiled and hesitated for a moment, then just blurted it out, "Was your brother Arthur Berenson?"

"Artie? Yes, Artie was my brother. He's been gone more than 50 years. Died in the army. He was the wild one, always in trouble. He would shoplift little things at the drug store. Candy, perfume, games, you name it. That's why they sent him away. Why do you ask about him?"

"Did he go to the Philippines?"

"Why, yes, he did. He had a choice: Jail or the military. That was the deal my dad arranged. For a Jewish family, jail would have been impossible."

I watched Dr. Berenson as he spoke, amazed that he might be my uncle. Our faces and our skin were so different. He stood up and moved next to a black and white photo on the wall. With my nearsighted eye, I was able to distinguish the faces: a man and his wife and two boys in their teens.

"Is that him?"

"Yep. That's us with our parents. I was thirteen. It was right after my Bar Mitzvah. He was sixteen." The doctor's face looked pensive.

"I think Artie might be my father," I said.

He shook his head without looking at me. "My brother never got married."

"Well, his name is on my birth certificate."

Dr. Berenson stared at the eye chart as if he were focusing on the letters. Finally, he took a deep breath. "I guess you might be him. You're not what I imagined. I imagined a baby! Isn't that something? I imagined a child…"

"No, I'm grown up now."

He turned to look at me. "My parents told me about you."

"They knew?"

"I don't know the whole story. They only told me after your adopted parents died. Someone called them from the Philippines. They thought you might show up and need money, and they didn't have much. I guess they were scared. My mother was considering contacting you, but then she decided it would be best if we left well enough alone. It might upset you to find out that you had this other family."

I nodded and stood up. We were almost of the same height. "No, I would have been glad."

"So, what do you want? Do you want to punch me in the nose?" he laughed. "Go ahead if it will make you feel better."

"That's not why I came here," I said. "I just wanted to meet you and know what my father was like. Whether I'm like him."

"He was wild. I don't sense that in you. He was always trying to figure things out – puzzles, games, poker. He loved poker and gambling. He liked the ladies. Are you married?"

"No," I said.

"He had the same kind of eyes as you. One nearsighted and one farsighted. He used to squint a lot and close one eye and then the other. Do you do that?"

"Yes."

"So that's one thing."

"Did you know anything about my mother?"

"All I know is that she was a Filipina lady, a real beauty, a teacher and a hostess at a club, no parents or family. That's what my parents said. That was all they told me."

I nodded slowly, wishing there was more.

"You're lucky," he said.

"How so?"

"Your eyes… You can see the world from two perspectives: Close one eye and you get all the details. Close the other and you get the big picture."

I tried it. I closed my left eye and now I could see the stubble of whiskers he had missed when he shaved in the morning. The deposits of fat on his eyelids that suggested a high risk for heart disease. Sun damage to his nose that was causing precancerous plaques. I closed my right eye. Now his face was a blur, too close for me to see any of the details. But the family photo was clear and distinct: two boys and their parents, frozen in time.

When I opened and closed each eye quickly, it was like watching black and white images racing across a movie screen.

"Don't ever get glasses," Dr. Berenson said.

"I'm not sure I've ever heard that from an optometrist!"

He smiled and walked over to a desk and opened a drawer. "I have something for you, Dr. Thames." He pulled out a sheaf of papers and sorted through them. "Here it is."

He held out an old photograph. It was a young man in a uniform with a Filipina. Even in the faded photo, I could see that she was extraordinarily beautiful. They were standing under a coconut palm tree with a motorcycle. The man was holding her hand delicately, as if they had just met. "That's your mother and dad. A week before he died."

I stared at them – the woman in a long, native wrap-around dress, my father in khaki pants and a leather jacket, both so young and hopeful. I ran my fingers over the surface of the photograph as if I could reach back into time and discover more.

"You can have it. Here's an envelope. It's an old picture. You have to be careful."

I slid the photograph slowly into the envelope. For a moment, I was afraid that the image would disappear and slipped it back out to check before replacing it back inside.

"Thank you." I clasped his hand and felt a slight tremor.

He walked me back down the hall to the empty waiting room. The receptionist was gone.

"What do I owe you… for the visit?"

"Nothing," he said. "It's on the house."

As I flew back to Washington, I debated calling Sarah. I wanted to find out how Steven was but feared the worst. So much had happened recently, generating the buzzing prelude of a new migraine. When I closed my eyes for take-off, the buzz became the roar of the plane's engines. The flashing lights in my skull became the ambulance lights carrying Steven to the hospital.

I opened my eyes and reached into my jacket for the envelope containing my parents. I pulled out the photo and turned it over. On the back was written "Artie and Melania, Eden Bayabas, Philippines."

They were in Eden; perhaps I was even conceived there. The plane strained to lift off from the ground and shook as it flew up over Boston Harbor. As I laid my head back against the window, the lights from the ground flickered. I closed my eyes and the next thing I remembered was the flight attendant, informing me that we had arrived in Washington.

Book 4

38

Death comes as an animal. Sometimes it attacks swiftly and violently in the guise of a lion as the victim is walking across a street, or sitting in a car, or playing with a gun after drinking and socializing at a bar. It is over almost before there is a realization that life is about to be replaced with death. Fear is sudden, brief, and quickly replaced by acceptance.

Sometimes it's the gradual accumulation of thousands of stings of wasps or the bites of ants, such as when thousands of bacteria seed a heart valve and disperse to the liver and kidneys and brain where they take root and grow and proliferate. Tumor cells also do this as they metastasize from a small black dot on the skin to spread throughout the body, gradually draining the body's vital forces. The body senses something; the walls of the blood vessels and organs collapse as the invaders overcome the defenses like a rising tide that washes the beach clean.

Sometimes it's the snake that injects its venom with one swift bite, and as the venom spreads there is time to anticipate the end, to have some final thoughts about life, and a conversation with God about death. The body gradually shrinks away, leaving a consciousness that remains tethered tenuously until it is released and floats freely away. This is the patient who suffers a sudden loss of blood from an ulcer that can occur in minutes, or a ruptured blood vessel.

Sometimes it's a loyal dog that comes for what is left of a body that is suffering irreversible decline and infirmity. The loyal dog wags its tail and snuggles in closer and closer until it suffocates and smothers the lungs with pneumonia. The end is merciful.

Sometimes death can float in air currents circling above the earth, like a pelican scanning the ocean for moving oval reflections before it plunges suddenly into the sea.

Or the hyena that tears off a limb here and there, devouring the body piece by piece, like the ravages of diabetes that can lead to amputations one after another, or AIDS, taking one organ and then another and another before it is finished. My patients ask why they are still here when that happens. *Why is it taking so long? It's going too slowly.* I have watched them die of AIDS and tuberculosis and various complications of old age that remove one piece after another, leaving a mutilated, empty shell.

I am not sure how Steven died in the end. Sarah called me after he was gone. I could tell from her voice, just by how she said my name, "Robert?"

"Yes," I answered.

But I knew. It had been two weeks since our visit and I hadn't expected him to last even that long. When I heard that he had survived the ICU and had gone back home, I half expected that he would find some drugs and overdose to spare himself the indignity of suffering the last days and weeks. I should have called Sarah. But instead, I retreated into the details of the life around me. Mr. Grundel had given me more papers to sign, and the pension people had visited me and suggested that I meet with a financial adviser. I was busy and had lots of excuses for not calling. But none of them were good enough. Each day that went by I felt worse.

"Steven just died," she said. "I thought you'd want to know."

"I'm sorry."

"I knew it was coming, but I still was surprised. There were so many times when I thought it might happen, but he just kept going. But last night he said he was cold, and I tried to put blankets on him. And then he just stopped breathing. We're having a service at the Alumni Chapel at Harvard on Saturday, nine o'clock."

"I'll be there," I said. "I can be there sooner. Tomorrow."

"It's okay. Just come up for the service. There are lots of people here now."

"How are you doing? I'm sorry I didn't call."

"It's okay. Now that it's over, it's sort of a relief." She paused and then added: "He talked about you when he came home from the hospital. He was worried about you."

"He was?"

"He remembered everything. Isn't that amazing? He remembered the card game and all of you being there. He felt so grateful. He didn't want you to give Danvers anything, not his file, not his picture. He wanted you to keep it."

"Don't worry. I'll never give the files to them. I'm still trying to figure out what to do with them. I'm still in shock from seeing the guys together after so many years, and Maiser..." I paused and tried to collect my thoughts and say something coherent, but my mind was blank. "And...and you."

And then I hung up the phone.

39

The memorial service felt like a play where the actors stroll onto the stage in a final rehearsal before they bring the set alive with their dialogue. The chapel itself was a simple set of wooden benches lined up in three rows and facing a crucifix and small podium to convey austerity and spiritual depth. Men and women in long coats spoke in whispers as they walked up and down the aisles. I could tell that many of them were only now learning the circumstances of Steven's death. They all gazed around, wondering if they would recognize a friend or classmate. I found a seat toward the front and kept my eyes on the floor.

I had decided that I would get up and speak about Steven. I wanted to be able to speak eloquently and support Sarah, but I didn't know if I had the right words or the courage. My chest felt heavy as I inhaled and exhaled. I tried to slow my breathing and empty my brain of thoughts, like a solitary tree in the wind. I swallowed and became the tree and closed my eyes for a few minutes. When I opened them I began to recognize people.

First I noticed Mark Harrison and Ann, his wife. I felt obliged to wave, but I still felt betrayed by Mark, who was responsible for bringing Maiser and Hobson to Steven's house. It was hard to forgive him. I imagined that he was there to represent Danvers and make some kind of official speech. He walked with the presence and solemnity of one accustomed to such events.

Sarah sat in the front, wearing a charcoal shawl over a purple dress.

Her hair was twisted into a French braid. There were two women sitting with her, one holding her hand. I kept expecting her to turn and greet people, but she maintained a steady gaze toward the podium in the front of the room.

Then I saw Tim Washington arriving. He was the only Black person at the service.

The room became quiet as a minister in a dark suit approached the podium. He had kind eyes and a calm, deep voice. His bald head reflected the light from a window, creating the illusion of godly presence.

"I'd like to welcome you to this memorial to celebrate the life of Steven Thompson. We will be sharing memories of Steven. I know some of you have requested to speak, and I want to assure all of you that there will be ample opportunity for everyone to do so. For now, let us pray."

As we stood, I heard the rustling of heavy coats and the coughs and deep sighs of mourners as they cleared their throats in preparation for prayer. When the room had become quiet again, the minister continued, "Oh, Heavenly Father, we are gathered today in your presence to celebrate a life and to ask that you receive Steven Thompson into everlasting peace. As we pray here today let our voices rise up to accompany his soul on its final mission. Thank you, Lord, for all that you have given to us and even in our darkest sorrow let us remember the joy that awaits each of us in your kingdom. From dust we cometh and to dust we shall return. For thine is the power and glory, in Christ's name, Amen."

The minister paused and there was a moment of silence. A tall man in a blue suit took this as his cue and walked to the podium.

"Good morning," he said. "I'm Ted Akins, one of Steven's partners from the law firm. We worked together for twenty years. I learned a lot about Steven in that time. He liked to cook. He would bring in food for our staff and everyone raved about it. He loved spaghetti. He was also a connoisseur of wine. He knew how to have fun and enjoy life. That is something I learned from him, how to slow down and have fun. There will always be more work waiting. You can never finish everything. But if you don't enjoy life, what is the point? Steven did that wholeheartedly. He was also a very accomplished lawyer. He took numerous cases pro bono. But all I want to say is, Steven, we will all miss you – your friendship, your caring attitude, even your wild side – which made us all a little more human. I'm sure you're sitting next to a nice case of those Apple Valley Cabernets that we used to enjoy and taking a long sip just about now."

The man began to cry and stopped talking for a moment to compose himself. "Well, that's all." He wiped his eyes with a tissue and walked off the podium.

Next, a round, short man with a cane ambled up to the podium. He seemed anxious and unaccustomed to speaking. He spoke in a singsong voice with a thick Boston accent. "Hello. My name is Billy Masters. I own Masters' Corner Coffee Shop. Mr. Thompson used to come there every day about ten and order coffee and a jelly donut. He liked to talk about the Sox and the Pats, but he really liked the Celtics. He knew all the stats for each of the guys. So one day we was talking about Larry Bird and this guy at one of the tables just keeled over dead in front of us. I thought it was a joke 'cause I never seen it before except on TV. But Mr. Thompson, he goes over and picks the guy up and like, he hugs him real tight on his back and front. I was going to stop him in case the cops come by, but then this big piece of donut comes out of the guy's mouth and he starts choking and and throwing up all over the place, must have been two or three donuts and other stuff too. He saved the guy's life! No doubt about it. When the paramedics came that was what they said. They took the guy to the Brigham and then Mr. Thompson, he helped me clean up the mess. He was laughing and smiling about it, and he said it was like Larry Bird hitting a three-pointer at the buzzer to win the game. I never seen him so happy. I told him he gets free coffee from now on 'cause it would've been bad for business if some guy dies in your shop. So after that, some of the other customers got mad 'cause he got his coffee for free, but I just told them that when they save some guy from dying in my shop, I'll give it to them too, and that would shut them up. When he got sick, he couldn't drink coffee no more so I changed the deal and gave him milk or tea or whatever the doctor ordered. Now at ten o'clock in my shop it isn't the same anymore. It's like when Ted Williams retired from the Sox. Something's missing that won't ever be the same. So when I saw it in the papers that he died, I wanted to pay my respects to his family. He was the best. I haven't come across too many like him and I see lots a guys come through there, even governors and mayors." He thought for a moment what more to say, and then nodded to Sarah and walked off the podium.

There was a lapse as we all looked around waiting for the next speaker. As I looked for someone to walk to the podium, I realized that there might not be another scheduled speaker, and that it was my time. I needed to say something. I knew that Steven would have wanted me to speak about our relationship. To me, it was about an awkward teenage friendship between two very different boys and a girl they loved, but for him it was something more. The meaning was different for each of us. Did that matter? And what of the randomness of how we met? I didn't know how to talk about any of that. I breathed deeply as I walked to the podium.

"My name is Robert Thames," I said. "Steven Thompson was my friend. We met in a line in high school where we were arranged alphabetically. Thompson and Thames were adjacent. There are many ways you could meet someone. We met because of the letter T. So I have been thinking that I would like to honor Steven in some meaningful way that recognizes our first meeting. I have decided to establish a scholarship for one student at Danvers Academy because in spite of all of its many shortcomings, a Danvers education provides the opportunity for the most amazing growth most of us experienced in our lives. But we can do better. We must do better. We cannot have growth if we are not safe. And that growth should be open to everyone, regardless of their financial or social class. This scholarship would go to a needy student whose last name begins with the letter 'T' in honor of Steven, and also the parents who adopted me and gave me their name. It brings to mind other things with the letter 'T' – like the thunder that awakens us in the night and reminds us we are still alive and not in a dream, or 'T' for the travel that allows us to leave our homes as I did and experience the world through the eyes of others, like Steven, or the 'T' for truth that can recede like a mirage on the horizon unless we have the courage to pursue it relentlessly, or 'T' for time that can stretch or contract like a spring, and never seems to be just right. We all run out of time eventually, just like words that begin with the letter 'T' eventually run out, but we never think about those words, just as we never think of all the people whose names begin with 'T' or all the seconds of life that run together and become our life until it is gone. Most scholarships and prizes are based upon what someone judges to be the best. The best Latin student, the fastest runner, the strongest body. But what do we know about what is best? Who is the judge? This scholarship would honor the luck of two boys who met each other in a line because their names began with the letter 'T'. I think that more things that are important in our lives can be traced to moments like that, than what we think of as 'the best.' And a scholarship would continue to remind us of our obligation to make Danvers and the world better than we found it."

I nodded at Sarah and looked out into the crowd. Tim Washington raised his index finger at me and smiled. Sarah shook her head and smiled. I walked back to my seat and waited for the other speakers.

Mark walked to the podium. He looked out over the crowd and seemed to breathe them in. Then he began, "My name is Mark Harrison and I'm here as the representative of Danvers, which Steven and Robert and I attended – as you just heard. Usually I have a pretty prepared speech, but this time I'm going to deviate because of what Robert just said." He turned and smiled at me.

I smiled back stiffly, wondering which card he was going to play.

"At first, as I was listening to him, I thought, Wow, dude, where are you headed with this stuff?" Mark laughed.

I was relieved that no one really laughed with him.

"But the more I think about it, the more it actually makes sense. I mean, what if 'T' was just the first of the letters chosen for a scholarship, and after that we picked 'H' and soon the entire alphabet. We could honor all of us. Why not? Who's to say what is most important? Why shouldn't we honor each one of us? So I am here to ask you to remember Steven in any way that you wish, perhaps to contribute to the Letter 'T' Scholarship Fund. But however you do it, consider the Danvers of the future, and all of the students, both boys and girls, who would keep his memory alive through their actions, because Steven Thompson helped to create a legacy. He was part of the first committee to address racial equality and justice at Danvers. The Danvers of the past was not perfect, and Steven experienced some of those flaws in the system. There were mistakes that we cannot change, but we can learn from them and get better. That's what Steven would want. Because of him and others here in this room, we have one of the most diverse private schools in the United States – Black, Asian, Hispanic, Native American, and recently, LGBTQ students. They need to all be safe and welcome. That's all I want to say. My condolences to Steven's wife, Sarah, and his other friends and family."

Sarah nodded her thanks and walked slowly to the podium. She seemed weighed down, hesitant, and fragile. I nodded my head to reassure her. Then I closed my eyes and tried to picture her running ahead of me through the park: a young, strong, self-assured girl.

"I wasn't sure I would be able to get up here and do this," she said. "It's been hard the last few months. When Steven was very sick, he decided he wanted me to read a message to you from him. I hope you will indulge me and not take this the wrong way. Those of you who know Steven will certainly understand."

She stopped and cleared her voice, leaned an elbow on the podium.

"Picture Steven downstairs in the bed, after a difficult night. He asks for a pen and paper; he wants to write something for the service. I have no idea what he is going to say, or even if it will make any sense. I want to tell him he is not going to die, because you are trained to say that, though I know it's almost time. He could say something profound, but, more likely, it will be incomprehensible – like some of the sounds he has been making. I have no idea. So he says: 'We have stopped just short of the gate...... Please remain seated with your seatbelts fastened...... We will be moving momentarily......The local time is 8 PM.....Welcome to ...your final destination.'"

A swell of respectful laughter and relief filled the chapel.

Sarah continued, "Well, that was it. He closed his eyes. And fell into a deep sleep. If you know Steven, you can imagine him saying that. Those were his last words."

Now there was the sound of muffled crying in the room.

"I think Steven is looking down on us from that final destination and encouraging us to keep going forward when we stop short. Keep your seat belts on, but don't be afraid to keep moving toward your final destination. There's so much we can do to make the world a better place before we reach the end. We need courage. And that's something Steven always had. And what he wanted to leave for us."

Music filled the room as she left the podium. I recognized one of Steven's favorites, "White Rabbit" from the Jefferson Airplane. The crowd and the music made conversation difficult. I could hear Tim Washington heading in my direction, speaking in a loud, preemptive voice. "Hey, that guy is amazing, isn't he? I saw him running through fire in the middle of Africa, with jackals and hyenas hiding in the grass. He saved my life; what can I say?"

I turned to stare at him. He was grinning.

"Well, he's exaggerating a bit, but not too much," I laughed.

Tim shook hands with a woman in a green dress in front of us. "Hey, nice to meet you, I'm Tim Washington." He acted as if he were still a professional football player, meeting fans and signing autographs after a game.

We bumped fists. "So, I got a surprise for you." He pointed to the back of the chapel. Near the door, waving his hand at me, was Dr. Tukutuba.

"What's he doing here?" I laughed.

"Well, my Foundation has some flexibility in funding. Tukutuba called me and told me about the fellowship you arranged, and so I pulled a few strings. He's all yours."

"But, nothing is arranged yet! I'm still working on it…"

"Well, at least we have him out of Africa. That is the difficult part. Now you can do your part. What do you think?"

"I think you just played a finesse on me," I said.

"That's what I like to hear. I like to win."

Sarah joined us and Tim wrapped his long arms around her. She almost disappeared for a moment. When she reappeared, I gave her a quick hug, too.

"If there is anything I can do, please let me know," I said, but it sounded hollow and insincere.

She nodded. "Actually I may be coming to Washington for a meeting in a few days. Maybe we can have lunch."

"Yes, sure, let me know."

As she was about to turn and move away, Tim introduced Tukutuba. "This is a friend of ours from Africa, Dr. Tukutuba. Thames here found him some kind of fellowship."

"I'm working on it," I said. "Tim's foundation flew him from Tanzania. I didn't know about it until today. Quite a surprise, Dr. Tukutuba!"

I shook his hand. He looked thrilled by everything around him.

"Didn't you say that you like surprises?" Tim laughed. "It was the best I could do at short notice. Hey, I like your idea for Danvers. 'T' is for Tim, did you know that? You can count on me for a thousand."

"Wow, that's wonderful," Sarah said.

"Thank you," I said, slapping him a high five.

"Refreshments anyone?" asked Tim. He and Sarah moved off toward the open door, where the sunlight was flooding into the chapel.

Tukutuba tugged at my coat. "Dr. Thames, you are surprised to see me?"

"Yes…the fellowship is still only a possibility."

"Yes, but a possibility is something!"

"Who's taking care of patients in your hospital?"

"My brother. Actually he is my cousin but we call each other brothers. He is also a doctor. When he heard of my opportunity, he came to help me."

"You must be very tired."

"Not at all. I am ready to start my new life here in America!"

Mark Harrison stopped me with a handshake as we moved toward the door.

"Hey, Robert – nice speech. I think you may have started a whole new movement in philanthropy. I already texted the alumni office to give them a heads up. Brilliant, really. Honoring your family and Thompson at the same time. Great idea: Two for one."

"Thanks."

"Hey, and I got a call from Tillman Hobson. He apologized for what happened with Dean Maiser. He wants to speak with you."

I shook my head slightly.

"I'm really sorry, too. Hobson said the Danvers Board had agreed to issue a formal apology to all of us. And they're going to issue a press release and tell the world about Goodson and Cheadle and the research study. And they are interviewing the twelve men that Steven mentioned and looking for others. They're going to pay for psychological therapy for anyone who wants it."

"Wow…that's better than I ever expected."

"Oh, and get this: They've rescinded the naming of the new building after Dean Maiser. If you're interested, they might have a position on the development committee for you. That's the first step to getting on the Board."

He handed me his card with Hobson's private number on the back. "You should call him. They need more color on the Board."

"I'm not sure I want to be anyone's 'color.'"

"Oh, gee. I just meant that – "

"Don't worry about it. I'm just not sure I can forget how Hobson barged in on us at Steven's."

"I'm really sorry. That was totally unexpected."

"I suppose we'll all get over it, except for Steven." I pocketed his card.

Mark smiled, shook my hand, and said, "*Non sibi.* Not for ourselves."

40

A few weeks later, Sarah arrived in Washington, D.C. She called and told me she had just interviewed for a job in the Justice Department's Civil Rights Division.

"It's something I've always wanted to do. And I need to get out of Boston and that house. They seem to want me, even though I'm older than most of them…and White."

"If it's what you want to do, then you should do it," I said. "I'll meet you at your hotel. There are parks and museums all over town; let's have some fun."

"Yes. That would be wonderful. My own private tour guide."

She was staying at the Renaissance Hotel near the Portrait Museum. After we met up, I suggested we take a quick walk through the museum. It was one of my favorite places in D.C., with portraits of the presidents and special exhibits of paintings and photography.

On that day there was an exhibit of photographs with haikus. The exhibit was meant to illustrate how linking the photographs with haikus changed our perceptions of the photographs.

One photograph was of two, identical twin men in their 60s with their wives, who were also identical twins, sitting at a table eating breakfast at a restaurant. Everyone was smiling and eating fried eggs and toast. The picture made me think about twins and what it would be like to know that there was someone who shared the same genes and probably had similar thoughts and feelings. Underneath was written,

We like the same things.

I guess that makes life simple.

We never argue.

I imagined my Danvers photo and what haiku a poet might have written underneath.

Where are you going?

You look so sad and so lost

Did you find your way?

Sarah and I walked past the presidential portraits: Washington, Lincoln, Kennedy, and Reagan. Over time, the styles of portrait painting had changed and so had the clothing fashions. But the portrait was still just one pose, at one point in time. How much could you tell about a person from a portrait? As we moved between rooms Sarah asked me, "Have you decided what you're going to do?"

"About what?"

"About your job? About your life? About those files?"

"I'm not sure. I'm thinking of taking the job offer in the Philippines. I'd like to help people who are like me, who were born in the wrong place, with the wrong parents, at the wrong time, but who don't give up. They're what Dr. Hart called the outliers."

"You don't really believe in all that trash do you?"

"I don't believe in physical determinants like body type. But I do believe that we get set on a path, whether through birth or other circumstances. It happens pretty early on in life, and there are only so many chances to alter that path."

After a moment, she said: "I'd like to see Steven's file if you don't mind. And the boxes. I'm curious."

"Really?"

She nodded.

"Okay. We'll go over to my house. It is just two stops on the Metro."

We had lunch and took the Metro to Dupont Circle and walked to my apartment. When I opened the door, the boxes of files greeted us, obstructing the hallway and giving off a faint musty odor.

"Sorry about the mess. I haven't gotten around to moving anything since the files arrived."

She stared at them in fascination. "So here are the infamous files."

"I've been going through them, bit by bit, but I haven't decided what to do with them. They're really interesting – more interesting than the exhibit at the museum."

My phone began to vibrate. I wouldn't have picked it up, but it was Mr. Grundel.

"Hello, Robert. The lab just called. That specimen you collected in Africa has shown activity against several bacteria. One of them is the multi drug-resistant Staphylococcus, the one we were looking for. Of course, this is preliminary information. We will need to verify the results. But this could be the breakthrough we've needed. I thought you'd want to know."

"That's great," I said. "Thanks for calling."

As I hung up it hit me: The news of a new antibiotic could prevent budget cuts at our office. My job would be secure. I would not have to leave Washington and go to the Philippines. My plans for retirement in ten years would be back on track.

I should have felt overjoyed, but I wasn't.

"Who was that?" asked Sarah.

I explained to her about the antibiotic and its implications. "I should be thrilled. My job would be saved. But for some reason, I'm not."

"You can still take the job in the Philippines. It would be a risk. But it would be your choice, not anyone else's. It could be liberating."

"You're right."

She held up a file. "I found Steven's. He's so young in the picture! I can barely remember when he was like that. All I can think of is what he looked like when he was sick. Do you mind if I look at your file?"

I found my file and clutched it to my chest for a moment, deliberating about whether I wanted to share it with her. Even now, I felt embarrassed and afraid to expose myself to scrutiny. I hesitantly handed it over and she turned the pages, nodding and smiling.

"Hmm. A rabbit. That's what they labeled you. Had I known that, I would have been afraid to go running with you."

"Do you want to go for a run now?" I suggested. I had not gone running for years. The joints in my knees had signs of arthritis and I avoided exercise that might inflame them. But the words had come out spontaneously. I regretted asking almost as soon as I said it.

"A run?" she laughed.

"I was just remembering that first time when we met. You used to like to run."

"I still do," she said. "But I don't think I've run with anyone else since college. Steven never liked to run. Do you still run?"

"Not much, anymore. My knees… but it was so nice when we ran together."

"Well, okay. Why not? I guess I could run in these tennies. But I don't have a good shirt."

"You can borrow one of mine," I said, and brought her a t-shirt that I had gotten at a fundraiser.

"This is going to be embarrassing – two old people like us running through the streets of Washington, D.C. The police will probably arrest us for stopping traffic," she laughed.

We stepped out the door and jogged down the street, past the dry cleaning stores, small groceries, and restaurants. We passed people at the bus stop who stared at us briefly before turning away – housecleaners, students, tourists from out of town. I decided to lead us to a jogging path along Rock Creek.

As we descended the path, I watched her gray and brown hair bob as her shoulders dipped with each stride. She moved with short, tentative steps, not the easy flowing gait I remembered. I imagined it was a caution developed over years of encounters with pot holes, along with the occasional scrapes and falls accrued while running on nature trails. Her pace was slower, her steps more deliberate. She looked back at me and waved.

I also jogged gingerly, trying to protect my knees. I wondered how I must look to her now, puffing and gasping for air as I had once done years ago.

We found a quiet stretch of trail away from the picnickers and children on bicycles. The trail entered an area of overgrown bushes. I watched my steps as we passed roots and rocks exposed in the dirt. I almost crashed into Sarah when she unexpectedly stopped.

"Look at that flower," she said, standing motionless. It was a small purple flower with yellow veins, barely visible in the brambles. I never would have noticed it if she had not stopped to show it to me. I was happy to gaze at it as I caught my breath.

"Yes, that's a pretty one."

I realized how rare it was for me to notice anything new and beautiful in the city, like the flower, or to feel the air on my face as I ran. We stood there for a moment, each in our own thoughts. She looked at me as if she were studying me like the flower. She had sweat on her forehead and neck.

"So what do you think? Do you think you'll leave your job?"

"I was ready to. I signed papers. I was about to retire."

"Don't just stay there because it's the path of least resistance."

"It's not that. I want to go to the Philippines, but..."

"What is it?"

"I know it's too soon to talk about this, but when we were together in that motel and I was holding you, I felt something that I thought I had lost. And I don't want to lose it again."

She moved closer and kissed me on the forehead and then on either cheek. She pulled me into an embrace and held me tightly.

"I don't know what I want now," she said into my neck. "I need to do some things for myself. But I think you should take that job in the Philippines. I think it's what you want."

"I want other things, too," I said. I was afraid to express how much.

"You can always come back. I'm not going anywhere for a while."

"You could stay in my house if you get the job."

"Really?"

"Sure, why not? I don't want to sell it. I'll come back here eventually, one way or another. Of course, I'd have to check your references."

"Hahaha." She punched me softly on the shoulder, and for a moment I felt like we were kids again, with great possibilities ahead of us.

We ran back up the hill and along the sidewalk. It was not a long run. Perhaps half an hour. And yet everything had changed. I opened the door and looked at the boxes.

"I think I want to burn the files," I said. "All of them. Now."

"Once you burn them, there won't be any proof of what they did to you. Shouldn't they at least admit it – take accountability? Shouldn't they acknowledge the truth?"

"They've admitted it. They're writing us all letters of apology and offering counseling."

"Well, that's a start…"

"What is the good of starting a scandal, hurting the students and teachers who are at Danvers now? These boxes of files are like ghosts keeping watch over me, morning and night. Just like Dean Maiser did at Danvers. Those measurements are not my truth. I need to get rid of them."

"All right," she said. "Let's do it."

I lit the fireplace in my living room, and soon the logs had caught and flames burned brightly, illuminating the photograph of my parents that my father's brother had given to me. I decided to burn the files alphabetically, just the way we had been photographed. I read the names on the files like the names of the dead from a war. "Thomas Morgan… Michael Mungar… Albert Munoz… Peter Nathanson…"

I handed each to Sarah, and she threw it into the fire.

I watched as the cover and the inner pages burst into flames. Sometimes the photograph curled into a ball before it burned. Sometimes it stretched out vertically, as if arising from a long sleep before darkening and burning. Sometimes I could make out a face or a torso, an arm or two legs.

As we were in the midst of burning the files, there was a knock at the door. It was Tukutuba. He was staying with me temporarily, sleeping on a blow-up bed in my study until I could arrange a placement for him. He still needed to get his medical license, but there were several promising opportunities in Utah, New York, and Baltimore. He had been out shopping and now, as he returned, I realized I had completely forgotten about him.

He observed the fire burning and Sarah sitting with me. Perhaps he imagined we were observing some type of ritual. He nodded his greeting to us and stood by the fireplace, even though we offered him a place to sit. It was as if he were a guardian of the flame. Soon we began to hand the files to him and he placed them carefully into the fire, each one separately, his deep voice echoing the name.

They burned so quickly. Fireplaces are not built for this type of fire. They are made to burn logs that produce orange and blue flames with sweet, pungent smoke. This harsh paper smoke drifted back into the living room making us cough and burning our eyes. Tukutuba opened the windows and poked at the embers to coax them up the chimney. When we got to Thames and Thompson, I held them together for a moment, remembering when our life paths had been joined, and how they had been torn apart. I thought of how Steven had waited for me at night in the shadows years later, and the translucent connection – like the thread of a spider's web – that had survived between us over the years.

But now it was time that Robert Thames of Danvers be laid to rest, just as we had done for Steven. It was time for a new Robert Thames of the Philippines.

I gave the files to Tukutuba and he read "Robert Thames" and "Steven Thompson," with his deep, sonorous British accent. Sarah grabbed my file and held it in her hand, running her fingers over the surface and then inside across the photograph and the sheaf of papers before throwing it into the fire. Then she held Steven's file and paged through it one last time. She took a deep breath and laughed. "I was just thinking of you as boys."

I looked at her silently.

"Steven told me that he would think about that weekend with the three of us at his house at the end. It was what gave him peace. Can you imagine?"

She dabbed at an isolated tear running down her cheek. Then she smiled and threw Steven's file into the flames.

Tukutuba continued to read the names, and Sarah and I took turns throwing them into the fire. Paul Zane was the last. I knew him as one of the boys in my Latin class. He had a thick file that smoldered in the ashes before bursting into flame. I caught a glimpse of his photo, just a fragment of his neck and back before he disappeared. All I remembered about him was that his last name began with a Z, and what a burden that must have been for him.

ACKNOWLEDGEMENTS

Thank you to Frank Huyler, Julie Mars, and Ethan Sklar
for their advice and encouragement.

ABOUT THE AUTHOR

From 1965 to 1968, David Sklar attended a private school where he was the unwitting subject of a research study that attempted to link body type to leadership potential. This disturbing experience inspired *Atlas of Men*. David's previous book, a memoir, explores his experience as a volunteer in a rural Mexican clinic prior to medical school and how it shaped his later career in healthcare. *La Clinica* was chosen as one of the Best Books of 2008. An emergency physician, researcher, editor of a medical education journal, and a professor at both Arizona State University and the University of New Mexico, David currently lives with his wife in Phoenix, Arizona.